PRAISE FOR NOVELS BY BRANDILYN COLLINS

One of the Best Books of 2007 ... Top

The excitement starts on page one and doesn't stop until the shocking
end ... [*Crimson Eve*] is fast-paced and thrilling.

Romantic Times

The action starts with a bang ... and the pace doesn't let up until this
fabulous racehorse of a story crosses the finish line.

Christian Retailing, for *Crimson Eve*

Collins crafts an unparalleled cat and mouse game wrought with
mystery and surprise.

TitleTrakk.com, for *Crimson Eve*

A ch   *Moon*

Thrilling   ost

...a fascinati   ching

                                                                  Moon

... fast-pace   me
scene in   *Dawn*

A sympathetic heroine ... effective flashbacks ... Collins knows how
to weave faith into a rich tale.

Library Journal, for *Violet Dawn*

Collins expertly melds flashbacks with present-day events to provide a smooth yet deliciously intense flow ... quirky townsfolk will help drive the next books in the series.

RT BOOKclub, for *Violet Dawn*

Skillfully written ... Imaginative style and exquisite suspense.

1340mag.com, for *Violet Dawn*

A master storyteller ... Collins deftly finesses the accelerator on this knuckle-chomping ride.

RT BOOKclub, for *Web of Lies*

... fast-paced ... mentally challenging and genuinely entertaining.

Christian Book Previews, for *Web of Lies*

Collins' polished plotting sparkles ... unique word twists on the psychotic serial killer mentality. Lock your doors, pull your shades—and read this book at noon.

RT BOOKclub, Top Pick for *Dead of Night*

This one is up there in the stratosphere ... Collins has it in her to give an author like Patricia Cornwell a run for her money.

Faithfulreader.com, for *Dead of Night*

... spine-tingling, hair-raising, edge-of-the-seat suspense.

Wordsmith Review, for *Dead of Night*

A page-turner I couldn't put down, except to check the locks on my doors.

Authors Choice Reviews

Collins keeps the reader gasping and guessing ... artistic prose paints vivid pictures ... High marks for original plotting and superb pacing.

RT BOOKclub, for *Stain of Guilt*

... a sinister, tense story with twists and turns that will keep you on the edge of your seat.

Wordsmith Shoppe, for *Stain of Guilt*

... an abundance of real-life faith as well as real-life fear, betrayal and evil. This one kept me gripped from beginning to end.

Contemporary Christian Music magazine, for *Brink of Death*

Collins' deft hand for suspense brings on the shivers.

RT BOOKclub, for *Brink of Death*

This gripping murder mystery thrills from page one.

christianbookpreviews.com, for *Brink of Death*

Compelling ... plenty of intrigue and false trails.

Publishers Weekly, for *Dread Champion*

Finely-crafted ... vivid ... another masterpiece that keeps the reader utterly engrossed.

RT BOOKclub, for *Dread Champion*

... riveting mystery and courtroom drama.

Library Journal, for *Dread Champion*

The cleverly complex plot, realistic courtroom drama, well-sketched secondary characters, and strong pacing make this book a fascinating read.

dancingword.com, for *Dread Champion*

Chilling ... a confusing, twisting trail that keeps pages turning.

Publishers Weekly, for *Eyes of Elisha*

A thriller that keeps the reader guessing until the end.

Library Journal, for *Eyes of Elisha*

Unique and intriguing ... filled with more turns than a winding mountain highway.

One of the top ten Christian novels of 2001.

Captivating ... An imaginative plot, rounded characters, and workmanlike prose.

dark pursuit

Brandilyn Collins
Seatbelt Suspense

OTHER BOOKS BY BRANDILYN COLLINS

Kanner Lake Series

1 | Violet Dawn

2 | Coral Moon

3 | Crimson Eve

4 | Amber Morn

Hidden Faces Series

1 | Brink of Death

2 | Stain of Guilt

3 | Dead of Night

4 | Web of Lies

Chelsea Adams Series

1 | Eyes of Elisha

2 | Dread Champion

Bradleyville Series

1 | Cast a Road before Me

2 | Color the Sidewalk for Me

3 | Capture the Wind for Me

BRANDILYN COLLINS

dark pursuit

ZONDERVAN.com/
AUTHORTRACKER
follow your favorite authors

Dark Pursuit
Copyright © 2008 by Brandilyn Collins

This title is also available as a Zondervan ebook.
Visit www.zondervan.com/ebooks.

Requests for information should be addressed to:
Zondervan, *Grand Rapids, Michigan* 49530

Library of Congress Cataloging-in-Publication Data

Collins, Brandilyn.
    Dark pursuit / Brandilyn Collins.
      p. cm.
    ISBN 978-0-310-27642-5
     1. Beauty operators — Fiction. 2. Grandparent and child — Fiction. 3.
    Authors — Fiction. 4. Serial murderers — Fiction. I. Title.
    PS3553.O4747815D37 2008
    813'.54 — dc22   200825025

Published in association with the literary agency of Alive Communications, Inc., 7680 Goddard Street, Suite 200, Colorado Springs, CO 80920. www.alivecommunications.com

Interior design by Michelle Espinoza

Printed in the United States of America

08 09 10 11 12 13 14 • 23 22 21 20 19 18 17 16 15 14 13 12 11 10 9 8 7 6 5 4 3 2 1

For Tony Lamanna,
for all your help
with the law enforcement aspects
in my Kanner Lake novels.

Want to Discuss *Dark Pursuit* with Your Book Club?

Insightful questions about the story and how it applies
to your life can be found on my website at:

www.brandilyncollins.com

Dear Reader:

In this first book after my Kanner Lake Series I take you on a new
and somewhat different rollercoaster ride. In these hills and plunges,
rocketing through the blackened tunnels, you will meet new characters
upon whose beleaguered heads I've wreaked my never-ending havoc.
(Poor things—that they should end up in one of my books.)

Those of you familiar with the Peninsula side of the northern California Bay Area will quickly see I've wedged a town into rural territory.
Gayner lies on the west side of Freeway 280, roughly between Edgewood Road and the town of Woodside. As long as I'm creating people,
why not create an entire town as well?

My thanks to Courtney Rants at Zi Spa in Coeur d'Alene, Idaho,
for her information about the workday and training of a hair stylist.
Somehow she managed to do my hair and answer my million pesky
questions at the same time. All you other stylists out there—be thankful you don't have me for a client.

And now, here we go again. You know the drill. Strap on that
seatbelt, keep your hands inside the car, and—

Don't forget to *breathe*...™

**Beelzebub, addressing the fallen angels
after being thrown out of Heaven:**

The King of Heaven hath doomed
This place our dungeon, . . .
                nor shall we need
                . . . to invade . . .
                What if we find
Some easier enterprise? There is a place . . .
Of some new race, called Man, . . .
Thither let us bend all our thoughts, to learn
                . . . where their weakness: . . .
Seduce them to our party, that their God
May prove their foe, . . .
                . . . Advise if this be worth
Attempting, or to sit in darkness here
Hatching vain empires.

Paradise Lost, Book II, John Milton

dark pursuit

Part 1

severed

She died so easily.

Sure she fought. And I had a time ge---

here I wanted. But when it comes right down to

choking the life out of them, I've learned some-

thing. The line between death and life—that final

breath—is painfully th--- ---g, this realit-

As before, the days leading up to it were intense

--- about my business, then wham. Days a

--- more. It called wit-

one

"Ever hear the dead knocking?"

Leland Hugh watches the psychiatrist ponder his question, no reaction on the man's lined, learned face. The doctor lists to one side in his chair, a fist under his sagging jowl. The picture of unshakable confidence.

"No, can't say I have."

Hugh nods and gazes at the floor. "I do. At night, always at night."

"Why do they knock?"

His eyes raise to look straight into the doctor's. "They want my soul."

No response but a mere inclining of the head. The intentional silence pulses, waiting for an explanation. Psychiatrists are good at that.

"I took theirs, you see. Put them in their graves early." Deep inside Hugh, the anger and fear begin to swirl. He swallows, voice tightening. "They're supposed to *stay* in the grave. Who'd ever think the dead would demand their revenge?"

From outside the door, at the windows,
in the closet, in the walls—they used to
knock. Now, in his jail cell the noises
come from beneath the floor. Harassing, insistent, hate-filled, and bitter sounds that
pound his ears and drill his brain until
sleep will not, *cannot* come.

"Do you ever answer?"

Shock twists Hugh's lips. "*Answer?*"

The psychiatrist's face remains placid.
The slight, knowing curve to his mouth
makes Hugh want to slug him.

"You think they're not real, don't you?"
Hugh steeples his fingers with mocking erudition. "Yes, esteemed colleagues." He affects an arrogant highbrow voice. "I have
determined the subject suffers from EGS—
Extreme Guilt Syndrome, the roots of which
run so deep as never to be extirpated, with
symptoms aggrandizing into myriad areas of
the subject's life and resulting in perceived paranormal phenomena."

He drops both hands in his lap, lowering his chin to look derisively at the good
doctor.

The man inhales slowly. "Do you feel
guilt for the murders?"

"Why should I? They *deserved* it."

He pushes to his feet.

~~He pushes to his feet.~~ He slumps back in
his chair.

~~He slumps back in his chair.~~ He aims a
hard look

~~He aims a hard look~~

~~The psychiatrist.~~
~~Hugh's hands fist,~~
~~He cannot~~
~~He can only~~
~~He~~

"Aaghh!" Novelist Darell Brooke smacked his keyboard and shoved away from the desk. All concentration drained from his mind like water from a leaky pan.

His characters froze.

He lowered his head, raking gnarled fingers into the front of his scalp. For a time there he'd almost had it—that ancient joy of thoughts flowing and fingers typing. In the last two hours he'd managed to write three or four paragraphs. Now—nothing.

Absolutely nothing.

King of Suspense. He laughed, a bitter sound that singed his throat. Ninety-nine novels written in forty-three years. Well over a hundred million copies sold. Twenty-one major motion pictures made from his books. Countless magazine articles about his career, fan letters, invitations to celebrity parties. Now look at him at age seventy-seven. Two years after the auto accident and still only half mobile. And wielding a mere fraction of the brain power he used to have.

What good is an author who can't hold a plot in his head?

As for his once-diehard fans, they were now happily reading King or Koontz or that upstart Patterson.

Betrayers, all. He made a gagging sound in his throat.

Darell stared at the monitor, reading over his strikeouts, struggling once more to settle into the story. He pictured the psychiatrist, his killer...

No use.

Face it, old man. You'll never write that hundredth book. You've been put out to pasture for good.

He wrenched his eyes from the screen and reached for his shiny black cane. With effort, he pushed himself out of his leather chair to unsteady feet. The broken bones in his left leg and ankle had long since healed, but the ligament damage had not. Despite painful physical therapy his foot had not regained its full flexibility. Amazing—the constant flexing of a foot to maintain equilibrium. He hadn't realized the importance of those muscles and tendons until his were torn apart.

Darell shuffled across the hardwood floor of his thirty-foot-long office, repelled by his writing desk and computer. Every day they wooed, then shunned him. At the tall, mullioned window near the far corner he stopped and spread his feet wide. Hunched over, both hands on his cane, he brooded over the green rolling hills of his estate, the untamed and capricious Pacific Ocean in the distance.

He used to go to the beach to write a couple times a week, tapping his laptop keys as the surf pounded in rhythm to his pulse. Now he never left the house except for doctor's appointments.

Darell Brooke had no use for a world that no longer had use for him.

His mouth puckered with disdain.

Characters' faces in shadow, snippets of scenes filtered through his mind. Fredda Lee. Now there was a delectable killer. Or Alfred Stone with his black hair and eyebrows, an intimidating figure much as Darell had appeared in his younger days. *Black Tie Affair*, that was Alfred's book.

No. Not that one.

Midnight Madness?

Darell shook his head. He used to know. Before the accident, he remembered every story he'd written, every character.

"You knocked your skull pretty badly," the doctor had said as Darell watched the hospital room spiral from his bed. "The dizziness will pass, but you might find it hard to concentrate ..."

Now here Darell stood, a shell of his former self. As the undisputed King of Suspense he'd reveled in playing the part. No longer was there a part to play. His once stern, confident countenance—now blank-faced. His black hair turned an unruly shock of white. The wild gray brows jutting over his deep-set, dark eyes no longer intimidating, merely strawlike. Oh, how he used to love to use those eyebrows! The muscular arms—even into his early seventies—sagging. Straight back now bent.

"Pshhh." His lips curled.

Slowly, with defiance, Darell raised his chin.

He focused through the glass once more. At least the gnarled trees on his property still looked formidable. And his mansion looked just as severe from afar, with its black shutters and multiple wings and gables. From the outside looking in, people would never guess ...

Darell glared at the phone near his computer. On impulse he clomped over to it and picked up the receiver. His gnarled forefinger hovered over the keys.

What was the number? The one he'd dialed countless times, year after year.

He lowered himself to the edge of his chair and flipped through his Rolodex. *There.*

Malcolm Featherling, agent to the country's top writers, answered his private line on the third ring. Clipped tone, terse greeting. Malcolm was always pushed for time.

"Hello, Malcolm. Just checking in to give you an update." Darell pushed the old confidence into his voice. After all, his agent worked for *him.*

"Well, Darell, nice to hear from you. It *has* been three days."

Darell blinked. He'd called three days ago? Surely it was at least a month. Maybe two.

He cleared his throat. It sounded phlegmy, like an old man's. He hated that. "I wrote some today. Almost a page. And another yesterday. You know what they say—write a page a day and you've got a novel in a year."

He used to write at least two a year. All of them brilliant.

"That's good, Darell, good ..."

"Maybe I can get that contract back. Just think, Malcolm, fifteen percent of ten million is a lot of dough. I'll make you rich. Again."

"You do that, man, you do that. Keep up the good work."

He could hear the disbelief in Malcolm's response. The agent was patronizing him. Darell's publisher had waited eight months after the accident, strung along on the promise that he would be able to write his one hundredth bestseller—the assumed milestone that had landed him on the cover of *Time* magazine. But a worldwide publishing conglomerate couldn't wait forever, even for Darell Brooke. Not with half the contract—five million dollars—already paid up front, and doctors advising he may never write again. The deal was canceled. Darell had been forced to give the money back. Malcolm had to cough up his fifteen percent.

I'll show you, Malcolm. Maybe I'll even get a new agent.

"All right. Well, got to get back to my writing. See you, Malcolm." Darell clicked off the line and stared at the phone in his hand.

Just three days ago he'd called?

With a loud sigh he hung up the receiver. He shifted his legs and focused on the half-empty page on his screen. An emptiness he used to love to fill. Now it mocked him. His killer was still on his feet, frozen. The psychiatrist watched from his chair.

What were they supposed to do next? Where had he been headed with this story?

What *was* the story?

Oh, to regain half the concentration he'd once had. A fourth. A tenth. The thought of spending day after day in this mansion-turned-prison, in this office, unproductive and used up, filled him with an emptiness as deep as staring into the face of eternal hell . . .

Straightening, Darell dredged up his will.

He placed his fingers on the keyboard, straining to turn the gears of his mind. One more paragraph, just one. He'd give anything to finish this book. To gain back his reputation, his *life*. Anything.

The gears refused to move.

two

Pregnant. She was *pregnant*.

And her queasy stomach wouldn't let her forget it.

Kaitlan Sering stopped her Toyota Corolla at the edge of the driveway she shared with the Jensons and reached out the open window to check her mailbox. The northern California September air was warm, sun heating her skin. She moved like some robot, her mind on her troubles. The infamous stick had turned pink just last night, and she was still trying to wrap her mind around it.

Would Craig be mad? Disappointed? They'd only been dating three months, but they were the best months of her life.

Kaitlan sifted through envelopes. Advertisements and bills. Bills she wouldn't be able to pay if her customers kept canceling their hair appointments at the last minute. Two of them today, right in a row. One of them an expensive cut and highlight. Altogether, she was out almost two hundred dollars.

And now she needed the money more than ever.

How was she going to pay for having a baby without health insurance? How was she going to raise a child on her own?

Maybe Craig would marry her. He'd certainly shown his dedication to family. His father and sister meant the world to him.

Kaitlan tossed the small stack of mail on her passenger seat. Then—dumb, dumb—checked herself in the rearview mirror. She looked *terrible*. More like forty than twenty-two. Well, twenty-three next week, but the birthday wasn't here yet. Her lips, usually curving up, were all drawn down. Dull brown eyes. Lids drooping, forehead wrinkled.

"Ugh." She tore her eyes away.

For one crazy second she wanted to lower her head onto the steering wheel and cry. How long had it been since she'd done that?

She had no idea how to be a mother. But she wanted the baby more than anything in the world. Unlike her own mother, she would be warm and loving. Never abandon her child. *Never*.

Kaitlan took a shaky breath. What an overwhelming day. Sick stomach and now a throbbing head. Fact is, if her clients hadn't canceled, she'd have been a basket case at those appointments. Three o'clock in the afternoon and all she wanted was some aspirin and a bed.

Wait, can you take aspirin when you're pregnant?

She drove down the long driveway, past the Jensons' large two-story house and to her renovated garage-turned-apartment at the back of their five-acre lot. The Jensons' property lay on the outskirts of Gayner in a rural area, the closest neighbor about a half-mile away. Kaitlan loved the quiet, the woods surrounding the place.

Beat the streets of L.A. any day.

She parked in the carport and slid out of the Corolla, toting her purse and the mail. Her footsteps dragged across the hard cement toward the door leading into the kitchen.

She pulled the key from her purse and slid it into the lock.

A noise.

Kaitlan's head came up, her hands stilling. Ears cocked, she listened. Her gaze roved beyond the carport, over the trees in the back of the lot, the large stump with raised and tangled roots.

A gray and white cat pranced into sight, proudly carrying a mouse in its jaws.

Kaitlan let out her breath. Boomer, a neighbor's pet who wandered far and wide.

He veered in her direction.

"No! Go on, shoo!" She stomped her foot, and he ran away.

"Oh." Kaitlan pressed a hand to her forehead. That jarring hadn't helped at all. With a sigh, she opened the door. She stepped inside and set her purse, mail, and keys on the table.

She looked around the kitchen. Pale yellow appliances. White sink with a chip in the left corner. Brown-flecked Formica countertops. The place wasn't fancy, but plenty big enough. Its high ceilings added to the feeling of space. Most of all, the apartment was hers.

Her gaze landed on the floor — and she spotted a blue pen. Frowning, she walked over to pick it up. She turned it over in her fingers and saw the familiar engraving of *Craig Barlow* along its side. Craig's expensive pen, a present from his father. He always carried it with him, in uniform or out, using it in spare moments to work on his novel.

Kaitlan was sure the pen hadn't been there when she left for work this morning.

She ran a finger over its slim smoothness. Why had Craig been here today? She'd given him a key, but he never just came over while she was at work.

Kaitlan checked the wall clock. Three-ten. At six-thirty Craig would be picking her up for his sister's birthday dinner at Schultz's restaurant. She should call him now and tell him she'd found his pen.

Laying it on a counter, Kaitlan first crossed to a cabinet for two aspirin and washed them down with water. Her glass clinked as she set it in the sink.

Kaitlan carried the pen over to the table and set it down. She reached into a side pocket in her purse for her cell phone.

A fleck of color in the living room caught her eye.

She focused through the doorway that led from the kitchen. Just within her line of vision — a bit of red.

Now what?

She walked to the threshold. Stopped.

Her red throw blanket was bunched on the floor. It should have been on the back of the couch. Her wooden coffee table sat at a funny angle. Two of its magazines were knocked off, one lying open. The small lamp on the end table — on its side on the carpet.

Electricity careened down Kaitlan's spine. Craig wouldn't have done this.

Maybe it was a burglar.

She gripped the door frame. Glanced left and right. Nothing missing. The TV was there, and her VCR and stereo. The CD tower.

What had happened?

Her jewelry—what little she had. The cash in her top drawer. Maybe somebody had come to steal that.

Kaitlan scurried through the kitchen, driven to see, afraid to know.

The doorway at the other end of the kitchen led to a short hall. Kaitlan first veered right toward the front door and checked to see if it was locked. It was. She retraced her steps, hurried to the left of the kitchen and toward her bedroom—the biggest room in the apartment, running from front to back.

She stopped just outside.

Her bedroom door was angled. Peering straight ahead, Kaitlan could only see the back part of the room. She gazed at the sliding glass door that led onto a small rear patio. Closed, like it should be. Black lever down—the locked position.

But there, next to it on the light blue carpet—a footprint. Almost parallel to the door. Craig's, or a burglar's?

Kaitlan's heart tripped into double time. She pressed against the doorframe.

What was that smell? Something flowery, like perfume. Mixed with ... urine?

The back of her neck tingled.

Kaitlan's feet propelled her into the room. Two steps in, she looked to the right.

On her bed—a woman.

Breath backed up in Kaitlan's throat.

The woman lay on her back, clearly dead, chin jutting into the air and mouth open. Clad in jeans and blue knit top, legs and arms askew.

Knotted around her neck—the telltale strip of black fabric with green stripes.

Kaitlan's knees turned to water. In the time it took for her to sink to the floor—in those staggering, life-altering seconds—two words screamed in her numbing brain.

The fabric.

three

From the armchair in his south-wing bedroom, Darell glowered out the window, heavy brows hanging into his vision. In the distance, under gloomy skies that matched his mood, spread San Francisco Bay.

His killer and psychiatrist, still frozen, taunted his thoughts. He'd gotten so angry he turned off the computer and stormed from the office. If you could call his cane shuffle *storming*.

Darell's mouth twisted.

Down a slope he could see Highway 35 leading to Highway 92. Follow 92 east and you'd end up in the Peninsula flats, teeming with people and cars like flies on a corpse. Take it west, and you'd come to Half Moon Bay, a small coastal town. From his mansion's perch at the apex of hills between the two vastly different areas, Darell could view all directions. Here in his bedroom he used to enjoy the city lights at night. Now he couldn't stand the sight of them. They symbolized people, the world in which he once reigned.

Footsteps on the hardwood floor signaled the approach of his assistant, Margaret Breckenridge. Darell did not turn his head.

"Hello, D.," she said with bounce in her voice. Margaret was always cheery.

He pulled in the corners of his mouth.

"Time for your afternoon pills."

"Oh, joy."

She set the small ebony tray on the table next to his chair. He wrinkled his nose.

Margaret chuckled. "I swear if you acted any different one day when I brought your medication, I'd fall over dead."

"What do you want me to do, woman, dance a jig?"

"Oh, stop." She patted his shoulder, then plucked three small pills from the tray. His antidepressant, a pain pill, and one for his sluggish brain. "Hold out your hand."

He obeyed, swinging his head toward the window. She placed the medicine in his palm.

"Bombs away." He threw the pills into his mouth, took a water glass from her efficient fingers, and swallowed.

Three times they repeated the process. Pills, always pills, day and night. He didn't even know what he took anymore. Most of them were vitamins and herbs. Did no good at all, except to keep snake oil salesmen in business. As for the inventor of the one that was supposed to make him think more clearly—Darell could imagine a million torturous ways to kill the shyster off in his next book.

If he ever had a next book.

Margaret nodded with satisfaction when he swallowed the last batch. She stood back, folding her arms across her ample chest. Darell tilted his head to view her with unspoken challenge. A weak ray of sun filtered through the window, showing up the crow's feet around her eyes. The woman was looking old.

She was only sixty-one. Compared to her he looked like death.

"Have you done your exercises this afternoon?" she asked.

"No."

Her lips pressed. "D., you know you should."

He shrugged. "They don't work anyway."

"They might, if you'd do them three times a day like you're supposed to."

"Aaah." He swatted the air with his hand.

She exhaled loudly. "What am I going to do with you?"

Put me out to pasture, like everyone else.

"Where's your Thera-Band?"

The hated thick rubbery band from the therapist. At first he'd worked hard with it, determined to regain all the movement he'd lost. But as time ticked by and progress proved slow, the choking cloud of depression set in.

"I don't know. Maybe in the office."

Margaret picked up the glass and tray. "I'll go get it."

Darell focused out the window, waiting until she was almost to the door, far enough away to allow him space.

"Margaret. Thank you."

She turned back. "You're welcome, D."

For some reason her smile — so loyal and loving — reminded him of his granddaughter when she was little.

A sudden brutal image of Kaitlan filled Darell's head — the last time he'd seen her, six years ago. The hard, bitter face that looked decades beyond her sixteen years.

"I *hate* you!" Spittle had sprayed from her mouth as she marched toward his front door.

"Good." White-hot rage at her treachery seared his veins. *No one* stole from him. "Then you won't care that I never want to see you again."

She'd turned back, lips curled. "I *don't* care. You never showed me any love anyway. Your writing — that's all you care about. And now you have nobody left. Nobody!"

In Darell's mind, he heard the door slam.

Margaret reappeared, toting the Thera-Band. She held it out to him, and he snatched it from her fingers. Why had he thought of Kaitlan? Anger at her betrayal swirled within him, and he didn't know what to do with it. He leaned over, slapped the long band around the ball of his foot, and pulled the ends up hard with both hands, forcing his toes downward.

"There," he said through gritted teeth. "See? I'm exercising."

Margaret studied him. "Good. Whatever you thought about just now — keep thinking it."

As she turned away, Darell pulled tighter, jaw clenched. His ligaments screamed. So did the memories. Maybe a little more pain would drive them away.

He relaxed for a second, then pulled again — harder.

four

Kaitlan's body shook. *How could this ... what ...?*

Somehow she pushed herself off the floor. *Call 911!* her mind screamed, but her stupid feet wouldn't move. She swayed like a drunk-ard, shoulders hunched and breathing ragged. Her gaze glued to the corpse on her bed — the woman's bugged eyes, drool coming out of her mouth. And her expression! Didn't faces go slack in death? This one was frozen in shock.

The glands around Kaitlan's mouth started to drain. She was going to throw up.

She lurched for the bathroom. Rounded the corner, fell on her knees before the toilet, and threw back the lids with a loud *crack*.

Kaitlan heaved, holding back her hair, eyes squeezed shut. Again and again until nothing was left in her stomach.

When it was over, she trembled from head to toe. She flushed the toilet and put down the lids. Washed out her mouth with toothpaste and water. Trying to tell herself none of this was true. She'd leave the bathroom to see nothing on her bed. She was just tired, that's all. Too stressed.

Clutching her arms, Kaitlan sidled back into the bedroom.

The body was still there.

She stared at it, mind bouncing. Looking for one rational thought she could grasp.

Why would anyone bring a body *here*?

Craig. He'd been in the apartment today.

But he couldn't have done this.

Who was this woman? Kaitlan had never seen her before. She looked ... maybe in her forties.

That cloth around her neck. Black with green stripes. It *was* silk, wasn't it? Kaitlan forced herself to move closer, peering at its shiny texture.

Yes. Silk.

She drew back, shuddering. This fabric had been used in two other killings in the area over the past year. The last one just two months ago.

Craig.

Kaitlan sagged against the wall, disbelief eating a deep, dark hole inside her. Craig had told her about the two killings. But he knew far too much for a mere beat cop, details only the investigators should know—like the black and green silk fabric. He'd claimed his father, the chief of police, had told him everything. She wasn't supposed to say a word to anyone.

Kaitlan shook her head. So what? So he knew too much. He and his father were close. Chief Barlow *would* have talked to him.

But Craig was the only person with a key to her place. And he'd been here. She'd found his pen.

No. He couldn't have done this.

Three months ago Craig Barlow had stolen her heart. He was charming and a little mysterious. Abercrombie model gorgeous, with deep blue eyes and grooves around his mouth when he smiled. Craig was private, not a lot of friends. Often he didn't open up as much as she'd like. But he'd been good to her. They'd fallen in love. With her past, finding someone stable and strong like him had been incredible.

Kaitlan shivered. She didn't care about the pen or the fact that he knew too much about the killings. Craig couldn't kill *anybody*. There had to be another explanation.

Maybe the body was here before he came.

But then why did he leave it? A police officer wouldn't just walk away from a crime scene. And why hadn't he called her?

Okay, then someone did it *after* he was here.

But who? And how did that person get in?

How long had the woman been dead?

Heart pounding, Kaitlan edged to the bed. She raised a hand to touch the body, to see if it was cold. Twice she pulled back. The third time she grazed the woman's wrist.

Still warm.

What did that mean? She died an hour ago? Two?

Craig would know. He lived for crime. He watched all the forensics shows on TV, wrote every chance he got on the suspense manuscript he never let anybody see ...

A memory reeled through Kaitlan, and her hands flew to her mouth. He'd told her his favorite scenes to write were about the killer. And he wrote those scenes in *first person.*

She swallowed hard. No. She still couldn't believe this.

Kaitlan glanced out the front window. Whoever did this must have thought she'd be at work all day. What if he came back?

She ran out of the room.

Kaitlan stumbled into the kitchen. She had to call 911. Head throbbing, she thrust a hand into her purse for her cell—and it rang just as she touched it. Craig's tone.

She jumped and snatched back her hand.

A second ring.

Kaitlan pulled out the phone and stared at it, eyes wide.

Third ring.

He expected her to be at work. There, she would answer the phone. Why was she afraid to answer? He *didn't* do this.

Kaitlan flipped the phone open, willing herself to sound calm. "Craig?"

"Hi. You sound out of breath."

And he sounded ... not right. Tight-throated.

"Oh." She laughed, gripping the edge of the table. "I was just coming out of the bathroom at the back of the shop and somebody said my cell was ringing."

Her eyes squeezed shut. Why had she lied?

Silence. "Really." Craig's voice lowered, heavy with suspicion. Like he *knew*.

Kaitlan stilled, that deep hole inside her widening. *No. This can't be.*

"I was just calling to check on you," he said.

During his shift? He'd never done that before.

"Oh. Well. Thanks." She swallowed. "Were you ... at my apartment today?"

"No." The word was clipped, hard. "Why do you ask?"

Kaitlan's heart flipped over. Her eyes fastened on his pen lying on the table. "No reason."

"Then why do you sound so funny?"

Why do you?

Her mind thrashed for something to say. "Your day going okay?"

"Yeah." Defensiveness crept into his tone. "Just out patrolling, giving speeding tickets. Pretty boring."

Out patrolling. Alone. He could have been here, done this, and nobody would know. Besides, the tone of his voice. Denying he'd been here. He was *lying*.

She picked up his pen and gripped it hard. "Oh. Sorry to hear that."

No response. Kaitlan could hear Craig breathing over the line, like he was waiting for her to admit she wasn't at work.

But how would he know that?

Her fingers curled around the phone. "Are we still on for tonight?"

"Why wouldn't we be?" he snapped. "You know I'd never miss my sister's birthday."

He'd never talked to her like that before. "Sure. Of course." No way could she face that dinner. Like she could eat.

His pen burned in her fingers. She tossed it down.

"Please be ready on time." His tone evened a little. "You know Dad hates it when people are late."

"Okay, I will. 'Bye."

Kaitlan threw the phone into her purse and fell into a chair. She dropped her head in her hands.

He'd just called to say hi. She'd imagined his suspicion.

No, you didn't. He'd called to make sure she was at work.

But this was crazy. Craig was no killer. She would find another explanation.

Please, God.

Kaitlan had experienced way too much deceit in the past. She knew it could look you in the face and swear it was one thing when it was totally another. Hadn't she manipulated enough people herself?

But Craig couldn't be so deeply deceptive. Never him.

She needed to call 911.

Kaitlan retrieved her phone once more and stared at the keypad. She clutched the cell until her knuckles went white. In her mind rose Chief Russ Barlow's wide, flat-nosed face—on the day they'd first met.

"So you're Kaitlan." The chief had slapped a protective hand on his son's shoulder. "Craig's told me a lot about you."

Kaitlan flicked a nervous look at Craig. Just *how* much? "He's told me a lot about you, too, sir. Good things."

"Well." Chief Barlow had given her a half smile that somehow managed to chill her. "Be good to my son now, hear? I'm watching out for him."

Kaitlan bit her lip. How could she call 911 now? She'd just lied to a police officer. How to explain that? And what would they say when she tried to tell them Craig had been here?

If he really did this, no one would ever believe her.

She threw a glance over her shoulder, as if the dead body might lurch through the doorway any minute. Craig could be patrolling—close. What if he was on his way back here *right now*?

Panic took over her body. She had to get out of here.

Kaitlan threw the cell in her purse, shoved to her feet, and ran for the door. There she pulled up short. Eased the door open and stuck her head out. Checked right and left.

No one.

Heart slamming around in her chest, Kaitlan slipped outside and into her car. She started the engine, thrust the car in reverse to turn around, and flew down the driveway.

Two minutes later she was headed up Freeway 280, on the run to nowhere. Who could she possibly go to for help?

Images of the woman's silently screaming face pulsed in her head.

She'd left a *body* in her apartment. She should call 911.

But—Craig. His pen on her floor. His detailed knowledge of the previous murders. The black silk fabric with green stripes.

Craig and his strange phone call. Craig and his continual intense focus on that suspense manuscript of his. Writing scenes about his fictional killer in *first person* . . .

Manuscript. The word shot light through Kaitlan's dimmed brain.

There was one place she could go.

Kaitlan blinked at her surroundings. She wasn't that far. In fact she'd automatically headed north from her apartment, as if in her subconscious she already knew. North toward the one person who had spent his life immersed in crime, who could see through this horrific puzzle and tell her what to do.

If he didn't meet her on his porch with a shotgun.

OBSESSION

five

She died so easily.

Sure she fought. And I had a time getting her where I wanted. But when it comes right down to choking the life out of them, I've learned something. The line between death and life—that final breath—is painfully thin.

Frightening, this reality.

As before, the days leading up to it were intense. I was going about my business, then wham. Days ago the fabric called to me once more. It called with a need—no, a *yearning*. Reached deep down in the pit of me, rattling my chains.

This time I knew it would be different. And I couldn't ignore it for long.

The call never comes at a good time. As if the fabric cares I have enough worries already. Family, friends, job. It seems to feed on these things, my daily challenges a sugar-water IV into its vein.

The yearning wouldn't die. I wanted to break something.

Where did this thing inside me come from?

The killers in movies are too self-assured. Too well informed. They all seem to understand the "why."

I understand nothing.

Logistical concerns terrify me. All the forensic details. DNA and fingerprints. A certain rare leaf stuck in my shoe. Victim's hair on my shirt. These things can convict you. Send you to jail for life. Or death.

I should know.

In the past few days the yearning became unbearable. I would explode if I did not let it out.

When I was a kid I caught the end of my finger in a collapsible chair. It hurt so bad I thought I was going out of my mind. My mom finally took me to the doctor. He punctured a hole in my fingernail. Instantly all the pressure from the swelling was released. It was amazing. The pain went away so fast. I could function. I could breathe.

And that, you see, is what killing is like. A heart-swelling, mind-blowing *relief.* I can breathe again.

Usually.

But not this time.

six

Kaitlan exited Freeway 280 onto Highway 92 west. She drove over the reservoir and wound up into the mountains. At Highway 35 she turned left and within a half-mile came to her grandfather's long private driveway. Guarding it was the heavy black gate she knew so well—a symbol of what her grandfather had become. Removed from the world. Not needing anybody.

During the drive she'd tried to convince herself Craig knew nothing about the murder.

So he sometimes had moody moments. Kaitlan of all people should understand. Craig's mother had walked away from the family when he was eight and his sister was six. Craig's life had fallen apart. His father almost had a nervous breakdown. Even now Craig harbored a lot of bitterness. Kaitlan had seen it burning in his eyes when he told her the story. A burning so like her own.

But his odd phone call. The hard, suspicious tone in his voice. He'd never talked to her like that. And Craig had a key to her place.

Plus he knew about the fabric.

Most of all, his pen on her floor.

"Were you at my apartment today?"

"No."

Kaitlan eased her car even with the gate's electric keypad and put the Corolla in park. What was the code?

The numbers wouldn't come. Too many years had passed.

Didn't matter, he'd probably changed it by now anyway—to keep *her* out.

She gazed at the gate. Beyond it the driveway climbed and curled through rolling green until it disappeared. Far up on the hill sat her grandfather's mansion, looking huge and haunted, just the way he wanted it. White with black shutters, a dark roof. Porches and gables that loomed mysterious and chilling, like Darell Brooke himself. A rambling north and south wing, each of their hallways over forty feet long.

Her grandfather was hard-nosed and selfish. His career, never his family, was his first love. Before Kaitlan was born he'd driven his long-suffering wife, Gretchen, to leave him. Three years after the divorce she died from a brain tumor. Their daughter, Kaitlan's mom, had soaked up Darell Brooke's selfishness like a sponge. At eighteen Sarah Brooke had changed her last name to Sering, distancing herself from her father. Her own single parenting of Kaitlan was cold and full of resentment. Kaitlan's rebellious early teen years gave Sarah the excuse she wanted to cut ties. When Kaitlan was fourteen her mother moved to England, leaving her to live with her grandfather.

What a disaster that turned out to be.

Kaitlan rolled down her window and focused on the intercom button. She couldn't bring herself to push it.

He would never let her in. Six years ago he'd kicked her out of his life, and when Darell Brooke made a decree, he meant it. And she had to admit she'd deserved it. Since then she hadn't contacted him, not even after his accident. Kaitlan had wanted to. She'd been worried about him. And she *needed* a family. So many times she'd picked up the phone only to lose courage. Truth was, she couldn't bear to hear his voice full of hatred and condemnation.

Kaitlan ran her fingers through her hair. She didn't even know what shape her grandfather was in. After two years the broken bones should be healed. But she'd heard all that publicity about how he'd lost his huge contract because he couldn't write. What if he wasn't any better?

She should just turn around and call the police.

Yeah, try to explain to Chief Barlow why a dead body was in her apartment—and she'd fled the scene. She'd never gotten the feeling he liked her all that much in the first place. He was too protective of Craig.

What if she was arrested? How was she supposed to prove she'd had nothing to do with this? The only other plausible person was Craig. And who'd believe *that*?

She could go to prison for years.

Kaitlan leaned her head on the steering wheel. She couldn't imagine going back to jail. It was a *horrible* place. Six months behind bars on a drug charge had been enough for her entire lifetime.

What about the baby? The thought pierced her soul. She'd have to give up her daughter. (Certainly it was a girl.)

No. Never. Her daughter would have a family.

Kaitlan bit her lip and gazed at the intercom button. She could just run. Go back to L.A. and hide out. The old friends were no doubt there—those who were still alive.

She might as well crawl into a black cave and die.

Her stomach flip-flopped. If anything had been in it, she'd have thrown up again.

She reached her arm out the window. This was the best choice. For her, for her baby.

Kaitlan punched the button.

seven

Margaret had just finished topping the chicken casserole with herbed bread crumbs when the gate bell sounded.

She stilled. Who was down there? The gardener? He came yesterday. A delivery? She hadn't ordered anything.

Quickly she rinsed her hands, drying them on a paper towel as she hurried to the gate intercom in the large front hall. She pushed down a silver button. Once she let go, for half a minute the visitor's response would be automatically picked up.

"Yes?"

Margaret heard vague noises of the outdoors. The distant zing of car tires against the highway. A bird chirping.

"Oh. Hi." Cautious relief tinged a female voice, as if a dreaded encounter had been postponed. "This is Kaitlan. I need—I'm here to see my grandfather."

Kaitlan?

Oh. *My.*

Margaret's chest prickled with heat. She so disliked confrontation. And if she let Kaitlan in, there would surely be one. D. would have a fit.

She listened for sound from the man. Was he in his office?

Her finger pushed the button. "Kaitlan. What a surprise."

A nonresponse, but it bought her a few seconds. *God, what should I do?* The estranged granddaughter had finally come. She and D. might have a yelling match, but maybe after they calmed down they could begin to reconnect ...

Talk about wishful thinking. The girl was a drug addict.

"Please." The voice caught. "Is this Margaret? Please let me in. I *have* to see him."

Protectiveness rose in Margaret. D. was as stubborn and irascible as a man could be, but he'd lived through so much. After Gretchen divorced him, he'd never been the same. Her death dealt another crushing blow, one that pummeled guilt so deeply into D. that he couldn't look at it, couldn't live with it. His only defense had been anger.

Margaret had prayed for his heart to be softened.

"What do you need, Kaitlan? Perhaps I can help you?"

A half sob filtered through the intercom. "No, you can't. Please, Margaret."

"Do you need money? Is that it?"

"I don't need money! I don't do drugs anymore, if that's what you're thinking. I've been clean for two years. Margaret, I have no family. I want to make things right. I can't *do* that if you won't let me in."

From down the hall, Margaret heard the distinctive sound of D.'s cane approaching.

Indecision froze her. Was this finally his chance to heal the rift with Kaitlan? What a change that could make in D.'s depressing life. Or was it a ruse on Kaitlan's part, merely to manipulate drug money out of him? Steal from him again?

"Who is that?" D. barked, his expression dark. The tension in his shoulders, that edge in his voice signaled his suspicions—and that he'd better be wrong. "What's going on?"

Margaret turned toward him, her finger sliding to the "gate open" button, almost of its own accord. She pushed in and held. Through the intercom, she heard the clank of the heavy gate responding.

With a deep breath Margaret prepared herself for the wrath of the King of Suspense. "It's your granddaughter."

eight

Kaitlan could hear him roaring before the front door opened. She stood weak-ankled on her grandfather's porch, clutching her resolve as tightly as the purse in her hands.

Her grandfather's shouts and curses blasted through the thick wood. "What did you let her in for? I'm not seeing her, understand? You can just send her right back to the streets where she belongs!"

A hard thump against the floor. "Never mind; I'll tell her myself!"

Footsteps and more thumping—just beyond the door. Kaitlan could feel his presence mere feet away.

She steeled herself.

A memory rushed at Kaitlan—herself at ten, peeking into her grandfather's office. He'd been hunched over his keyboard, typing like mad and muttering to himself. She just wanted to talk to him. She knew he was famous. People said so. They said it almost breathlessly, like they couldn't believe she was related to him. Kaitlan was so proud of him. It took a long time for her to get her courage up. Finally she whispered, "Grandfather?" He jerked up straight like somebody jammed a rod through his spine. He swung around, thick brows mashed together in a fierce frown. "*Don't* bother me, can't you see I'm *working*?" He shooed her away with a hard swipe of his hand. Kaitlan had melted back, eyes burning. She never tried that again.

On the porch Kaitlan heard the click of a handle. The front door flung open.

Darell Brooke glared at her, his wild gray brows knitted, gnarled hands on a cane. His cheeks were wizened and hollowed. And his shoulders—not straight and proud like she remembered. Now they hunched like an old man's.

Kaitlan felt shock flit across her face. This couldn't be her grandfather.

"I told you I never wanted to see you again!" His long bony fingers grasped the door, ready to slam it shut. "Now get out of here!"

Kaitlan flung herself across the threshold.

She pressed against the wall, chest heaving, hardly knowing how she'd gotten there. To her right spread the wide entrance to the TV room.

Her grandfather's head rotated toward her like a buzzard following prey. The sheer hatred on his face. His cold eyes and twisted mouth. Darell Brooke looked meaner than ever. Kaitlan tried to speak. Nothing came out.

She glanced past him at Margaret, some five feet back. Anxiety crisscrossed the woman's face, her hands tightly clutched to her neck.

Kaitlan's grandfather flung a hand toward the porch. "How dare you enter this house! Get out!"

The old grief stirred in Kaitlan. Her mind flashed on nights of sleeping in doorways, wondering how she'd sunk so low. Her hard jail cot. How she'd wished with all her might for a family.

"Please. I'm just here to talk to you."

"Talk?" He sneered. "We talked six years ago. You showed up here, so repentant after running away, remember? I let you in. And the minute I turned my back, you stole from me."

His gold Rolex watch—the special gift Kaitlan's grandmother had given him in celebration of his first number-one bestseller. Kaitlan knew that watch meant the world to him, especially after Grandmother died. She'd stolen it anyway.

Spittle flew from his lips. "A twenty-five-thousand-dollar watch. How much did you get when you pawned it, huh? Five hundred? Enough for one lowly fix?"

"I didn't ... I was wrong. But I'm different now. I'm clean. I have a new life—"

"That's what you said last time."

Kaitlan's mouth snapped shut. It was true. Cold-blooded manipulation then earned her no trust now.

Margaret took a step forward. "Maybe if you just—"

"Shut up, Margaret."

Her head jerked as if she'd been slapped.

Darell Brooke's eyes bored into Kaitlan. "You've got fifteen seconds. Either you leave or I call the police."

"No!" Kaitlan flung out her hands. Her purse dropped to the floor. "You can't. I need your help, *please*. They'll never believe me. I came home and found a dead woman on my bed. Strangled. With a piece of black fabric with green stripes. And I'm afraid my boyfriend did it. But he's a cop and the son of Russ Barlow, Gayner chief of police. No way will the police believe he's responsible. They'll arrest me for it; I know they will." She leaned toward her grandfather. "You have to tell me what to do. You know crime; you've written suspense—all of a sudden I'm *living* it!"

Margaret's mouth hung open.

Kaitlan sagged against the wall, drained of energy. Her heart thudded in her ears.

Her grandfather stared at her, emotions moving across his face. Shock ... disbelief ... suspicion. His eyes widened then narrowed, and his lips trembled. For the first time in her life, Kaitlan saw her grandfather at a loss for words.

No one moved. Outside a bird chirped. In some distant room a fluorescent light hummed.

Her grandfather's neck arched like a snake ready to strike. "How dare you." He shoved the front door closed. The slam rattled Kaitlan's bones. He breathed in long and hard, nostrils flaring. "How did you do it? How?"

Kaitlan darted a glance at Margaret—*what's he talking about?* Margaret lifted a shoulder.

Darell Brooke pushed his grizzled face into Kaitlan's. His lips pulled back and his cheeks were mottled. She could smell his musty breath. "Answer me."

"I ... don't know what you mean."

"The cloth!" He spat the word. "How did you know? What have you done—hacked into my computer? Not enough to steal my watch, now you want to take my work?"

Kaitlan threw another helpless look at Margaret. The woman's face creased in sadness. She closed her eyes and shook her head.

Oh. *No.*

The horrible truth sank into Kaitlan. Her grandfather was talking nonsense. Forget not being able to write—the King of Suspense was now nothing but a mindless old man.

Kaitlan's heart folded up. She couldn't bear this. She wanted to run out the door and forget she'd ever come.

"Kaitlan!" He shook his fist at her. "Answer me. How did you know?"

She licked her lips. "I'm sorry, I don't know what you're talking about."

"Don't lie to me!" He reared back, cheeks flaming. "I see what you're doing. You're playing with me. You want me put away so you can get my money." He creaked around toward Margaret. "And you're in on it. The two of you, planning against me. *You* told her about the cloth. You both want me to believe I've lost my mind."

Margaret stuck her palms out. "Now calm down, D. You don't know what you're—"

"I know exactly what I'm saying! Strangled, using black fabric with green stripes—that's what!" A ragged vein popped out on his neck. "I'm calling my lawyer. I'll tell him you two are conspiring." He jabbed his finger from Margaret to Kaitlan. "You won't get away with it!"

Kaitlan started to protest, but her mouth snapped closed. A tingle started down in her gut. *The cloth.* Was there something here for real? Not just the raving of an old man?

"Wait." She caught her grandfather's bony wrist. "What do you know about the fabric? All I know is—this is the third victim in Gayner it's been used on in the past year."

"Third? In a *year*?" He gaped at her, eyebrows jammed together over his nose.

"Please. Lives may depend on it. Including mine. What do you know?"

Her grandfather's forehead flattened. He pulled back and looked to Margaret. She nodded in encouragement. His eyelids flickered. In that little motion, Kaitlan saw his vulnerability. He wanted to believe them.

He straightened his shoulders. Lifting his arm from Kaitlan's grasp with all the dignity he could muster, he raised his chin, surveying her with the haughty expression she knew so well. For a moment he looked like the grandfather she remembered.

Relief burst in Kaitlan's chest.

"The fabric you spoke of. Silk, is it?"

Her eyes widened. "Yes."

He nodded. "Of course. Because it's straight from the manuscript I've been working on for the past year. My antagonist's MO—the crazed killer who hears the dead knocking. He strangles his victims using a black silk cloth with green stripes."

UNTITLED MS.

nine

The fabric silks across Hugh's palms like
the soft kiss of a lover.

Black with green stripes. An alluring
sight, fraught with familiarity. He balls
the long, enticing strip, raises it to his
nostrils. Breathes in deeply. The scent of
promise and lust, joy and betrayal, ecstasy
and revenge.

The scent of death.

His eyes consume her lithe form across
the dim and crowded bar. She leans with
nonchalance against a railing, wine glass
in hand, held up and crooked toward her
bare décolletage. So casual, so cool. In a
motion of pure fluidity her left fingers
ease a strand of blonde hair from her temple. Her glossed red lips are parted, bent
in a slight smile of amusement at the story
of the hopeful male before her. Her lashes
are feathery, thick. When she laughs her
head tilts back, exposing the tan supple-
ness of her throat.

Hugh's fingers flex.

She is a goddess.

She is a witch.

No one pays the slightest attention to him, but that's the story of his life. No matter. He has learned to edit its once stuttered prose. He sits in a corner on a three-legged stool, his face and torso beyond the umbra of light. Pale white rays from an overhead lamp spill across his jeaned legs, puddling on the hardwood floor. His hands, rubbing the black and green vesture of his vengeance, rest against his chest. Hugh arches his shoulder blades against the wall, imagining the mystery his half-illumed body must surely project—should anyone notice.

No one will.

They don't see, though they seek him. They don't know, though the criminal profilers have psychoanalyzed him to the core.

The cloth brought him here. To *her*.

Whenever he lifts it from his dresser drawer, cradles it in his arms, Hugh feels the power. It electrifies his veins with desire. Always, always it sings him into the night, and he follows, captive to its siren song. Until it leads him to the one who must die.

Across the bar, for no apparent reason her head turns—and she gazes in Hugh's direction.

~~What thought made her~~
~~He stills.~~
~~Emotion wells within him.~~
~~His hands~~

~~No. Not yet~~

~~He is~~

~~A~~

~~Her~~

~~He~~

~~jjjjjjjjjjjjjjjjjj~~

ten

Darell studied his granddaughter's reaction. She may have fooled him before but not this time. He wasn't a doddering old man. He still had his wits about him.

Kaitlan's cheeks washed white. She stared at him, arms sliding up to cross against her chest. A protective gesture.

Her grandmother used to do that.

Darell's heart cramped.

Kaitlan had grown to look so much like Gretchen. She was no longer the ragged, hard-faced teenager with movements jerky from crack. Her features had softened, filled out. And she had a new confidence. Those wide-set brown eyes held light in them, even now through her fear. Her shoulder-length hair was lustrous, stylishly cut in layers with bangs. That upturned nose, the oval face—all Gretchen.

Don't get sucked in. She still could be a lying little thief.

Darell's fingers tightened on his cane. He set his jaw, casting a sideways glance at Margaret. No deceit on that face he knew so well. She looked completely flummoxed. He could practically hear the wheels turning in her head. She held his gaze, obviously trying to read him, trying to figure out if this was one of his "loose goose" moments.

Stupid woman.

"Your manuscript?" Kaitlan swallowed. "I don't ... what do you mean?"

He looked down his nose, surveying his granddaughter under half-hooded eyes.

No sign of her lying either.

It hit him then—a punch in the solar plexus. Breath snagged in his throat. Could this be true? A real-life killer, copycatting his newest antagonist?

The killings—she said they'd started a year ago. Just about the time he began to write.

But *how* could anyone get hold of the manuscript?

If you could even call it that. Scattered, unfinished, frustration-producing scenes was more like it.

No. A manuscript. The plot will come.

Sudden weariness blanketed Darell. This was too much; his brain couldn't hold it all. His shoulders drooped. Quickly then he caught himself and straightened as best he could. Whatever was happening here, he must remain in control.

"Kaitlan," he spoke her name harshly, "I will hear you out. But I want to sit down. Follow me into the library."

He turned and headed toward the north wing.

Behind his back he sensed the exchanged questioning looks, the bonding of females in their shared confusion. So be it. He could handle them both.

His heart fluttered. *Who has gotten hold of my manuscript?*

Darell crossed the entryway and headed toward the long hall. He passed the formal living room on his left. Ten feet from the end of the hall he turned left into his stately library.

He had chosen to meet in this room where he still reigned King. Darell Brooke novels lined the shelves—in over twenty languages and multiple formats. Hardcover, paperback, audio tape, CD, large print. Special editions, book-club issues. Not to mention an entire case of awards he'd won. On other shelves were other authors' books—classics and contemporary, some cheaply bound, some in leather. A sea of books, symbolic of the literary world in which the King of Suspense lived and moved and had his being.

Kaitlan and Margaret trailing, he thumped over to his burgundy leather armchair and lowered himself down. He sat with back straight, palms on top of his cane. So many thoughts in his head. There had to be an explanation for this.

Maybe these women *were* lying.

Was his online data storage not secure? The company declared it was. The system automatically backed up any changed files in his computer. He'd used it since before the accident with never a problem.

Heat flamed his nerves. If someone was reading his manuscript, they'd know he couldn't write.

Was it his agent? His publisher?

But what would *they* have to do with a killer?

Darell's throat ran dry. "Margaret, get me a glass of water."

She scurried off, her footsteps pattering against the floor like a nervous child's.

Kaitlan stood before him, empty handed and trembling. She'd left her purse in the hallway.

"Sit." He waved the back of his hand at her.

She sidled over to the matching couch and perched on its edge.

Margaret returned with the water, placing it on a coaster on the table beside Darell. She faded back and sat on the opposite end of the couch from Kaitlan.

"Now." Darell gave his granddaughter a stern look. "Tell me your story, and I'll decide whether or not to believe it."

She bit the inside of her cheek. "It started this afternoon when I came home early from work ..."

Time stalled for Darell as she rattled out her tale. A crazy, heart-stopping scenario that sounded as if it had been pulled from one of his novels. The young, unsuspecting woman returning to her out-of-the-way apartment. The noise outside. *Was it the cat?* Signs of an obvious intruder. A body. Victim's identity unknown. The boyfriend with a key to her place. Who knew too much. His pen on the floor.

Somewhere along the way Darell's disbelief faded. Kaitlan, with her wildly gesturing hands, the round eyes and uneven voice, was not spinning a lie. She was *reliving*.

Panic trailed down his spine. Kaitlan was indeed in terrible trouble. What if he couldn't help her? What if puzzling through the mystery lay beyond him? *Wait, slow down!* he wanted to cry as she hurried on. So many details for his mushy mind to remember.

Even so, excitement began to sing in his veins.

He gripped the arms of his chair, torso bent forward, listening for all he was worth.

"... then I looked away from the footprint toward—"

"Stop." Darell lifted his hand. "Explain the print."

"Um." Kaitlan blinked. "It was just inside the sliding door that leads to the little patio off my bedroom, like I said."

"Pointed what direction?"

"Oh. Sort of like parallel to the doorway, but not quite."

"Explain 'not quite.'"

"It was like the heel was closer to the threshold than the toes. So maybe at a ... forty-degree angle to it?" She scrunched her face. "Does that make sense?"

"How big was it?"

"Bigger than mine. I think it was Craig's."

"Left foot or right?"

She thought a minute. "Left."

Darell closed his eyes, picturing. *Forty-degree angle.* As if someone had hurried outside, then stepped his left foot back in, not intending to enter but merely leaning in to listen ...

For what?

The sound of a key in the lock?

"Grandfather?"

He grunted impatiently. "Yes, yes. Did you see an unknown car in the area?"

"No."

"And this area is pretty rural, you say."

"Well, on the edge of town. Neighbors are kind of scattered. We're backed up to woods."

Woods. Nice place to hide things. Maybe the victim's car?

"Describe the body."

Kaitlan did. Darell pulled from her every nuance. Position of the victim's arms and legs. Marks on her skin. Was she warm or cold to the touch? He shivered to hear she'd been still warm. The woman hadn't been dead long. Kaitlan might have been able to establish an alibi for time of death had the woman died much earlier. But if it was soon before she came in the door . . .

"How wide are they?" he asked.

"Huh?"

"The stripes on the cloth. Tiny? Medium? Large?"

"I don't know. Medium, I guess."

"And green."

"Yes."

"Grass green?"

Kaitlan stilled. "Yes." Her eyes swept over Margaret's face, then pulled back to Darell's. "Is all of this . . . ? I mean, is it really from your manuscript? The body and everything?"

"Not the body. Nothing about the scene. Just the cloth. But it's a perfect match. *Perfect.*"

Kaitlan's gaze roamed the library, as if searching for an answer to this madness. "Craig talks about you a lot." She looked to Darell. "You're his favorite author. He dreams of meeting you—having you look at the manuscript he's writing."

Darell tilted his head—*of course.* "Does he know you're my granddaughter?"

A pause. "No."

"*No?*"

She licked her lips. "I . . . no one knows. You and I weren't talking. I moved to this area, hoping some day . . . But I was afraid to come see you. I knew you'd throw me out. If I told my friends who I was, they'd ask questions." Kaitlan's voice lowered and she hugged herself. "Questions that would have been too painful to answer."

Margaret caught Darell's eye as if to say, see what your stubbornness has done?

Darell grimaced at Kaitlan. "How long have you lived here?"

She swallowed. "Four months."

"Four months. And you're only now coming to see me."

"I'm sorry. I should have—"

"Only because you need something."

She shook her head hard. "Not 'only.' I missed you. I want my family. Please believe that."

Darell sniffed.

Silence rang in the room.

Kaitlan lifted her hand in a helpless gesture. "Craig's writing a suspense novel. He won't let anyone read it, but I know he scribbles on it whenever he gets the chance. He told me the scenes in the killer's point of view come easily. Now I think about that and just ..." She shuddered.

How very interesting.

Darell ran his tongue behind his teeth. "When did he start writing?"

"I think about a year ago."

A year. When the first murder occurred. And when Darell started his own manuscript. As soon as Kaitlan spoke the words, he saw the revelation on her face.

Is that boy stealing my work? If Craig thought he would never recover from his injuries ... Easy thing to believe, after all the salacious news articles to that effect.

But Craig had used the fabric to kill for real.

Was he using it in his book as well?

Which came first, fiction or reality?

Darell struggled to unwind the vicious circle and found only confusion. The gears in his head gummed up as if an unseen hand squeezed glue into the cogs. His thoughts creaked and groaned.

Margaret's hand lay against her cheek. "I've heard about the murders from local news. They must have mentioned the cloth."

Kaitlan shook her head. "No. Craig said only a few people working the case know."

"The police would withhold the information in case they ever got a confession," Darell said distractedly. He still struggled with the conundrum of Craig Barlow. "Too many crazies confess to crimes they didn't commit. This way only the real killer could describe the full MO."

"Oh." Margaret frowned. "But I ..."

The puzzlement in her voice caught Darell's attention. He pierced her with a look.

Understanding poured like ice water over his head. She'd heard of the fabric. And there was only one place that could have come from.

Indignation rolled up his back. His face went hot. "You've been reading my manuscript, haven't you."

"Well, I—"

"How *dare* you!" She may as well have laid his soul bare. Checking on his damaged brain, was that it? Critiquing his ability to write. "You stay *away* from my computer."

Margaret spread her hands. "D.—"

"Do you see what you've done?"

Her eyes darted from him to Kaitlan. She shook her head.

"You told somebody about my story." Darell's voice rose. "Who was it? A friend? Some big mouth at that church you attend? What if that person told another and another—until it got to Craig Barlow? And now, thanks to your big mouth, he's imitating Leland Hugh. And three women are dead."

Margaret's face blanched white.

eleven

Yesterday I talked to a mother of two young kids. She's on drugs. Meth. Pure vileness. "Hey," I told her, "why give the dealers your money? You want to ingest poison, just mix up some bleach, ammonia, and gasoline. About as good for your system."

Her kids were put in foster care. They screamed when they were taken from their mother. I wanted to hit something.

The woman's pretty in a hardened way. She was probably once beautiful. Three months from now, if she keeps doing the methamphetamine, she'll look like death walking.

"Why?" I asked her.

"I don't know." And she started to cry.

Her words haunted me.

That night I watched local TV news, hoping to see something about the second murder. Nothing. As if it carried no importance at all. One life gone five days ago. The world turns on.

I paced around, ill at ease, restless.

In time I picked up a magazine. Read an article about a football player who'd made it to the top of his game. He couldn't stop gambling. Ended up losing his house, his wife. All that money he made—*all that money*. And it wasn't enough.

"Why?" the interviewer pressed him.

"I don't know."

Disgusted, I threw the magazine in the trash.

What is *wrong* with these people?

twelve

Darell glared daggers at Margaret. "Well?"

Slowly the color returned to her cheeks. She stared back with rank indignation. "I have not told *anyone* what you're writing."

Blood whooshed in his ears. "So you did read my manuscript."

"Only the beginning pages. I was just—"

"I know very well what you were trying to do." He threw the words at her, cold and accusing.

Kaitlan's eyes darted from him to Margaret, bottom lip drawn between her teeth.

Margaret pulled her head back and looked him square in the eye. "D., we can talk about this later. Right now you want to help Kaitlan, don't you? Then listen to me—search somewhere else. I'm not your leak."

She held his gaze until the ice flow of his anger broke up and drifted out to sea.

His thoughts floated back to Craig Barlow.

"Then he's hacked into my computer somehow. Or my online data storage. Craig has read my manuscript."

Silence throbbed. The three of them focused on the floor, across the room, as the reality settled in their minds.

Darell forced himself to regroup.

He turned to Kaitlan. "I've been out of touch with local news in the past year." All news, for that fact. Except for Googling his own name in masochistic curiosity to see what they were saying about his demise. "I've heard nothing about these murders. Are the women sexually assaulted?"

"No. The police have said that much."

Darell calculated the information.

Kaitlan thrust both hands into her hair. "Look, I can't imagine how Craig knows what you're writing. Even with so much pointing to him, I just can't believe he killed those women. He's a good person and I . . . I love him." She aimed a pleading look at Darell. "Tell me how he can be innocent. I must be missing something."

His heart squeezed. "What about your landlords? Wouldn't they also have a key to your place?"

"Yeah, the Jensons have one. But they left for Europe a week ago."

"Anyone else they might have given a key to? Family in the area?"

"Their kids are grown and live across the country. I don't know who in this area they would allow to have a key to a rented apartment."

Margaret spread her hands. "If Craig killed these women, why would he tell Kaitlan about the cloth when he's not supposed to know?"

"Don't you know anything after reading my novels, woman?" Darell shot her a withering look. "Three reasons why criminals get caught: greed, ego, or drugs. Ego—that's a big one. The criminal thinks he's smarter than everyone else. That he'll never get caught. And then he gets so full of himself he just has to talk about it."

Kaitlan closed her eyes, a sick expression on her face. "But how could Craig read your manuscript? And why would he use your writing in real life anyway?"

Darell pulled his head back. "Because *I* wrote it, that's why. I know crime. I know the psychology of killers, forensic techniques, law enforcement policies and procedures. I know motivation, the court system, attorneys, and timing and plot. Why devise your own MO when I've created the best of them?"

Kaitlan drew her top lip between her teeth and shot Margaret a nonplussed look.

They were silent for a moment. Darell's brain shuffled through the evidence. Everything pointed to Craig Barlow. Darell wished he could tell his granddaughter it wasn't so. But the truth was the truth.

If this were a novel, what would he write next?

He'd be stuck, that's what.

He needed a better sense of this killer.

"What about Craig's mother? You haven't mentioned her."

"She ran off with some other man when Craig was eight. Abandoned her kids. Craig's father ended up raising him and his sister, Hallie."

Ah. Childhood troubles. "He still have issues with that?"

"Yes, he's bitter. I don't think the pain has ever gone away."

"How old is he?"

"Twenty-five."

"How long has he been a cop?"

"Three years."

Darell's thoughts were flowing freely now. "How long have you been dating him?"

"Three months."

Darell tapped his cane. "And the last known victim was two months ago."

"Yes."

"Where was Craig at the time of that murder?"

She focused on the far wall. "I don't know. I think that one and the one before it happened at night. "

At night. So this one was an anomaly. Perhaps because he now could lure the victim to Kaitlan's rural apartment?

"What about this afternoon? Was Craig on duty?"

"Yes, patrolling. Alone in his car. Which, really, could give him time to …" Kaitlan crossed her arms and gazed at the floor.

Darell's brain picked up speed. How terrible yet fascinating this was. Exhilarating. He felt the creative juices begin to flow. It felt *good*, like the old days.

Could these real-life murders spur his faltering story?

Darell recoiled at the selfish thought. Three women dead and his granddaughter in dire trouble — and he was thinking about his need for a plot?

Still …

If he could just learn more about this real killer. Get into Craig's mind—if, indeed, he was responsible, which seemed highly likely. Manipulate him. *Catch* him—that would be the main goal. At the same time ... if Craig Barlow had used Darell Brooke's fiction to create reality, why couldn't Darell Brooke use that reality to spark his fiction?

Darell's mind hummed. What serendipity. Just think of the novel he'd get out of this. Based on real events. Imagine the publicity! He'd reclaim his reputation, climb even higher—

The story needs a twist.

The creaking gears in Darell's brain shuddered to a halt. In the racking quiet, the old emptiness rushed back.

No, no, no. Not yet.

Darell's shoulders slumped. He dropped his head low.

"What is it?" Kaitlan demanded.

He raised up, his face slack. "It's too easy."

Stunned silence. Margaret and Kaitlan exclaimed in stereo, "*Huh?*"

Darell turned a weary gaze on his granddaughter. How could he have thought for one minute this would work? "The perpetrator, the bad guy. It should never be who readers first suspect. They'll be disappointed."

Kaitlan's brow knitted. She stared at him, lips parted. Then her eyes rounded, her cheeks draining of color. "Grandfather." Her voice fell to a thick whisper. "This isn't one of your novels. This is *real.*"

The words hung in the air, heavy with sorrow and dread, as if she'd gazed into his brain and seen its flimsy barrier between clarity and confusion.

Just what did she think he was, a demented old man?

Darell drew himself up with a huff. "Of course it's real, girl, you think I don't know that?"

Kaitlan cast a pleading glance at Margaret. "It's just ... you said ..."

He puffed out his chest. "Tell me—why did you come here?"

"I thought you could—"

"Was it not because I have the keen mind, the wits to guide you?" His voice rose. "Was it not because of *who I am*? My experience, my cunning, my knowledge of psychology and crime?"

She nodded.

"And just where does that come from?" he shouted. "From writing suspense novels!"

Kaitlan bit her lip. "I'm sorry. I didn't mean ..."

Margaret tilted her head. "Now, D.—"

He threw her a steely look—*shut up*. She closed her mouth.

Kaitlan stared at her lap. A tear dropped onto her cheek, and she brushed it away. "Grandfather, please. I don't know who else to turn to. I'm scared, and ..." She raised her head, mouth trembling. "Can you tell me what to do?"

Darell's heart twinged. Even now his mind phased in and out. *Could* he logic through this puzzle?

Leland Hugh. Finding the truth here would give motivation for Leland Hugh.

Darell took a long breath and straightened. He summoned what remained of the man he had been—both for Kaitlan's sake and his own. The strong voice, the confidence. That brilliant writer who *knew* how to plot suspense. "Of course I can help you. But you must not question my decisions. You must do exactly as I say."

thirteen

Kaitlan could only nod. Yes, she'd do whatever her grandfather said. No way in her own confusion could she think straight. And she had to admit, she wanted to believe Craig was innocent. She couldn't look at the facts objectively.

Margaret shifted on her end of the couch. Kaitlan glanced at her. Margaret's shoulders were drawn in, her lips pressed. Almost like she was biting her tongue to keep quiet. Kaitlan raised her eyebrows—*what?*

The woman looked away.

Kaitlan drew a ragged breath and focused on her grandfather. "I'm running out of time. Craig's supposed to pick me up for Hallie's birthday party at six-thirty. I need to call and give him some excuse for not going. And what are we going to do about the body?"

Her grandfather rubbed his cheek with a gnarled finger. "It's too late to go to the police. Even with Craig's ties to the force, it may have worked if you'd called right away. But you fled the scene. They won't buy your explanations."

"Wait, they can't pin the murders on her." Margaret leaned forward. "The first one happened before she even moved to town."

Kaitlan's grandfather gave her a long-suffering look. "They'd say she was copycatting on this one. Craig would quickly admit he'd told her about the cloth—better that than become a suspect himself."

"Oh." Margaret's face fell.

"But I don't even know who the woman is!" Kaitlan burst.

Her grandfather scoffed. "She's in your apartment. She's dead. What more do they need?"

Kaitlan gripped the edge of the couch. "I'll prove I didn't do it. They *have* to believe me, I'm innocent!"

"Yes, you might prove it eventually. But in the meantime you'll be arrested and denied bail. You'll sit in jail for months while the newspapers parade all the 'evidence' before the public. They'll convict you before the case ever goes to trial. Is that what you want?"

Kaitlan squeezed her eyes shut and shook her head.

Her grandfather rapped his cane against the floor. He focused across the room, brow furrowed. Interminable seconds passed by . . . a full minute. Still he said nothing.

"Grandfather—"

"*Quiet!*"

Kaitlan edged back against the couch.

Her grandfather focused on the wall.

Terror wormed its way through Kaitlan's gut. Was he stumped already? Maybe he really couldn't do this. Hadn't Margaret indicated his mind wasn't so sharp? And the way he talked about all this like it was some novel . . .

Her grandfather's head snapped toward her. "I need fifteen minutes to sort this out. Get out, both of you." He shooed a hand at them.

"But—"

"Go!"

Kaitlan looked at Margaret. Together they pushed off the couch. Kaitlan's knees wobbled as she left the room.

Margaret closed the library door. "This way." She pointed with her chin.

Kaitlan followed.

The kitchen smelled like a hot oven. "Oh." Margaret made a face. "I was just putting together a casserole when you rang the bell." She crossed to a counter with purpose, as if glad for something to do. She picked up a filled square glass pan, stuck it in the oven, and set the timer. Then she turned to face Kaitlan.

Like boxers at the ropes they leaned against opposite counters, eyeing each other. The large center cooking island stood between them. Kaitlan stole a glance at the stove clock. Five-fifteen. So little time . . .

Margaret's forehead zigzagged with worry. Not good. Kaitlan ran a hand over her face. "You're wishing I'd never come."

"That's not it." Margaret stared at the floor, both hands gripping the tile counter. She sighed deeply. "Your grandfather's condition is called MTBI. Mild traumatic brain injury. It happened when his head was hit hard. The skull didn't crack, but his brain was shoved around inside. *Contre coup* trauma, they call it." Margaret shifted from one foot to the other. "He's a lot better than he used to be. For the first year he struggled with balance. His concentration was nil. No sleep—unless he took pills. Terrible depression. Then he slowly started getting better. It was a major milestone when he tried to write again. Now antidepressants are keeping his mood more level." She lifted a shoulder. "But he still can't always think clearly. It's strange how he comes in and out of it. At any time he might just ... go blank. And he gets confused. Mixes things up."

Kaitlan's chest tightened. No way could she lose this last hope. "But he's writing. He must be able to concentrate if he's writing."

Margaret shook her head. "Kaitlan, the last time I sneaked onto his computer to check, he'd done thirty pages at most. Thirty pages in an entire year. He used to complete two full books in that time. And by the way, despite his accusations, I've barely read any of that manuscript. I just wanted to see how much he'd written."

Fear rattled through Kaitlan. "Are you telling me he can't help me?"

"I don't know." Margaret gazed around the room, looking ready to cry. "He wants to."

"Wanting isn't enough." Kaitlan's voice turned off key. Nausea rolled through her stomach. This couldn't be. What had she done? If she left here with no help, with that body still lying in her apartment, she was done for.

"Well." Margaret fiddled with the neck of her blouse. "Let's see what he comes up with."

Kaitlan flung herself to the center island. "But you're telling me he may not come through! What am I supposed to do then, just go home and wait for Craig to show up? I don't have *time*, Margaret."

"But none of this makes sense. Craig couldn't really be planning to pick you up tonight. If he saw a body at your place he'd have to arrest you."

"Exactly! Maybe that's what he planned all along. What a way to throw everybody off his trail."

Where had that thought come from? Kaitlan sagged against the island, trying to breathe. Could it possibly be true? He *was* a murderer—and planned to pin this crime on her? She pictured the scene. Her coming home from work, finding the body just before he showed up. What would an honest cop do but arrest his own girlfriend?

No. Craig wouldn't, *couldn't* do that to her.

But even now she felt the Craig she knew slipping away. Too much evidence stared her in the face.

Margaret pressed her fingers to the base of her throat. "You'll just have to stay here. Hide out."

"Fine, but there's a body in my apartment!"

Margaret gave a distracted nod. "Well, I ... we'll just ..." She looked around helplessly, hands rising to her cheeks. "D. will figure it out. He will. He'll come through for you."

Let's hope so.

They waited.

Kaitlan sank into a chair at the table, head down, her mind like sludge. Margaret busied herself at the sink. After five long minutes Kaitlan pushed to her feet. "I'm going to the restroom."

In the bathroom mirror she stared at herself with horror. Hollowed cheeks, makeup smeared, fear written all over her face. Panic rose up, closing her throat. Pregnant and now this. Trapped.

This couldn't be happening. She loved Craig. She longed for him to step up and be a good father to their baby. Finally she was close to having the family she'd always wanted.

Some good it had done, pulling herself out of the gutter. Might as well go back to snorting crack.

What a stupid thought.

Still, it echoed in her head. Remember the elation? One hit and she'd forget all of this. She wouldn't even care.

Know what? She should do it. Just go back to the streets. Lose herself in the cement jungle where no one would find her. Maybe some big city across the country, where they wouldn't think to look. Atlanta. D.C. New York.

If her grandfather couldn't help, that's what she would do.

Kaitlan leaned her head against the cool glass, feeling her dreams blow away like rose petals in a fierce wind.

She'd believed she could stay clean forever. Going through the Twelve Step program, she'd found God, that "Higher Power," and clung to Him for help. She'd prayed and prayed, turned herself around. She'd thought God was giving her a second chance, bringing someone like Craig into her life.

"I messed up, God, didn't I? Are you punishing me for not going to church? For not being as close to you as I should? And now I'm pregnant—"

A knock on the door. "Kaitlan?"

She jerked up. Sweat popped out on her brow. "Yeah?"

"Your grandfather's calling for you."

"Coming."

She gazed at her reflection once more. Funny how life turned out. You work hard to make something of yourself, then *wham*, you get hit upside the head.

What's this life for, anyway? What's the point?

Kaitlan took a drink and patted cool water against her face. She opened the door, ready to descend to her fate.

fourteen

The angled footprint—that was the key. Darell felt it in his gut.

Plus, the body had still been warm. And the objects out of place in the living room—evidence that a struggle had occurred.

The noise Kaitlan heard while in her carport. The cat? Not likely. Cats didn't tend to knock into things while carrying their prey.

Darell's mind had sharpened as he wandered the library, his cane thumping. Cunning plot points now bounced around in his brain, details of the murder creating a visual in his head. He'd calculated what had happened at Kaitlan's apartment. Her boyfriend, Craig, was the perp, all right. His clean-cut police officer persona meant nothing. The most cunning killers fooled everyone around them. Darell had looked at the evidence forward and backward, and everything fit. Any homicide detective with their knowledge of the evidence would zero in on Craig Barlow.

But first they had to convince the police Kaitlan was telling the truth.

He didn't believe Craig had merely used the black and green fabric from his manuscript. To some extent Craig actually *saw* himself as Leland Hugh.

Darell had been stuck for months on Hugh's motives. Why did Hugh choose a certain victim?

Craig was going to show him why.

Darell pulled to a halt, overcome. Joy and power welled in his chest. His heart beat with new life, new confidence. He hadn't felt this like in years. Like he could sit down right now, write page after page, long into the night.

He threw his head back and laughed. Raised his fist in victory.

The King of Suspense was back.

All these years Darell Brooke had guided his protagonists to safety, even when they faced certain death. He was about to do the same for Kaitlan. He would save her from this disaster. And through saving her, he would pen the best novel he'd ever written.

Darell walked to the doorway. Even his gait felt stronger. "Margaret! Kaitlan!"

Pulse tripping, he resettled himself in the leather chair. A tremble in his fingers threatened to betray his excitement. He placed his cane on the floor, leaned back, and folded his arms.

Footsteps. They were coming.

Darell took a deep breath. He couldn't wait to call his agent, tell the man of his surge in energy. Good old Malcolm. He'd be thrilled to hear from his favorite client, Darell Brooke.

They hadn't spoken in at least a month.

fifteen

Kaitlan slumped onto the same end of the couch as before. Hopelessness and defeat sat in her chest. She felt old and heavy and dry. The only way to breathe was to put her mind on hold.

Margaret sat down, her nervous gaze on Kaitlan's grandfather.

Kaitlan looked him over. He sat back, arms folded. Very still. Except for his eyes. They bounced between her and Margaret, glimmering. Weird. His vibes reminded her of eating at his table as a little girl. He'd often be distracted, impatient, his gaze flitting about. Kaitlan knew those signs—he was in his fiction world, wanting to get back to his desk and write.

Hope flickered. Maybe his mind was functioning just fine. Maybe this would work out.

"All right," he announced. "I've looked at all the facts, examined the evidence. I know what happened."

Margaret threw Kaitlan an encouraging glance.

"Kaitlan." Her grandfather focused upon her. "Craig *is* the murderer."

The words sank through her like boulders.

"Today Craig was driven to kill—again. *Why* he murders, I don't know. We must discover the reason. But we'll get back to that."

That black hole within Kaitlan spread and gobbled up her insides until she would fall headlong into it.

"He used your apartment because he *could*. It's a quiet, out-of-the-way place to commit a murder during the day. Somehow he lured his victim there. It will be interesting to see how far away her car is discovered. He got her inside and a struggle ensued. Not a long one apparently, since only a few items were knocked around in your living room. At some point she fell on the couch, grabbing the blanket. He yanked her off, and it ended up on the floor."

No, someone else. Not Craig. Kaitlan drew goosebumped arms across her chest.

"He dragged his victim into your room, strangled her on the bed. I imagine it was over quickly. With no sexual assault, no apparent beating, he simply wants to get the job done. Which," her grandfather raised his eyebrows, "I find quite telling. These are crimes of *cold* passion rather than hot."

"What do you mean?" Kaitlan whispered.

"He kills his victims quickly and efficiently. He seems to take no warped joy in the act. Rape, you see, is an act of power and hatred against women. It has little to do with sex. Craig kills not in a rage, wielding such power, but with the quiet calculation that the woman—for some reason only his disturbed mind knows—deserves to die."

Margaret frowned. "Wouldn't he know not to rape because of the DNA evidence he'd leave behind? He *is* the police chief's son."

Kaitlan's grandfather shook his head. "Killers like this are driven by their twisted desires. Even with all they might know about crime-scene evidence, they don't think in those terms when they give way to passion. Besides, they have the ego to believe they'll never be caught."

"But ..." Kaitlan swallowed. She still couldn't grasp this. "He's been so nice to me, and I just can't ..."

Her grandfather's expression softened. "Girl, listen to me. Too often there's a mighty fine line between truth and fiction. In my stories, the murderer is always someone you'd never expect. Those stories are a reflection of the real world. How many times have you heard about a serial killer being apprehended, and everyone who knew him is shocked?"

"I know, but still ..."

"Kaitlan. *Do* you want me to save your life? Because that's what's at stake here."

She clutched her hands, running one thumb over another until it whitened. Deep inside a part of herself was shriveling up and dying.

"But the book he's writing," she blurted. "How would he ever expect to publish it? All those scenes in the killer's head. If he did this, if those scenes are true, readers from around here would *know*."

"Vanity, granddaughter. A person like this does not think of getting caught. Besides, don't believe everything he's writing is true. Or even fifty percent of it. The scenes could be predicated on his own experience and motivation for killing. But details will be masked, many completely changed. That's what I'm telling you about fiction — it arises from truth about humanity, the world, but then veers off into imagination. In reading a novel, you may form a picture of the author's worldview, but don't forget the characters are fictional."

"I just thought ... I don't know." Kaitlan tried to imagine reading Craig's manuscript. If he was a real killer, would reading his work help her understand him better or only throw her off course, since she wouldn't know what was true and what wasn't? Especially if over fifty percent turned out to be made up ...

She fisted both hands and pressed them underneath her chin. This whole thing was too awful. She couldn't grasp it.

The party. Kaitlan checked her watch. Oh, no, it was *late.* She had no time to wrestle with this.

She took a deep breath. "So what do we do about the body? And I have to call Craig. How do I keep him from coming over and 'discovering' it?"

"No."

"No, what?"

"You're not going to call him."

"I have —"

"Stop." Her grandfather raised his hand. "Listen to me. You were right about Craig's suspicious tone when he called you. He doesn't think you're coming home from work soon. He knows you found the body two and a half hours ago."

"But —"

"He knows, Kaitlan." Her grandfather leaned forward, his words coming more rapidly. "He was there when you got home. He had just killed the woman. You wonder why he left her in your apartment? The answer—it was never his plan. He heard you coming and slipped out the back. When he phoned you, he was somewhere close to your house."

"Oh!" Margaret's hand flew to her mouth.

Kaitlan's lungs swelled. "Then he'll kill me too! Why would he let me live?"

Her grandfather ignored her. "The reason he called you? He wanted to see how you'd react. What you were thinking."

"What I was *thinking?* Like—congratulations on your latest success?"

"Don't be stupid," her grandfather snapped. "He needed to know how pliable you'd be. Were you quick to suspect him, or had you already convinced yourself he could never do such a thing? And you failed his test. Had you screamed about the body in your house, he'd have come to your rescue, played the innocent. But you claimed you were still at work. You acted normal. Which immediately told him you suspected he was responsible and were too petrified of what he'd do if you let on."

Kaitlan covered her face. This couldn't be. Even though everything made so much sense. Even as she realized the sickening truth had screamed at her from the moment she'd answered that call.

Heat radiated down her limbs. One thing she could cling to. Her grandfather had figured this out while she hadn't. He *was* thinking clearly. "What am I supposed to do?"

"What time is it?"

"Um." Her body felt so flushed, so hot. "Five-forty."

"Then you'll have to hurry. You need time to fix your makeup."

"Wh-where am I going?"

"Home. You have a dinner party to attend."

She stared at him. "There's a body on my bed!"

"It'll be gone. Your place will be cleaned up, just like you left it this morning."

This was insane. "But if he knows I saw it—"

"Craig's waiting to see what you'll do. He knows you ran from your place like a scared rabbit. Believe me, the minute you were gone, he took care of all the evidence, so even if you did go to the police there'd be no proof. You failed his first test—your life depends on passing the second. You play your part now, he'll play his. As long as he believes you'll keep his secret, you'll be safe."

"Safe? Dating a *killer*?"

"D.," Margaret sounded aghast, "you can't possibly—"

"Silence!" His face darkened. He glared from Margaret to Kaitlan. "Your charade won't have to last long. Wherever he dumped the body, it will soon be found. This time he'll be caught, no matter whose son he is. Because we"—he pointed from himself to Kaitlan—"are going to flush him out. We're going to play his game, all the while planning to expose him in a way that leaves no doubt he's the killer. And no one on the force, including his father, will be able to cover for him."

"And just how are we going to do that?"

Her grandfather lifted his chin. "I haven't figured that out yet. It will come."

"It'll come." Kaitlan almost laughed. She shoved off the couch, feeling like an escaped fly told to return to the spider's web. "So while you sit here and 'figure it out,' I'm supposed to play lovebird with a maniac!"

"You got a better idea?"

"Yeah! Forget this. I go to the police right now!"

"And what are you going to say when you take them to your apartment and there's no body?"

"It'll be there. It will!"

"No, Kaitlan." His voice sharpened. "It won't. And you'll have lost all chance of credibility with the police. Plus Craig will see the need to silence you."

Kaitlan's eyes filled with tears. She swiveled toward Margaret. "Tell him I can't do this."

Margaret's mouth flopped open like a fish out of water. She spread her hands in helplessness.

Kaitlan's grandfather slid forward in his chair. "Kaitlan, go. If you don't leave right now it'll be too late."

"No, I'm not going." To even think of being alone with Craig. Letting him touch her. Kiss her ...

"Margaret, see her to the door."

"I'm not going!"

Anger flicked across her grandfather's face. He snatched his cane from the floor, fumbled to his feet. "Don't trust me above your boyfriend, do you?" His tone could have cut steel. "Think I'm a doddering old man? One who'd play with his only granddaughter's life? Fine, then. But you're not staying here. Run off again—you obviously know how to do that. But if you have an ounce of brain in your head, you'll at least return to your apartment and see if I'm right. I dare you. Go see if you find a body. If it's gone—you just might want to believe me and do what I say!"

He turned and stalked from the room.

"Oh, Lord help us," Margaret whispered.

Kaitlan stared at the floor. Her brain wouldn't work.

She had no time to think. The clock just ran out. It was either run away to the streets, not knowing the truth, or follow this crazy plan.

Nausea knifed her stomach. *The baby.*

If she fell back in with her old friends, returned to drugs, what would happen to her baby?

I dare you. See if you find a body ...

Maybe she would find it still on her bed. Maybe even now there was hope Craig didn't do this.

Mind and body numb, Kaitlan walked out of the library.

"No, don't go!" Margaret cried.

Kaitlan ignored her.

At the front door she picked up her purse.

"Wait, wait." Margaret hustled to her. "At least listen for a minute ..."

Moments later Kaitlan perched stiff-backed behind the wheel of her Corolla, gunning its engine to life.

Part 2

conspiring

She died so easily.

Sure she fought. And I had a time ge—

here I wanted. But when it comes right down to

hoking the life out of them, I've learned some-

thing. The line between death and life—that final

breath—is painfully this realit

As before, the days leading up to it re intense

about my business, then wham. Days a

more. It called wit

sixteen

Margaret stood on the porch, watching Kaitlan drive away. Her heart beat double-time, making her lightheaded. She couldn't believe this was happening.

Kaitlan had promised to call as soon as she got home. "If nothing's changed," Margaret told her, "drive right back here."

"And if the body's gone?" Kaitlan asked.

Margaret had tried to keep her voice even. "Then your grandfather will be right, won't he."

Inside the house—a slammed door. D. had walled himself in his office, seething. He hadn't even waited to see what his granddaughter would do.

Kaitlan's car disappeared around the driveway's curve. Margaret listened for the distant gears of the gate opening. Maybe that sound wouldn't come. Maybe Kaitlan would change her mind and turn around.

But no. Faintly—the metallic whir. Moments later, the clank of the gate's closing.

On wooden legs Margaret returned to the kitchen. The smell of her casserole filled the room. She idled near the center island trying to think. What to do to fill the time? Before Kaitlan arrived she'd meant to go to the store but now couldn't even remember what she needed. Soon it would be time for dinner, but she couldn't imagine eating a bite.

She pulled out a kitchen chair and fell into it. Braced her elbows on the table, her head in her hands.

Imagine if she hadn't let Kaitlan come in through the gate.

Margaret breathed into her palms, feeling the heat of her cheeks. *How* had this happened? Why did this family face one trauma after another when she'd prayed so hard for them, and for so many years?

"God, I know You see what's going on. Why don't You do something?"

Truth was, there were plenty of times when God hadn't seemed to answer her prayers. Her own life hadn't been easy either. She'd never been able to have children, as much as she and her husband, Robert, had tried. Then she lost him at forty-nine to pancreatic cancer. The Brooke family had become her own. After D.'s accident he needed full-time supervision. She gave up her house in Half Moon Bay and moved into the suite at the end of his mansion's north wing, casting off her administrative assistant role for one of caretaker and nurse. She missed having her own time, her own space. Missed editing D.'s manuscripts, keeping up with his fans. Oh, sure, some still wrote him, but for the most part, they'd fallen away. At least she was able to attend church each Sunday—and those worship times had seen her through.

"Dear Lord," Margaret whispered, "please protect Kaitlan. Please show D. what to do next. Oh, God, protect us all."

She checked the stove clock. Five-fifty. In ten minutes Kaitlan would be home. Fear gripped Margaret. She stared at the clock hands, willing them to move. How was she going to stand the waiting?

She pushed back from the table and stood. The casserole would be done in seven minutes. She still needed to make a vegetable, a salad. Set the table.

Oh, for D.'s sake she hoped he was right! What it would do to him to hear he'd figured everything wrong. He'd likely never write again.

But to wish that Kaitlan found a clean apartment, had to go to dinner with a killer ...

If something happened to Kaitlan, whether right or wrong, D. would never forgive himself.

Margaret forced herself to the refrigerator and pulled out lettuce and tomato, some green beans. She fetched other ingredients by rote and placed them on the counter.

Five minutes.

Chopping lettuce and tomato, Margaret fought back fear. Salad done, she cut ends off the green beans and poured oil into a skillet for stir frying. As the beans sizzled, Margaret's eyes glued to the clock.

Kaitlan should be home by now.

seventeen

The description captivated me.

Black silk cloth with green stripes.

I stared at the words, a flush spreading across my skin. Like the warmth of a campfire on a cold night, the way it reaches out, envelops you, and you don't want to leave, don't want to move.

Black silk. Green stripes.

I could *feel* this cloth in my hands.

The smoothness of it. Its delicate strength, one rough fingernail enough to snag a thread, ruin its perfection.

My heart thudded.

I closed my eyes and imagined the exposed neck, its fluttering pulse. My hands rose, fingers spreading, curling. Longing, *aching* for the black silk.

What was happening to me?

The last couple of months I'd been restless. I did my work, went about my business. Nobody would know. But my insides felt ... unsteady. Mushy. Like concrete trying to harden but missing some major ingredient.

My sleep had been affected too. I had vague, dark dreams of childhood, never able to remember the

details when I awoke, but filled with foreboding and
dread. Of what, I didn't know.

I sensed a blackness in the world that I hadn't
before. And somehow I understood it wasn't new, was
in fact ancient. But only now had I become aware. I
wasn't sure of my place in it. But I did know I was
fully bound to it and helpless to escape on my own.

And now—this. The black silk cloth.

A sudden yearning for it rose in me, lifting me
out of my chair. I glanced at the time. Shortly after
four. How late did fabric stores stay open?

Where *was* a fabric store?

I snatched up a phone book and checked its yellow pages. Found a shop about five miles away. I
hurried to my car and headed for it, feeling antsy
and compelled and oddly out of place in my own
neighborhood. Here was this store now so essential
to my very life, on a street I'd driven countless
times—and I'd never even noticed it before.

How strange I felt going inside. Like everyone
was looking at me, wondering what in the world I was
doing there.

I wandered the aisles, trying to take it slow,
appear normal, while my mind revved like an overpowered engine. My nerves tingled as I looked at
all that cloth, thinking *no, no, wrong, wrong.* I
saw cotton and polyester, all kinds of colors. Some
designs with stripes, even green ones. But nothing
other than the black silk would do.

It wasn't there. That whole store, with hundreds
of different designs, offering everything some seam-
stress could ever want. Except the one cloth that I
wanted. *Needed.*

The urge overpowered me, possessed me. I went home and paced the rooms, unnerved and having no idea what to do.

I found myself at the computer. All that evening I searched online for the fabric. I scoured dozens of sites, thousands of designs. The longer I looked the more desperate I became. The fabric obsessed me, taunted me, and I still *didn't know why.*

And suddenly—there it was.

Black silk. Green stripes.

"Ah!" My hand flew up from the keyboard and pressed hard against the screen. My heart beat in my throat. I wanted to climb inside the monitor, curl up with that bolt of fabric. Feel it, hear the swish of it, smell it.

I was going mad.

I ordered five yards. Express delivery.

The next two days are a blur. My life felt on hold, the world stopped on its axis, waiting for the cloth to arrive.

When it came I tore into the package, shaking, petrified at what was happening to me yet helpless to stop it. At first sight of the fabric I froze, overwhelmed at being in its presence. I reached out to touch it, afraid, so afraid it would be less than my imaginings.

The cloth was silky. Cool. Utterly mesmerizing.

I balled up a corner of it and pressed it to my nose. It had a tangy, vaguely sharp smell I hadn't expected. Exotic. Heady.

My legs trembled.

I unwrapped all five yards from the bolt and gathered them to my chest.

That night I slept with the cloth.

I told myself the next day I would be back to normal. Whatever this . . . thing was, it couldn't last. I would toss the cloth in a dumpster. A few days later I'd be laughing at my own idiocy.

Morning dawned. Time came to leave for work.

I couldn't leave the cloth.

I cut a piece of it and slipped it in my pocket.

Throughout the day whenever I was alone I pulled it out, felt it, smelled it. Luxuriated in it.

What was *happening* to me?

That night I cut a bigger piece. A strip about ten inches wide, running the fabric's width of three feet. I laid it out across the kitchen table and stared at it.

This was it. What I had longed for.

Cut this way, the fabric vibrated heat. For a minute I had the crazy idea it would self-ignite, burn up right before my eyes.

The piece seemed too big to keep in my pocket. The next morning I folded it carefully and placed it in the glove compartment of my car.

There it called to me. All day as I worked. And the next, and the next. Wooing me but keeping its secrets.

One day—soon, I hoped, or I would go completely insane—it would answer my questions.

It would tell me *why*.

eighteen

Kaitlan pulled into her carport and shut off the engine. Her brain had stayed numb all the way home. She'd driven like a total robot.

The engine ticked as she got out of the car, purse in hand. She glanced around, half expecting Craig to jump out at her. But there was no sign of him.

Wait! If Craig was here when she'd gotten home around three o'clock, where had he left his car?

Kaitlan froze.

A narrow private road formed the Jensons' east property line, leading to three houses about a half mile down. Craig could have parked there, out of Kaitlan's sight. But then how would he have gotten his victim here?

Grandfather hadn't mentioned Craig's vehicle at all. Hadn't he thought of it?

Kaitlan's hope soared. This was *huge.* If Craig had been here when she arrived unexpectedly, *where was his car?*

Why hadn't she thought of this before? It was so obvious.

If her grandfather missed it—what else had he missed? He couldn't even possibly know if Craig was the killer.

But if he wasn't, wouldn't the body still be on her bed? *Then* what would she do?

Kaitlan tried the door. Locked. As it should be.

She pulled the key from her purse and inserted it. Pushed open the door. For a moment she stood there, listening. *Feeling.*

She stepped into the kitchen, her body turning to lead. Whatever she found in the next sixty seconds was going to change her life. Either she would become the most desperate actress on earth or the most desperate fugitive.

Kaitlan put her purse on the table. She took a deep breath and turned around. Walked to the doorway into the living room.

Everything looked in perfect order.

The red throw blanket—draped over the couch. Her lamp sat on its end table. The coffee table and magazines—all as she'd left them this morning.

Panic and disbelief punched her in the stomach. She sagged against the doorway, face in her hands. Maybe she was crazy. Maybe she'd come home, nauseated and tired, and imagined the whole—

Craig's pen. She'd left it on the kitchen table.

Kaitlan whirled around. It wasn't there.

She strode back to her purse and picked it up. No pen underneath.

With a cry she dropped the purse and ran for the bedroom. She swiveled around its angled entrance.

Her bed was empty. Coverlet smoothed, pillows at the top. No strangled woman, no black fabric with green stripes.

The memory of the smell hit her—the flowery perfume mixed with urine. She lifted her face and sniffed.

No scent remained.

In a half-daze Kaitlan sidled to her bed and ran her hand across the coverlet where the woman's hips had lain.

Dry.

She placed her palms on the mattress, leaned over and breathed in. The faint smell of urine wafted up her nose.

Kaitlan jerked up and stumbled two steps backward. She stood, hands clenched, air stuttering in her throat, as panic rappelled down her spine. She wasn't crazy. That woman had been here.

And so had Craig.

Kaitlan turned toward the sliding glass door, her focus landing on the carpet. The footprint. He'd forgotten to clean it up.

She stared at it, visualizing Craig's flurry of activity as he restored the apartment, his fear of being caught. Or had he been methodical, so confident he could control her that he hadn't bothered with the print?

Maybe he thought she was too dumb to notice it.

She couldn't believe this.

She *had* to believe it.

Margaret. She and Kaitlan's grandfather would be waiting to hear what happened.

Kaitlan hurried back to the kitchen. She fumbled in her purse for her cell phone. With shaking fingers she dialed the unlisted number she'd never forgotten.

"Kaitlan?" Margaret's voice pinched.

"She's gone." Kaitlan's tone sounded flat. "Everything's in place."

Margaret sucked in a breath. The sound chilled Kaitlan's blood. It was a sound squeezed by fear.

Her grandfather had been right. Craig was a killer. Now her life depended on what she did next.

You play your charade, he'll play his.

Kaitlan's eyes bounced to the clock on the kitchen wall. Ten after six. Craig would arrive in twenty minutes.

This was *insane.*

"Gotta go, Margaret. I'll call you tonight when I get back home."

"I'll be praying for you."

"Thanks. I believe in that."

She snapped the phone shut and dropped it in her purse. With a deep breath, Kaitlan swiveled toward the bathroom to make herself presentable for her boyfriend—a man who had killed three women.

nineteen

He was right. Darell *knew* it. He was right!

Perched in his office chair, back erect, he stared at his monitor. But his mind barely registered the empty page that had once taunted him so. The angst of the past year, that gut-churning fear of a career in the dust—now stunningly behind him. The freedom he felt! How true the saying—one didn't know how heavy the burden until it was gone. His fingers weren't flying over the keys just yet. But the story would come as this true-life trauma unfolded. He need only wait and watch.

And catch this killer.

Darell crossed his arms and focused out the window. The straggly end of an oak branch pushed against the edge of the glass, its leaves trembling in the breeze. He narrowed his eyes, listening to the scratch of wood. *Skreek, skreek.* A nerve-whittling sound. One he might use in a dark and threatening climactic scene . . .

Why did Craig Barlow kill?

Darell pondered that. His gaze returned to the white of the screen—and in that second, out of nowhere, the shock of reality hit.

This wasn't a novel. This was real.

Kaitlan wasn't a character, she was his granddaughter. Her boyfriend had killed three women. And he—who knew the criminal mind—had forced her right back to the man.

What was he *thinking?*

Fear curdled Darell's blood. He sagged back in his chair, palms pressed against his chest. Air clogged his throat like mud.

He had sent his only granddaughter off to die.

How was he supposed to protect her from here? As if he could guide an aberrant criminal mind from afar.

Dread encased Darell in a blanket of metal. He put a hand to his sweating forehead. How had he allowed this to happen? Just this morning a mere fictional murderer had outwitted him. Oh, to have that back as his only problem.

Darell fumbled for his cane and pulled to his feet. "Margaret!" He thudded across the office. "Marrrgaarettt!"

The door flew open and she rushed in. "What? What is it?"

"I need ..." His arm flailed. He could barely breathe. "I need Kaitlan's cell number. Have to call her, tell her to get out of that apartment—now!"

"It's too late, D. It's six-forty. He picked her up ten minutes ago."

No. Darell shook his head until his brain rattled. "No. Not too late. We have to reach her. We have to get her *out* of there."

Margaret's cheeks paled. "Come on now, let's get you to your chair." She nudged him back toward the desk.

No, no rest in the chair. He had to move, do something!

But his body betrayed him. Sickness oozed through Darell's limbs. Like an old man he allowed himself to be propelled to the desk. He half fell into his seat, beaten and worn. Dropped his head into his hands.

"Listen to me." Margaret knelt down, pushing her face close to his. Her words came in short breaths. "You are going to help Kaitlan. You can do this, D. I believe in you." She squeezed his wrists. "You were right about the empty apartment, weren't you? Saw straight into that crazed mind. You started this; now you have to finish it."

Darell felt stripped to the soul. "But she's with him right now. She might already be dead."

"No. You read him right. He's playing the game he started. We have time to figure this out. "

"But I—"

Margaret made a furious sound in her throat. She grabbed Darell's shoulders and shook him. He ogled her in dull surprise. "Listen to me, Darell Brooke. You can't afford to lose yourself in confusion now. You have no right. This isn't about you anymore. You sent Kaitlan back there. You're in this now, and you have to finish it!"

The words sank into Darell. Down ... down until they took hold.

He sat back, spent. Blinking rapidly.

Margaret was right. He had to do this.

Darell cleared his throat. He searched within himself for the King of Suspense. What would that man do?

"I need more data," he said. "I need to know about the other two murders."

Relief fluttered across Margaret's face. "We can look up news stories online."

"You'll help?"

"Of course."

He nodded. "Okay."

Margaret stood up and backed away a few steps, still watching him — as if he might collapse any minute.

He straightened his shoulders. What did she think he was — some flighty invalid?

Darell turned to look at his computer monitor. The white page stared at him.

In all the novels he'd finished, he'd known the story's ending from the very first page. He just wasn't always quite sure how to get there. Same with Kaitlan's story, right? He knew the ending: Craig was caught. Solidly. Irrevocably. Darell just hadn't figured out how to make that happen yet.

But it would come.

It would come.

"Kaitlan promised to call when she gets back home," Margaret said.

That could be hours from now. If she made it home safely at all.

Darell's stomach growled.

He focused on the clock. Six-forty-five. Dinner was late.

"You ever going to feed me, woman?"

She blinked then almost smiled. "It's ready. Come on into the kitchen."

Darell shuffled out behind her, following the smell of baked chicken and rice. Something about that comforting scent got his mind chugging again.

This latest victim needed to be discovered. Immediately. Two victims may not be enough to connect every dot as to what commonalities they shared—and which were important. Three would be much more effective.

Besides, they needed to tie Craig to this third body.

Darell entered the kitchen and settled himself in his chair. Margaret filled a plate.

He'd been right about the body. He'd been *right*.

Darell ate without tasting, thinking of Craig. Those thoughts soon drifted to plot points ... and characters ... and his lagging manuscript.

Why did Leland Hugh kill?

twenty

Deep in the night Leland Hugh walks the town.

Darkness is his ally.

In movies and in books the dark has been unworthily portrayed. Unpredictable, ferocious, protector of evil and ugliness. The hour of vampires and witches and goblins. Hider of sins.

The velvet blackness drapes soft on the back of Hugh's neck.

This night the pavement sheens from recent rain. Lamp post light glides across asphalt as he passes, a ghost galleon in a shallow sea.

Although the air is warm, Hugh detects a whisper of coming autumn.

He traverses the central downtown street, nerves thrumming to the music of its silence. Twelve hours ago shoppers and lunchers filled these blocks, fiercely intent on their useless errands and gossip of the absurd. Their absence fills Hugh with a quiet joy. He entertains the thought of himself as sole survivor of the town,

an unbridled and brilliant founder of new
beginnings.

The world according to Leland Hugh.

He reaches an intersection and swerves
diagonally to the opposite curb.

His footsteps strike without noise.
This is an art he has perfected. Fear may
be unleashed through the shriek of power,
but nothing is as terrifying as soundless
dread.

On the other side of the street he
approaches the coffee shop where he first
saw tonight's victim. He pauses, peering
into the café's shadows. Round wood tables
and straight-backed chairs speak of the
day-timers who fill the place, the bustling
chrome galley now polished and sparse. At
the far table—*there*—she sat two days ago,
leaning over a latte in deep conversation
with a girlfriend. She was black-haired,
slender-shouldered, a small silver locket
around her neck. Full pink-glossed lips. A
trace of their color pressed into the tip of
the straw protruding from her drink.

His eyes riveted, fascinated, to that
tinted plastic. To the piece of her it had
claimed as its own.

When his gaze lifted to her face, she
glanced up and caught his stare. Her eyelids flickered, mouth curving slightly before she looked away.

Feeble female, mistaking his attention
as admiration.

Hugh smiles as he turns from the window.

Her name is Mariah. Not surprising to
Hugh, she works at a dress boutique cater-
ing to the wealthier of clientele over on
Second Avenue. Mariah is twenty-eight and
single. She lives a mere three blocks from
where Hugh now walks. Alone—in a single-
bedroom apartment on the ground floor of a
three-story building. Yesterday he slipped
through her place while she was at work,
quiet and efficient, leaving nothing to
hint of his exploration.

Her bedroom is pink. Hugh finds that
highly appropriate.

At the next curb he veers right. Two
blocks to go.

The familiar electricity in his veins
powers on.

~~Were it not for~~

~~Somewhere in the recesses~~

~~A new and strange premonition rises in
his~~

~~At sight of her place Hugh stops. Something is wrong.~~

He

twenty-
one

Wrapped in cellophane, the half dozen red roses lay on the passenger seat of Craig Barlow's convertible Mustang.

The engine roared to life. Craig backed out of his designated space at the apartment complex. Rolling through the parking lot with the car top down, he caught the scent of grilling steaks.

He wasn't the least bit hungry.

His nerves still teemed with crawling insects. Anger, disbelief, and defense twitched along his limbs, just below the surface. Look at him wrong and he'd explode.

It would take every ounce of willpower he possessed to make it through his sister's party.

Containment. This was now about containment.

Craig pulled onto the street, and the cellophane crunched in the wind.

He had bought the flowers during his lunch hour. He'd never given Kaitlan flowers before. Figured it was time.

Following this afternoon's nightmare he'd nearly wrenched them apart in fury.

But no. They were right. They were good. Women liked roses.

This evening he had to keep Kaitlan unsettled. Frightened enough to keep her mouth shut.

Reaching an intersection, Craig turned right on red. Gayner was a small town. He'd reach Kaitlan's place in minutes.

She'd lied to him on the phone. He'd never, ever expected she would do that. Never expected she would so quickly finger him as the killer.

Funny how your life could be turned upside down in one wretched moment. Who he was he could be no longer. The things he used to worry about, hope for—all gone.

He'd thought he loved Kaitlan. Maybe he still did. Right now he just couldn't feel it.

But it was better this way. If the emotion came flooding back, he might waver, and that he couldn't afford.

Craig already knew what had to be done. He'd considered it and, aghast, quickly discarded the thought. When he found no alternative, it boomeranged.

But not yet. First they had a birthday party to attend. For Hallie. For her friends. So all would seem well.

After the party he'd have to do it. He'd have to take care of Kaitlan.

twenty-two

Craig arrived bearing a half dozen red roses. Looking like he sat on a razor's edge but was trying not to show it.

Kaitlan had opened the front door, skin on fire, her senses hyper-aware. Her feet were unsteady, like maneuvering the deck of a rocking ship, and her heart fluttered.

She wasn't really doing this—facing a man she could no longer deny was a killer, pretending everything was all right. She stood outside herself, looking on. Watching the movie unfold.

Craig wore khaki pants and a tucked-in blue shirt. His hair was slightly windblown, as if he'd stepped out of a modeling shot. His lips spread in that smile that used to turn her insides to mush. No more. "I brought you a present." His blue eyes held hers as he stepped over the threshold.

The same one he crossed hours ago, luring his latest victim.

Who was that woman?

"Oh. Thank you." Kaitlan took the flowers and lifted them to her nose. "They're so pretty."

The smell of perfume and urine.

Kaitlan's eyes bounced to Craig's. He surveyed her like a sculptor studying a flawed creation. The look laid her bare.

These flowers were no present. They were a bribe.

The thought was so insane. Roses—for keeping quiet about a *dead woman*?

Something flicked across Craig's face. His eyes narrowed, but his ever-dazzling smile remained. "You look good."

"Thank you."

Kaitlan couldn't even remember getting ready. Somehow she'd found herself in beige pants and a short-sleeved coral blouse.

Maybe this was all a dream.

"I'll just ... put these in some water." Kaitlan scurried into the kitchen, feeling his eyes on her back and his shadow at her heels. She didn't like him behind her but couldn't let him see her fear. She fought not to turn around.

Kaitlan fetched a tall glass from a cabinet. At the sink, the running water sounded so loud. Her fingers shook as she slid the rose stems into their holder.

Craig moved in behind her and put both hands on her shoulders.

Kaitlan turned to ice.

She caught herself, then forced her body into motion. *You play your part, he'll play his.*

Kaitlan turned off the tap and set the flowers on the cabinet. She turned around. Craig's fingers slid toward her neck with intimacy, one thumb coming to rest at the base of her throat.

Her heart nearly stopped.

His head tilted, his eyes filling with suspicion. "You love me, don't you?"

"I ... of course." Kaitlan's pulse surged back to life, startling her veins with heat.

His hands pressed against her skin. Dizziness swirled in Kaitlan's head.

"Then why did you lie to me?" Craig's voice lowered.

"What do you mean?"

"Don't play with me, Kaitlan. You told me you were at work when I called. You weren't."

At any other time, with any other guy she would have stood up for herself, given it right back to him. *And just what were you doing checking up on me?* Now she trembled like a trapped bird.

"Oh?" She forced a little smile. "How'd you know that?"

He slapped her.

Kaitlan's head ricocheted back. Her left cheek blazed with the sting of a hundred fire ants. She stared at Craig, mouth open, shock glazing her brain. He'd never hit her before. Had never come anywhere close.

Her hand floated up to her face, tears biting her eyes.

"*Don't*" — his forefinger jabbed at her, stiff and full of fury — "*ever* lie to me. Understand?"

Her head bobbed up and down. One tear slipped out of her eye.

He saw it, and the anger on his face unraveled. "Come on now." His voice gentled. "Stop crying."

Kaitlan gulped. Her hand pressed harder against her cheek.

Craig rested his weight on one leg, a hand on his hip. His breathing came unevenly. "Tell me why you lied."

He hit me, he hit me! was all Kaitlan could think. Where had this come from?

Yeah, like she should be surprised. He'd killed a woman, hadn't he? What was hitting his girlfriend compared to that?

But it wasn't supposed to be like this. Her grandfather said they were supposed to play their parts . . .

Craig pulled her hand away from her burning cheek. "I asked you a question."

"I . . ." She swallowed. "Two of my clients canceled at the last minute. And I was feeling sick. I didn't want you to worry about me, so I just . . ."

"You just decided to lie."

"Yes." Her voice squeaked. "I'm sorry."

"Because you thought I wouldn't find out?"

"I don't know. I guess I really didn't think."

They surveyed each other.

"No. Apparently you didn't."

Kaitlan's breathing shallowed. Was he going to hit her again?

Craig stepped back. "Time to go. We're going to be late, thanks to you. Do you think you can pull it together? My father will expect us to be in a party mood."

She nodded.

He studied her with half-closed eyes. "The redness will be gone by the time we get there."

The words sounded so casual, as if he'd commented on the weather. But their meaning hit Kaitlan in the gut. The dead woman's body was gone, the mark on her cheek would be gone. All was right in Craig Barlow's world. As long as he kept her under control.

If she said a word against him ...

"Get your purse." Craig turned away. "And don't forget your present for Hallie."

Present. Kaitlan's mind flashed white. Oh, no. Had she forgotten to buy Craig's sister a birthday gift?

Hallie wouldn't care if Kaitlan didn't show up with a gift. She'd wave her hand in the air and say, "Hey, no worries. Bring me chocolate tomorrow, I'm happy." But Chief Barlow was hardly Kaitlan's greatest ally. He wouldn't like it.

"You told me you bought her a bracelet." Craig's tone sharpened. "Is it even wrapped?"

"Oh. I ... yeah. It's in my bedroom. On the dresser."

Had it been there the whole time? While that dead woman lay on her bed?

"Well, go get it. Hurry up!"

She hustled into the bedroom, telling herself to think nothing, nothing at all. Not about the sight she'd seen here just hours earlier. Or the sounds that would have filled these walls. Muffled screams, Craig's grunts as he cinched a striped cloth around the woman's neck ...

What that must feel like — to have the life choked out of you. To struggle for that last breath.

A whimper escaped Kaitlan's throat.

She spied the small wrapped box, complete with white ribbon. She grabbed it and returned to the kitchen.

Craig tilted his head. "Kaitlan, don't look so frightened."

She dropped the gift into her purse. Pushed the terror down her throat, down, down to her toes. "I'm ready."

As she slid into Craig's car, Kaitlan wondered if she'd live to see morning.

twenty-three

Seven-thirty.

Outside his office window night drew a sullen, gray blanket over the shoulders of the hills.

Darell faced his computer, belly full of casserole and salad, and his mind fairly alert. Normally he'd be fading by this time of day. But he couldn't afford to do that tonight. He had to stay awake until Kaitlan called.

As he ate dinner Margaret's words had fully taken hold of him, giving him confidence. She was right—he had no time to fret about his inabilities. Besides, he *had* been right in predicting Craig Barlow's actions. Now he needed to proceed with his instinct. Hadn't he done that many times when faced with a novel that refused to be finished?

Margaret had searched online for news articles on the two previous Gayner homicides, looking particularly for information about the victims. She'd flagged stories for him to read. Darell now opened the first, an article in the *San Jose Mercury News*.

July 19, 2008

BODY OF SECOND STRANGLED WOMAN FOUND

The body of an alleged homicide victim, the second in ten months, was discovered yesterday in Gayner near Edgewood and Cañada roads, at the town's northern border. The victim has been identified as Linda Davila, Hispanic, age thirty-one, a Redwood City resident who worked as a receptionist in the dental office of Dr. Harvin Coutz in Palo Alto.

Davila's body was found by Gayner residents Marty and Tricia Darton as they jogged a trail off Cañada Road. Gayner police and the San Mateo County coroner's office responded to the scene.

Gayner law enforcement have been tight-lipped about details of the two murders due to their ongoing investigation. In a press conference late yesterday Chief of Police Russ Barlow refused to identify specific similarities between the two murders, saying only, "We do have reason to believe they are linked."

Some Gayner residents are now demanding that Gayner police step up their efforts in solving these murders. Tina Arbuckle, president of Gayner Women's League, spoke with reporters after the press conference. "This is a small town, and we know for a fact the police department has little experience with homicides," she said. "Before these recent murders, Gayner hadn't seen a homicide in thirteen years. So why aren't Gayner police calling in other, more experienced departments for help?"

Chief Barlow responded, "That kind of talk is what happens when a citizen, who has no inside knowledge of the crimes, thinks she knows more than local law enforcement, whose members are working night and day to solve these murders. I suggest she keep quiet and let us do our work."

Contacted for his opinion, Samuel Buckman, a San Mateo County veteran homicide detective of seventeen years, noted the "telling circumstances" of both victims being killed in Gayner, population 18,000. "The Bay Area Peninsula is a huge mass of people," he said, "one town running into the next. When you get two similar homicides in a town as small as Gayner, chances are high that the perpetrator lives in the area. If I were on the Gayner force I'd be looking for a suspect in my own backyard."

First victim Tamara Strait was discovered last September in the hills on the south side of Gayner. Strait, twenty-seven, Caucasian, was a checker at the Sequoia Station Safeway in Redwood City. Recently divorced, she was new to the area, living alone in a one-bedroom apartment at Hampton Place. Strait's daughter, age five, lives with Strait's mother in Los Angeles. According to police her ex-husband, Samuel Strait, also living in the L.A. area, was questioned and determined to have been in Southern California at the time of the murder.

Linda Davila was a single mother of two children with no other family in the northern California area. The children's father, Tom Gerritson of Reno, Nevada, is being questioned today by Gayner Police.

Darell read the article twice, one hand plucking at his lip.

Victim's ages were fairly close. Varied ethnicities. Both divorced. Both mothers. Worked very different kinds of jobs in different towns.

Strait was new to the Bay Area. Was Davila?

Did they both know Craig Barlow?

That may not matter, considering Craig was a cop on patrol. He would see many women come and go from their homes and could track them with immunity.

As for his father, the man sounded like a real hothead. A police chief should keep his cool under fire. Lashing back at a concerned citizen would not win him any points with the public or media.

Darell rubbed his chin, thinking of his novels. If he placed a murder in a small town under the jurisdiction of a police force inexperienced with investigating homicides — wouldn't he have a smart police chief request help from outside sources?

Of course he would. In fact his police chief had done just that in *Sweetriver Affair.*

No, not that one. *Sideswiped.*

No, not *Sideswiped.*

What *was* the title of that novel?

Maybe *Sidetracked* ...

"Pssh," he muttered. Didn't matter.

Darell stared at the screen, trying to retrace his line of thought.

The chief.

Why would he not ask for help? Especially after the second murder.

A horrific thought surfaced. Did Chief Barlow know about his son?

Prickles hotfooted between Darell's shoulder blades — the sensation he used to feel at the rise of an unexpected plot twist. His thoughts snagged on the feeling, the excitement it generated. Yes, yes, this was right. Just what he'd do in a book!

He'd reveal the twist ... halfway through the story.

No. In the crisis/climax.

Maybe Leland Hugh was the son of a police chief.

No, too close to this real case. The son of a ... county sheriff.

Or the coroner.

107 ~ dark pursuit

A state senator.

Yes—a state senator immersed in pushing through tougher legislation on crime ...

Darell's gaze drifted out the window. Thoughts of his story swirled and dipped like leaves in a mercurial wind.

Sometime later—he didn't know how long—the gusts abruptly died. Images of Hugh, the senator, the psychiatrist plummeted to earth and stilled.

Darell blinked.

He swung his focus back to the monitor. What was ...?

The news article. He'd been reading about the Gayner homicides. The chief.

Did the man know his son was the murderer?

Darell's eyes narrowed as he considered the possibility.

Perhaps. It would explain why the chief hadn't asked for help. He didn't *want* the murders solved. As months dragged on, evidence could lie uninvestigated or even disappear. Meanwhile the chief would be trying to rein in his son.

Had anyone explored links between the victims? Or sought the origin of the black and green fabric? It could be sent to an outside lab, tests run to determine its unique makeup. From there they could discover what company made the cloth, where it was sold. Try to track down who purchased it.

Darell gazed at his keyboard, a realization dawning. For two years he'd cut himself off from the world. What a disservice to his career. Just fifteen minutes' drive away this fascinating case had been playing out for the past twelve months. Real life that could have fueled the fire of his creativity. Were novels not slices of life, reflections of the world?

Little wonder his imaginative flame had barely flickered.

Tiredness seeped into Darell's veins.

He sighed. Dinner was hitting his digestive system. He took deep breaths, scowling at his weakness. It could be hours yet before Kaitlan phoned.

If she called at all.

The hair on his arms nudged up.

He wrenched his eyes back to the screen. He must help her. He needed to concentrate. Read another article.

Before Darell's hand could click the mouse, Leland Hugh pulsed again into his thoughts. Trailed by his senator father ...

Chief Barlow ...

The fabric and a body on the bed ...

Hugh's psychiatrist ... Kaitlan ... Craig ...

Darell's brain floundered. It turned in futile circles, seeking direction. He was lost.

Darell pressed both hands to his temples and closed his eyes. *Why* had he thought he could do this?

Even in his halcyon days he'd struggled. His suspense plots were Daedalean labyrinths, fraught with red herrings and foreshadow and innuendo and assumptions, both right and wrong. Some tunnels misled readers. Others ended in truth. Theme and metaphor lay in yet other passages. Each fed off the other, creating an intricate and precarious maze. One tiny change in plot, veer two degrees instead of four—and everything shifted. Every character motive, every word and thought. How then to retrace his steps to the beginning, rewrite everything as required?

Sometimes his writing had wandered for days, searching for the silken thread of Theseus to lead it back.

Darell's head flopped to one side. His tiredness now surged on a high, dark tide.

Maybe after a good night's sleep he could think again.

But Kaitlan needed him now.

He stared at the monitor. With mouth-firming determination he clicked to a second news article. He hunched forward, fighting to read it.

The words blurred.

Darell sagged back against his chair. His gaze floated to the edge of his screen, then out the window ...

With a sigh he pushed away from his keyboard and stared dully at the soulless night.

twenty-four

They spoke little in the car.

Craig drove a souped-up blue Mustang, the final touch to the perfect picture of muscled cop with good looks and charm. Or so Kaitlan once thought. Now that picture looked mottled and ugly, acid-stained.

Her pulse skimmed.

The Mustang's top was down, and cold wind whipped hair against her tingling cheek. She tensed in the chill. Northern California was so different from L.A. When the sun set, the temperature dropped. Kaitlan gathered her hair in one hand and held it against the nape of her neck. The leather upholstery beneath her whispered a tale of horror. Had this seat been the last thing that woman's body warmed?

Kaitlan shivered.

Craig's jaw was set, his mouth a thin line. His left hand gripped the steering wheel, the right shifting with hard movements. He wouldn't look at her.

She leaned her head back against the seat rest and closed her eyes. Her stomach fluttered, and she knew the nausea would soon return. Probably about the time they sat down to eat.

Craig had *hit* her.

Kind of stupid how that had thrown her, in light of everything else she now knew about him.

Maybe abuse ran in the family. Had Craig's father mistreated his wife? Is that why she'd walked away from him and her kids?

But what kind of woman would leave her children with an abusive man?

They wound down Edgewood Road, the divide between Redwood City and San Carlos, hit Alameda and turned left. Craig's father lived in a three-bedroom white wood house in the Belmont Hills. Craig and Hallie had grown up there. Schultz's restaurant, one of the family's favorites, was in a strip mall in Belmont, less than a mile from the house. The party was being held in a private room.

Kaitlan touched her cheek. Had the redness faded?

She spotted the strip mall a few blocks up. Kaitlan dug her fingers into the seat. Everything within her wanted to jump out of the car and run away. How was she supposed to get through this party?

Kaitlan didn't know how many people would be attending. Plenty, she hoped. All the more easily she could avoid Chief Barlow.

Craig pulled into the parking lot of the mall and cut the engine. He turned toward her and nudged hair off her cheek—almost like the old Craig. "You might want to comb it."

Her fingers fumbled as she opened her purse.

He watched until she finished, then touched her shoulder and smiled—the expression that sparkled his eyes and deepened the grooves in his cheek. Pain and longing shot through Kaitlan. Was he trying to torture her? The way he looked right now, she could almost convince herself ...

She tried to smile back. It came out crooked.

Craig reached in the back seat for Hallie's present. "What'd you get her?" Kaitlan asked. She just wanted to sit here. She dreaded going into that restaurant, especially facing Chief Barlow. She'd never figured out how to read the man. If she stayed here long enough with Craig, maybe she could talk herself out of everything. Her grandfather was wrong about Craig. He was no killer, and his hand had just slipped. He hadn't really meant to hit her.

"Scrapbooking stuff. A binder and pages, plus headlines and picture frames and graphics. You know how much she's into all that."

"Oh. Yeah."

That's what a killer did on an ordinary day. Bought scrapbooking materials for his little sister's birthday.

Kaitlan's mind flashed to her grandfather. Was he figuring out what to do? She couldn't take much more of this.

They got out of the car. Craig put his arm around Kaitlan's waist as they walked toward the restaurant. An arm that had strangled a woman just hours earlier. It took every ounce of willpower Kaitlan had not to draw away.

Schultz's—odd name for an Italian eatery—smelled of garlic and olive oil. Kaitlan's stomach recoiled. The place was brightly lit, with ferns and gold metal railings and lots of glass. Shine and animated voices. Background music, too loud. Her senses overloaded. She wanted to close her eyes, stop up her ears. Most of all, get away from the smell of food.

How was she going to eat?

The host directed them into a party room at the back of the restaurant with large double doors open wide. People milled inside. Loud, laughing people.

Guided by Craig, Kaitlan walked numbly into the room.

Her eyes flicked over the group of about fifteen people. Some she didn't know. There were three friends of both Craig and Hallie from the Gayner police force—Steve Arden, Joe Babisi, and Eddie Sanchez. The Three Musketeers, Craig called them. Steve was tall, lanky, and loud. Brown hair, coarse and curly, cut short. He was the clown of every party. Or at least he tried to be. Kaitlan had wondered at his antics. It seemed like they were almost driven, as if hiding a hungry soul that craved attention.

Joe's hair was thick and dark, almost black, his body muscular. He didn't talk much and was kind of a mystery to Kaitlan. She'd tried to figure what was going on behind those thoughtful eyes. He looked at her a lot. Something told her if she wasn't dating Craig, Joe would have made a move.

What would he do if he knew Craig had hit her?

Eddie, a detective, was older, around thirty. Divorced, with three kids. He had a friendly face and quick smile, but he pulled no punches. Eddie had a way of looking you straight in the eye and saying just what he thought, good or bad.

Was he one of the investigators on the murders? Did he know about Craig?

"There you are. It's about time." Chief Barlow strode over, his hard brown eyes landing on Kaitlan. "You're late."

"I'm sorry," she said. "It's my fault."

Like frames from a movie, scenes flashed in her head. The body on her bed, the footprint, Craig's expression as he slapped her.

"You know women, Dad," Craig said lightly. "Always have to wait while they get ready."

Chief Barlow grunted. He raised his hand, holding a bottle of beer, and gestured. "Your sister's in fine form."

Hallie stood near the far wall, surrounded by chattering friends and their dates. Her pixie face was full of animation as she told a story complete with wild hand gestures. She delivered an apparent punch line, and everyone around her broke into laughter.

Kaitlan liked Hallie. She was unassuming and laid back, and loved to have fun. Much more outgoing than her brother, with a wider circle of friends. Hallie worked in a nonprofit organization as a counselor for dysfunctional families. Her clients loved her.

Craig touched Kaitlan's arm. "Let's go say hello."

"Not so fast." Chief Barlow stepped closer. She could see the faint scar across his bulldog chin, the veins in his nose. His left hand found his hip, and he leaned forward, making a point of looking down at Kaitlan. "I want to talk to her."

Her. Why wouldn't he even say her name?

Craig surveyed his father. His lips pressed, his gaze moving from Chief Barlow to Kaitlan. Animosity glinted in his eye. Craig's relationship with his father seemed complicated. On one hand they were close enough for Craig to follow in his dad's footsteps. And Kaitlan didn't doubt for a minute that the chief would turn into a raging bull to protect Craig if he had to. Lie for him, cover up for him. Kaitlan could see that.

But a part of Craig clearly resented his father.

Maybe Chief Barlow *had* abused him as a child.

On the outside Craig wasn't anything like his dad. He was reserved instead of blustery. Compliant under his dad's bossiness. Craig still grieved over his mom's leaving, while his dad hated Ellen Barlow with his whole being. At least that's what Craig had told Kaitlan. "Don't ever bring up my mom to him. Ever."

But underneath maybe father and son were just alike. Both boiling with rage over being abandoned.

"Now, Dad, don't be hard on her." Craig pressed a playful fist against his father's shoulder. "She's had a rough day." He turned and locked warning eyes with Kaitlan — *keep yourself in line.* Then he walked away.

Kaitlan faced Chief Barlow, insides trembling. She slid her purse off her shoulder and held it with both hands at her chest.

"So." He smiled — an expression that didn't reach his eyes. "How was hair styling today?"

"Fine."

He ran his tongue below his top lip. "Craig said you had a rough day. You work long hours?"

The question startled her. He'd backed into it nonchalantly enough, but . . .

"I — I had some cancellations at the last minute. Not good. I lose money when that happens."

"I see."

He looked down on her with heavy-lidded eyes. "I've been doing a little checking on you."

Her breathing hitched.

The chief sniffed, and his large nostrils flared. "Seems you've done some time. For drugs."

She should leave this party *now.* Just walk home.

The chief raised his thick finger and pointed at her. "I don't like that kind of background dating my son. You could bring him down. And I won't let that happen. He's going to be chief some day."

Kaitlan swallowed.

"Unfortunately I can't control my grown son's choices." The chief gave Kaitlan a penetrating look. "I raised him. Now he's his own man. He's going to do what he's going to do."

His gaze dumped ice in the pit of her stomach. What was he really saying?

"So I'm telling you, Kaitlan. Watch yourself. Don't *do anything*, don't *say anything* that would give Craig trouble." He thrust his head forward—and for one second fear gripped his features. "Am I making myself clear, young lady?"

Kaitlan had gone numb.

He knows.

The hard, meaningful stare screamed his story—sleepless nights, the decisions he'd made, and chances he'd taken to sweep his son's guilt under the rug.

Craig must have told his father she'd found out. Driven by the fear of being caught, he'd confessed he'd killed again—and begged his dad to help him keep her quiet ...

How easily they could. Given her history, one planted package of drugs in her car could send her away for years.

Or worse. Craig would kill her.

"Kaitlan. Answer me."

She willed full understanding into her expression. "Yes, you've made yourself clear. *Completely.*"

Chief Barlow pulled back with a slow smile of satisfaction. He nodded once and raised his bottle of beer in a toast.

"Enjoy the party."

twenty-five

My first kill happened the night of a party.

A friend of mine and his wife found out she was pregnant. They were ecstatic after trying for over three years. His wife wanted to wait to tell people until she was sure the pregnancy would last. Women always seem to be more cautious about such things than men. My friend—forget it. He wanted to tell the world. And he did.

That weekend they threw the celebration. "Everybody, come over! Bring a bottle of wine, let's celebrate!"

Of course I went. Of course I was happy for them. Bringing a baby into this world. Messed up as it is. Going to hell as it is.

You can always hope. Maybe redemption's out there somewhere.

It had been a week since I bought the fabric. I was still running on automatic, my insides twisted and waiting for . . . something.

At the party I watched his wife, knowing she shouldn't be drinking. The thought of alcohol mixing

into that tiny little baby's blood made my own boil.
You don't mess with kids. You don't want to screw
their lives up—before they're born or after. They
just might turn into something you wouldn't like.

She drank three glasses of wine.

At her first sip I told her she shouldn't. "It's
not good for the baby. All the warnings tell you not
to drink."

She grinned at me and raised her glass. "I know!
But it's only tonight. I'm *so* happy. Just one night
won't hurt."

How do you know?

After that I moved through the house like a
robot. I did everything right. Talked to people,
raised toasts to the parents-to-be. But every move
I made, every word I spoke tremored with vibrations from that new mom. Even with my back to her,
I knew where she was at all times. I *felt* her walk,
sit down on the couch, get up. I swear I could even
hear her think. When she touched her husband, I was
aware. When she leaned against the kitchen counter,
I felt the tiles under my own palms.

Every time she took a drink, it burned my
throat.

Weird, I thought, as I stood in the corner of
the living room, watching her. What was happening to
me? Since when did I feel so in tune with a *pregnant
woman*?

Only then did the realization hit me. It wasn't
the mom I identified with.

By the time I left the party—early—I wanted to
kill that new mother. Wanted to feel my hands around
her throat. Watch the life choke out of her. Wanted
to see in her eyes the regret, the guilt over her
supreme selfishness.

I drove the streets randomly, chaotically, not wanting to go home. Knowing I would only claw the walls if I did. But I didn't understand what was happening inside me. As if the cloth thing a week ago hadn't been enough. Now a ball burned in my stomach, churning, churning. Felt like the Hyde coming out of Jekyll. Memories of childhood and my mother flashed in my head. Memories of Dad. I didn't know why, didn't understand how they were connected.

It was barely ten o'clock.

I drove along the south end of town. Saw a woman coming out of a bar. Alone. No one else was in the parking lot. She vaguely resembled my friend's wife. Medium-length brown hair. About the same build, same height. A small purse slung on her shoulder. She had a haughty walk, as if saying to the world, "I'll do as I please, just see if you can stop me."

Everything in my being fastened on that woman. My hands gripped the steering wheel, my eyes glued to her. I watched her cross toward a car and get in. Throw her purse on the passenger seat.

And then I knew what I would do.

My body relaxed. I fell into a state of heightened numbness, if that makes any sense. Very aware but emotions turned off. Except for a vague anticipation in carrying out justice.

How I would go about my business I didn't know. Somehow. That night. Before the woman got home.

I would follow her.

Sometimes the world turns on its axis right. Sometimes it gives up the deserving.

The woman's car wouldn't start.

I drove up beside her and offered help. Told her who I was. Who wouldn't trust me?

"I have Triple A," she said. "I'll call for a tow truck."

"Let me take you home. You don't want to be waiting out here in the dark. Tomorrow's Sunday anyway. It's safer to take care of this in the daylight."

"Okay."

Just like that—"Okay."

She picked up her purse, locked her car doors, and slid into my passenger seat. Told me where she lived.

We talked as I drove. I asked if she had children. A young daughter, she told me.

"Oh. Who's watching her now?"

"Her grandmother."

Her grandmother. While Mom went out to bars. The ball in my stomach flamed.

"You lived here long?" I asked.

"No."

How had I known that? Instinct. Bubbling up from deep inside me.

"I know a quicker back way to your house."

I turned on a road headed west, toward the hills. Past some houses and into a rural area framed by woods.

"You sure you know where you're going?" She didn't even have the sense to be scared.

"Don't you think I would know this town?"

There's an old dirt road in that area. Teenagers used to park there until too many of them were caught on a slew of drug raids. After that word got around to avoid the place. Now on a Saturday night it was pitch dark and empty.

I turned into it, shoved my car in park, and lunged for her throat.

They say pit bulls don't let go once they bite. My fingers were like that. No matter what she did to me, they weren't about to let loose.

She fought. I rammed my head down against her chest, shielding my face from her nails. With long sleeves on, I wasn't worried about my arms.

The silence surprised me. I expected gurgles, choking. But those require air, and I gave her none. She thrashed in her seat like a mute, her only sound the rustle of her clothes.

Without warning she fell slack.

"Playing dead," a voice told me.

I squeezed even tighter. My fingers hung on until they cramped. Even then I wouldn't let go. Another thirty seconds, another minute ...

When I pulled away she slumped over like a puppet with its strings cut.

I gazed at her for a very long time. I hated what I saw.

She looked much uglier than she had in life. Worthless. I wanted her dirty body out of my car. And yet ... something. Something wasn't right.

The fabric.

That thought screamed at me, froze my limbs. My mouth unhinged. I stared at the sack of flesh, that bent neck—and I *understood.*

My life opened up before me.

I reached for the glove compartment and reverently removed the black silk cloth. Suddenly it was no longer a mystical unknown. It had become my purpose.

I ran it through my hands. Closed my eyes and smelled it.

Yes. *Yes.*

I pushed the woman's body up straight. Wound the cloth tight around her neck and tied a knot.

Sitting back, I surveyed my work.

No. Still not right.

My fingers found the fabric again. Over the knot I formed an awkward bow.

Again I pulled away and gazed, like an art critic before a painting.

Yes. This was it. Perfection. I felt it in my gut. She looked like a wrapped present. A gift. To *me*.

I smiled.

For a moment I leaned back in my seat and simply *breathed*.

Logistical details began to surface in my head. I forced the body down over the console, where it couldn't be seen by anyone else. Just in case. I drove farther into the woods. Dragged her out of the car and into the trees about a hundred feet from the dirt road.

I laid her on her back, chin tilted up. My last lingering look focused on the cloth. Even though I had more, much more, I felt sorry leaving it behind.

Under the sliver moon, I made my way back to the car and drove off.

My heart floated. Relief and joy wrapped around me like an oven-warmed blanket.

On the way home I threw the woman's purse in a dumpster behind a closed grocery store.

By the time I reached my place, I was exhausted. That night I enjoyed the best sleep I'd had in the past week. Before going to bed I felt compelled to cut another strip of the black silk.

The next day I awoke wondering if it was all a dream.

Reality hit. I had *killed*.

Why would I do that?

The fabric. It was the fabric.

On a gut level I knew this. Yet still that cloth sang to me. I couldn't imagine getting rid of it.

By noon I would talk myself out of the silly notion that it was to blame.

In my car I found a couple brown hairs. Dirt on the floor. I'd just washed and vacuumed the car the day before. I washed and vacuumed it again. Removed the vacuum bag, took it across town and threw it in a dumpster.

I worried about the parking lot. Had anyone seen me pick up the woman? But I knew it had been empty.

Leaving her car there was good. Very good. That would throw detectives off the trail. They'd think she left with someone in the bar. They'd question everyone there that night. If I were investigating, that's the first thing I'd do.

Why did I kill her?

Too much to drink at the party maybe.

No matter, it wouldn't happen again. I'd been driven beyond myself, the victim of some sinister compulsion. But no more. Now I was in charge of my own life.

The next day I went back to work feeling *normal*.

On the news that night I heard the story. A couple of hikers headed up into the hills saw a flash of color some distance off the dirt road. Something made them check it out.

No report of the most crucial detail. A bow of black silk cloth with green stripes tied around the victim's neck.

Of course I understood why.

twenty-six

As Kaitlan walked away from Chief Barlow, Craig lasered her with his eyes. Hand at her back, he steered her toward Hallie.

"Kaitlaaaan!" Hallie sang the name in that lilt of hers, flinging an arm around Kaitlan's neck. "Thanks for coming to my party!"

Hallie was tanned and athletic, with large brown eyes. Coarsely textured and straight, her hair was highlighted in varying shades of honey blonde. She'd starting coming to Kaitlan for styling two months ago. Good thing. Her cut had been all wrong for the shape of her face.

Hallie, if you knew the trouble I was in, would you help me?

"Wouldn't miss it." Kaitlan managed a smile.

Craig kissed Hallie's cheek. "Happy birthday, Sis."

Kaitlan shuddered at the thought of those lips on her own skin.

"Thanks." Hallie rolled her hand in the air. "Everybodyyyy! Does everyone know Kaitlan, the very best hairstylist *in* the world? I should know because she made me look terrific." She pushed up one side of her hair in an animated primp.

Kaitlan heard laughs and a chorus of "Hi, Kaitlans." She tried to nod to each person.

Hallie bounced her hand from one friend to the next, introducing each one. Patty from work and her husband, Mike. Sheila and Leslie, also from the counseling service. And their dates, somebody and somebody. Then seven or eight more people. Kaitlan tried to focus, but the faces and names started to run together.

"And of course my wonderful dad, who's paying for this night on the town!" Hallie picked up a glass from a nearby table and raised it high in the air.

"Hear, hear!" The others joined in her toast.

"Thank you," Chief Barlow boomed. "It's costing me a fortune, but hey. Anything for family."

He slid a look at Kaitlan.

"So go ahead, Hallie." Patty waved her fingers in the air. "You were telling us about the crazy guy at work."

"Oh, yeah." Hallie looked to Kaitlan. "This was a few years ago, and the people are long gone, so I can tell the story."

Sheila shook her head. "We counsel some of the nuttiest people."

Hallie guzzled a quick drink. "So like I was saying this woman and her husband come in, say they can't pay the bills, are always fighting about money, blah, blah. The husband says the wife's spending too much, and the wife says well maybe if he'd get a *job* ..."

Her audience laughed.

"So I say to him, 'You're not working?' 'No,' he says, 'I don't see the need.'" Hallie rolled her eyes. "Right. 'I don't see the need.' Then I turn to the wife. 'You working?' 'Yes, two jobs.' '*Two jobs?*' I point to the husband. 'And he's not doing anything?' Hubby speaks up. 'I'm doing something. I'm cutting out coupons.'"

"Oh, good grief." Eddie shook his head.

"See what I mean?" Sheila's eyebrows raised.

Hallie pushed hair off her forehead. "'Coupons,' I say. 'You mean like for the grocery store?' 'Yeah.' He looks proud. 'I save us a good twenty dollars a week.'"

She cocked her head with an "I can't believe this" expression. "'Twenty whole dollars.' I drag out the words, like—wow, you know. 'Wonder how much you'd *make* if you *worked* all week.' He looks at me like I'm crazy. 'But then I couldn't clip coupons.'" Hallie gurgled a laugh. "'Try clippin' 'em at night,' I tell him. 'Working moms do that all the time.' 'Oh,' he says, 'but I read too slow.'"

"Read too slow!" Steve guffawed.

Hallie giggled. "No, no, wait, doesn't stop there. He says, 'And my fingers are stiff, so I cut slow too.'"

Everyone howled.

"Oh, get outta here," Joe said. "I don't believe this."

"I'm telling you, it's true!" Hallie pushed his shoulder. "This is the kind of idiots we have to deal with."

"Yeah, well, try working on the police force," Chief Barlow said. "You see a few nuts there too."

Not to mention a murderer . . .

A few latecomers arrived, interrupting the conversation. People broke into smaller groups. Kaitlan didn't know where to go. She didn't want to stay near Craig, and Hallie was in too much of a party mood.

Craig gestured toward the open bar. "I'll get us some wine."

"No. Thanks, but . . . I'll take some 7UP."

He gave her a long look. "You never drink 7UP."

"My stomach's kind of queasy. Maybe that'll settle it."

Oh, no, why'd you say that?

Craig scratched his jaw, eyes still on her. Like he was looking right into her soul. "I've never known you to have stomach trouble before."

Surely he couldn't know she was pregnant. Could he?

Kaitlan went hot. *The pregnancy test kit.* He'd been in her apartment . . .

No, no wait. She'd taken the garbage out this morning.

Kaitlan suppressed a shudder. "I haven't exactly had the easiest day."

No response.

Craig moved away to get their drinks. She watched him approach the bar, trying to hear what he ordered. What if he didn't come back with 7UP? She wasn't about to drink alcohol, not now.

Joe appeared at her side, navy blue T-shirt showing off the biceps he spent every day in the gym maintaining. His block-shaped face and one-inch flat top added to the don't-mess-with-me look, but Kaitlan saw concern in his brown eyes. "You okay?" he asked.

"Yeah, sure. Why?"

"You seem a little tense."

Was she that obvious? Kaitlan glanced across the room at Chief Barlow—and their eyes met. She looked away.

"I'm fine." And she smiled. Widely.

Craig returned and handed her a glass. "7UP." He shook his head at Joe. "Girl's gone nonalcoholic on me."

Joe shrugged. "Happens to the best of us."

Was it just Kaitlan's imagination, or did she sense underlying meaning in their casual comments?

Craig—she's acting different. Should I be worried?

Joe—It's nothing, relax.

Did Joe know about Craig too?

Would he do that—protect Craig? Would Steve and Eddie?

Cops were so tight. Day in, day out, they protected each other, laid their lives on the line for each other. Hard to turn that around when one of their own became the criminal.

Waiters entered bearing platters of food. Garlic bread, pasta, chicken wings, pizza. Their smells filled the room. Kaitlan buried her nose in the glass of 7UP. As everyone else loaded their plates, she took a little salad and managed a few bites.

Conversation swirled around her—stories from the Gayner police force, Ed showing pictures of his oldest son playing soccer, Patty shaking her head over some family she'd counseled that day. Kaitlan tried to laugh in all the right places and add a comment when she could. Joe's words echoed in her head. She didn't want anyone else asking if she was okay because she just might lose it, just might not be able to play the part another minute.

She longed to go home, but the thought scared her to death. She'd be going with Craig. Alone.

If only Joe could take her.

That is, if Joe was really her friend.

Hallie announced she couldn't wait any longer to open her presents and dug in, oohing and aahing over each one. One thing about Hallie—she knew how to make a person feel special. "Oh, I *love* this bracelet!" she trilled upon opening Kaitlan's gift. Hallie stopped to put it on and held it up to sparkle blue in the light. "Thank you, girl!"

Kaitlan smiled. "You're welcome."

By nine-thirty she was exhausted from stumbling over lines, an actress on the wrong stage. Her thoughts kept returning to her grandfather. Were he and Margaret sitting by the phone, waiting for her call? Had he figured out what to do?

"Yo!" Steve whooped to Chief Barlow. "You hear what happened when Big Daddy here"—he jabbed a thumb at Ed—"took his kids camping last weekend?"

What if she couldn't call for hours? What if Craig wanted to stay at her apartment?

Chief Barlow shoved a final bit of birthday cake into his mouth, crumbs sticking to his lips. "No, but I bet I'm about to."

Kaitlan's heart tumbled. She couldn't be close to Craig, couldn't kiss him, surely couldn't sleep with him. The thought of even lying with him on her bed made her shudder. The bed, where he'd killed.

Steve guffawed. "First he couldn't get the fire going ..."

What did it matter what her grandfather came up with? Tomorrow was too late. She needed rescuing *now*.

"... then he dropped all the marshmallows in the dirt ..."

Kaitlan fled to the restroom.

She barricaded herself in a stall, leaning her forehead against the door. Six and a half hours, that was all. Her whole life had changed in six and a half hours. It seemed like an eternity. She couldn't do this.

"God," she closed her eyes, "I know I've made some mistakes. But please—help me."

She exited the stall. Standing next to a woman at the sink, she washed her hands. Kaitlan took her time until the woman left. Then she faced herself in the mirror, wondering how she'd gotten here, where she'd gone wrong. The day she'd walked out of jail she vowed to change her life. She joined a Twelve Step program and committed fully to getting clean. For a year she held two jobs, barely making it, saving every penny she could toward cosmetology school. Some days she wanted to get high so badly she nearly climbed the walls. That's when prayer helped the most. A California license required six hundred hours of school—thirteen to fourteen months if she worked real hard. Not to mention tuition of around ten thousand dollars. She applied for federal grants. Most went to single moms, but amazingly she got one. *God*, she thought.

In cosmetology school over a third of her classmates dropped out after the first four months. It was way more demanding than many of them thought—herself included. At first she found it hard to concentrate, the drugs had so messed up her brain. But slowly her head cleared. She pressed on, determined. When her old car broke down, she took the bus. When she didn't have money for the bus, she walked. No help from her mother in England, who couldn't care less. And she was too afraid to ask her grandfather.

The day she earned her license was the happiest day of her life. Moving to Gayner, finding a place to work, meeting Craig—blessings beyond belief.

Now it was all about to be taken away.

The restroom door opened. Sheila and Leslie pushed in, chattering away.

"Hi." Kaitlan forced a smile.

"Hey, Kaitlan!" They disappeared into stalls.

Straightening her shoulders, Kaitlan returned to the party and Craig.

An interminable half hour later as they prepared to leave the restaurant, Chief Barlow closed in. "Son." He shook hands with Craig. "You say goodbye to your sister?"

Resentment flicked across Craig's face. "Twice."

"Then go say goodbye to Joe."

Craig shoved his jaw forward, turned and left.

The chief leaned toward Kaitlan. "Keep yourself out of trouble now."

She gave him a tight smile.

Craig returned and put his arm around her shoulder. "We're leaving, Dad." He spoke the words flatly—*I can handle her.*

The chief gave them a mock salute. "Good seeing you both."

Craig ushered Kaitlan out the door.

As they crossed the parking lot he kept his head down, hands in his pockets. "Nice party."

"Yeah." Kaitlan hugged herself against the cold.

In the Mustang, Craig put the top up for the drive home.

Kaitlan focused out the window, watching familiar streets go by. They no longer looked friendly.

Somewhere out there lay a woman's body. Kaitlan realized she hadn't noticed if the woman wore a wedding ring. Was some husband going crazy with worry? Children?

Surely by now she'd been reported missing.

They reached Kaitlan's apartment. Her heart pounded and her limbs felt brittle. If Craig touched her she'd break apart.

Please stay in the car.

He pulled up behind her Corolla and cut the engine. "I'll see you inside."

The words hit like stones. She opened her door and got out.

Crickets' pulsing songs grated her ears. A chilling breeze lifted a strand of her hair, popping goose bumps down her arms.

The surrounding forest was so dark.

How had she ever felt safe here? The night seemed to have a thousand eyes.

Her footsteps sounded loud as she approached the door and unlocked it. Stepping inside her kitchen, she could feel Craig's looming presence at her back.

This was insanity. She never should have listened to her grandfather.

"I won't be staying," Craig said as she placed her keys and purse on the table. "Tomorrow I'm on the 6:00 a.m. shift."

Relief weakened her knees. She nodded.

"I'll just check your place out. Make sure you're safe."

Kaitlan stood like granite as he walked through the living room, into the hall. She clutched the top of a chair, the fingers of her other hand curling into her palm. *Get out, Craig, get out!* she wanted to scream. The minute he drove away she would throw what she needed into a suitcase and drive like a madwoman to her grandfather's—

"Kaitlan. Come here." He called from the door to her bedroom.

Something cold and slimy unfolded in Kaitlan's chest. For a wild moment she pictured herself tearing out the door and into the black forest.

Where she'd get maybe one hundred feet before Craig caught her. And he'd be *furious*.

"Hey! Come *here*."

If he tried to hurt her, she'd fight. She'd tell him that others knew what he'd done, and if anything happened to her, they'd go to the police.

Yeah, right. The Gayner police.

Kaitlan did the only thing she could. She walked toward the bedroom.

twenty-seven

Silence echoed through the house. A silence that mocked as Margaret waited for the phone to ring.

She had become accustomed to small noises amid the quiet. The heater kicking on in winter. A newly made ice cube falling in the freezer. The creak of a wall for who knows why, except that the house was old and perched on a hilltop where the wind whirled between ocean and bay.

Tonight Margaret heard none of these. Only the ticking, aching silence.

Dear God, protect Kaitlan.

Shortly after eight Margaret had tiptoed across the hardwood floor to D.'s office and leaned an ear against the door. No sound from within. Holding her breath she eased open the door, tensing against his sure anger at her intrusion. But she found him in his chair at the computer, legs splayed, head lolled to one side and mouth open. Sleeping.

On his monitor—a randomly rolling ball against black void.

She leaned against the door, its knob in her hand as hard as the fist of a corpse.

Through dinner, while cleaning the kitchen and mopping its floor, she'd clung to the hope that the clear mind D. had displayed with Kaitlan would remain. That given this deadline of all deadlines, he would rise above his weaknesses—because he *had* to.

How foolish she'd been.

Repelled and angered by the futility of the room, she'd shut the office door and hurried away.

Now Margaret stood in the library, facing the bookcase containing the first editions of D.'s novels. She'd been driven to this place with the sense that something here could help their situation. But what?

She scanned the ninety-nine books, shelved in order of publication. Margaret's eyes landed on *Fractions*, D.'s first in his Ben Seitz mathematician-turned-detective series. It was followed by *Division* and *Decimal Point*. Margaret's gaze skipped around then, from *Tumult* to *Ransacked*, *Perilous Hope* to *Midnight Vision*, *In the Making*, *Out of Madness*, *Last Speck of Dawn*, *Black Over Water*, *Sky Bright*, *From the Mist*. She knew them all. Many she had edited. Those written before she'd started working for D. she'd read on her own. Ninety-nine inciting incidents and story arcs and resolutions, spanning over forty years of work.

They say a writer's worldview emerges through his stories. Over the years Margaret had seen an element repeat in D.'s books. After Gretchen died it appeared even more strongly. Through symbolism and subtext throbbed what Margaret had come to call his "vain empires" doctrine, the phrase taken from her favorite passage in *Paradise Lost*. Always D.'s main characters were in one way or another bent on the dark pursuit of some obsession in their lives—only to discover that their private little empires were all in vain and brought only emptiness.

A truth about Darell Brooke himself that he could not, *would* not see.

Out of the Blue. Lights Across the Water. River's Edge.

Margaret stuck a hand in her hair. Why was she here?

On impulse she pulled out *All But Dead*, not remembering the story. She read the prologue. Oh, yes. Coal miner Ed Bramley and his nightmares, his epileptic daughter.

Margaret replaced the novel and opened a second—one of D.'s earlier works on the top shelf—and scanned the first two pages. This one she barely remembered.

Wind gusted at the windows. Margaret lifted her head to gaze into the night. The lights of Half Moon Bay dimmed, then disappeared. Fog was rolling in.

She checked the clock. Just past nine. Was Kaitlan still at the restaurant? Was she safe?

Margaret's limbs fairly trembled with tension, anticipating the phone.

A clue.

Her eyebrows raised. Yes, that was it. She was looking for a clue in one of D.'s books. Some plot point that would ignite an idea of what they should do—one he had surely forgotten. His past novels were nothing now but a jumble in his head.

Had he ever written a story about a female protagonist trapped as Kaitlan was—one who couldn't go to the police and had no evidence to present if she did . . .

Margaret slid out another novel and read the first chapter until the story surfaced in her memory.

No. Nothing here.

She lowered the book and focused out the window again, seeing only her dulled and anxious reflection. The fog now blocked out all view.

The wind had died down. The house was so very still.

Kaitlan.

This bookcase held thousands upon thousands of pages. Where to begin? It could take weeks to find what Margaret needed—if she found it at all.

She put the book back on the shelf and buffed her upper arms, chilled in the warm room of rich wood and leather.

Frustration balled in her throat. She should be moving, working, doing something. Tearing down the hill to the restaurant—did Margaret even know which one it was?—and rescuing Kaitlan. Just barge in and take her, who cared which people saw?

And what then, Margaret, after tipping your hand to Craig? What then?

She gazed at D.'s novels—the very reason Kaitlan had come to him for help in the first place. Somewhere in one of them must lay a crucial piece to this puzzle. A piece that had slipped into the milky waters below her and Darell's consciousness.

Random reading wouldn't do. She needed a systematic approach. The oldest books first. These were the least familiar.

Margaret reached for D.'s first novel on the far left of the top shelf.

twenty-eight

Kaitlan's legs felt rubbery as she walked through the kitchen. At each step her brain screamed there must be some way out of this nightmare. Something beyond this world, a rescue swooping out of the clouds . . .

Craig stood in her bedroom doorway, simmering with impatience. "Where's your vacuum cleaner?"

Vacuum cleaner? Kaitlan stared at him.

Craig gestured with his head toward the sliding glass door behind him. "Your carpet's dirty."

The footprint. Kaitlan's eyes cut toward it.

"We need to clean it up."

We.

The word sank to the depths of her. *We*—a team. Hiding evidence that could be used against him.

She could go to jail for that.

He nudged her arm. "Go get it."

Zombie-like, she turned and headed for the closet near her front door. There she pulled out her small portable vacuum. She returned to Craig.

He gave her a smug smile. "Thanks."

A realization spun through her. He'd planned this moment of entrapment.

The thought sent her back to a scene in her childhood. At the age of eight she'd been playing with a neighborhood boy when he caught a

134

moth. He stuck one of his mother's sewing needles through the moth's body and pinned it to cardboard. As it fluttered in a death dance she begged him to let it go. But he'd merely looked on, fascinated.

Now she was the moth.

Craig took the vacuum. "Go sit in the living room."

Heart scudding, she obeyed.

We.

Kaitlan perched on her couch and waited.

The vacuum surged on. She listened to the rise and fall of its whine as it pushed across the carpet. She imagined the dirt particles it was picking up, the footprint pulled apart. Obliterated.

The noise cut off. Kaitlan heard the sound of a plug pulled from a socket, the whizzing grate of the automatic cord roll-up. Craig's footsteps in the hall. A thunk of vacuum against floor. The closet door closing.

Kaitlan focused on a magazine upon her coffee table. Filling its cover — the perfect face of a laughing model. An article heading: "Six Secrets to Make Yourself Irresistible."

Craig approached. She tensed. He laid both hands on her shoulders.

Kaitlan thought she would crack in two. Right down the middle, between those hands. Between those fingers that had strangled three women.

"Thanks for helping," Craig said.

We.

"Get up, Kaitlan. Come with me into the bedroom."

She stared at the magazine. A second article — "Budget Now for Christmas."

A holiday she would never see.

Quiet despair uncoiled in her chest. The way he was doing this. Drawing it out, like he enjoyed every minute.

She stood and turned to face him, the couch as a barrier. "You going to kill me now too?"

His jaw flexed. "Just do as I say."

Her eyes teared up. "Where did this *come* from, Craig? *Why?*"

Silence.

"Does your father know?"

Anger shrank his eyes. "Leave my father out of it."

"He does, doesn't he. That's why he threatened me tonight."

"I said *leave him out of it*!" He lunged for her over the couch.

Kaitlan reared out of his reach, hit the coffee table. Almost fell.

Craig cursed. He pulled back, face darkening, and strode toward the end of the sofa.

Kaitlan turned and ran. Around the coffee table, into the kitchen. She flung herself at the door.

Craig caught her left arm at the elbow and yanked her backward.

"No!" Kaitlan writhed from his grip. She pulled toward the door with all her might, her right hand reaching, flailing for the knob, fingers almost touching—

He grasped her right shoulder and whirled her around.

Kaitlan's arms flew out, pummeled his chest. Sickly little sobs spilled from her lips. He spat curses, hands slicing the air, trying to catch her wrists.

"Stop!" Kaitlan aimed a knee at his groin.

He swiveled to one side, raked up a handful of her hair and wrenched her head toward the floor. Her body twisted in on itself. She fell forward into his waist. He gripped her shoulders hard, shoved her upright and back against the door. The knob hit her left kidney, knocking the wind clean out of her. Kaitlan gasped.

"Want to try that again, huh?" Craig pushed himself into her, breathing hard. Rage hardened his features into a face she couldn't recognize.

Kaitlan slumped in his arms and cried.

"Now you listen to me." Craig's words flattened to steel. "We are going *in the bedroom*. You can walk or I can drag you. But we are going. Got it?"

Kaitlan's world blurred. She looked down at his feet. The shoes that had left the footprint, now swept away.

Craig stepped back, still gripping her shoulders. "Go." He pushed her.

She moved.

At the angled entrance of the bedroom he shoved her forward until she could see the whole room. "Look around. Anything else that needs to be cleaned up?"

Now he wanted *her* to find lingering evidence?

Kaitlan gazed dully.

The body was gone. The bed straightened. But the smell of urine on her bedspread—that Kaitlan would keep to herself.

Craig raised an eyebrow—*well?*

"You're the cop, Craig. What are you asking me for?"

He hit her hard with the back of his hand. She reeled, fell to the carpet. Her cheek flamed with fire, slugged twice in the same night. She struggled up on one elbow, head lolling, sucking air. Craig loomed over her, legs spread apart.

"Get up."

She closed her eyes.

"Get up!" Craig kicked her side.

Slowly Kaitlan gathered both arms beneath her and pushed to her knees. She staggered to stand.

The world tipped.

Craig grabbed her chin, and Kaitlan flinched. He jerked her face to one side, examining her cheek.

In that moment a change swept over him. His fingers loosened, emotions rippling over his features like wind over water.

He let go of her. Stepped back.

"That'll bruise by tomorrow." Craig spoke the words as if he couldn't believe what he'd done. He pressed a hand to his forehead. "Okay, look. When people ask, you'll say you got up in the night to go to the bathroom and ran into the door. Got it?"

She nodded.

"Say it. Say the words."

"I got up at night to go to the bathroom and ran into the door."

"You don't sound very convincing. Say it again."

A tremor jagged down Kaitlan's spine. "I got up at night to—"

"No! Laugh first. Shrug, wave your hand in the air. *Something* to make the story believable."

Kaitlan swayed. Craig steadied her with stone fingers. "Try again."

"I can't."

"Yes, you can."

She swished her hand and forced a chilling little laugh. Reached down inside for the words he wanted to hear, but in her righteous indignation the wrong ones blurted out. "Oh, silly me. I ran into my boyfriend's fist."

She shrank back, shocked at herself.

Craig's jaw moved to one side. He took a slow, deep breath. "You think you're smarter than me? Think I can't shut you up?"

Kaitlan threw her hands up, palms out. "I'm sorry. Really. I'll say whatever you want."

His expression relaxed. Hints of the Craig she once knew softened his face. He gathered her hands in his and brought them to his chest. "Nothing needs to change between you and me. I still love you. You just have to keep quiet."

Her cheek throbbed. Kaitlan tried to draw away, but Craig wouldn't let go. The fierce control etched back into his eyes.

"Why?" she whispered. "Why did you kill them?"

His gaze drifted over her shoulder. For a drawn out moment she thought he wouldn't answer.

"I don't know."

The words writhed between them. Kaitlan couldn't breathe.

Defensiveness carved into Craig's face. "It's not going to happen again." He gripped her hands until they hurt. "You are not going to tell anyone." His gaze flicked around the room. "As you can see, there's nothing to tell."

"Where is she?"

"Who?"

139 ~ dark pursuit

"The woman on my bed, Craig."

"Gone."

"They'll find her soon, like they did the rest."

"Not this time."

"Why did you bring her here?"

"Shut up, Kaitlan."

"*Why?*"

"I said shut up!" He shoved her backward.

Kaitlan stumbled two steps and turned away from Craig. Crossing her forearms, she laid her palms on opposite shoulders. She focused out the sliding door to the black forest beyond. Was the woman buried out there?

If the body wasn't found, what could she and her grandfather do? They'd have nothing for the police.

"I'm leaving." Craig jerked her around to face him. "Tomorrow you'll go to work as normal. Tell the door story to anyone who asks about your face." His eyes narrowed. "Do you fully understand the situation you're in, Kaitlan? Telling anyone, *anyone*, will do no good. Because no one will believe you. Even if they did, they'd be as powerless as you to prove it. And then"—he pushed a finger against the base of her throat—"I'd have to take care of *both* of you, wouldn't I."

He was going to get away with this. And there wasn't a thing she could do. Her grandfather's schemes—useless.

Craig exhaled and ran a hand down his face. "Please, Kaitlan, don't even think of running away. Don't ruin *us*. If you try running, I'll have to stop you. Before you know it, you'll have a warrant on your head for drugs found in your apartment." Determination flattened his features. "That is, *if* I don't catch up to you first."

He surveyed her. "Plan on running?"

"No."

"Telling someone?"

She shook her head.

"Good girl."

Abruptly he turned away. "I'm taking your cell phone with me. And your car keys."

"No! How am I supposed to —"

"Supposed to what?" He halted in the doorway. "Call someone tonight? Go somewhere?"

If she couldn't phone her grandfather . . . "No, I wouldn't. But how do I get to work in the morning?"

"My shift starts at six. I'll drive by on patrol and give them back to you. Just for the day."

Kaitlan stared at him, picturing the face of her childhood friend as he gloated over the pinned and dying moth.

"See you then." Craig shot her a tight smile. "Sleep well."

twenty-nine

In the weeks that passed after that infamous night, my mind dulled out. Scenes of what happened after the party sank to the bottom of my memory. Not gone. Just covered by the daily issues of life. Sometimes when I fell into a masochistic mood, I'd fish out the memory, turn it over in my hand. Examine it like some disinterested onlooker, barely able to connect myself to the events.

I hid the black and green silk fabric in the bottom of a box of books in my bedroom closet. Out of sight, out of mind.

It was some months before the cloth called to me again.

One night I came across an envelope of old family pictures. Didn't even know I had them. I dumped them out on a table, started flipping through the stack.

One stabbed my attention.

I felt the pierce go right through me—even before my brain registered what I'd seen. Mouth open, unable to move, I stared at the photo. Sweat popped from my pores, chilling on my skin.

141

The picture taunted me.

Thoughts flitted and knocked through my brain. Why was I rendered so helpless at the sight of that photo? Why did it have such power over me? I couldn't find the answers, only knew the strength of the questions. This picture held the key to who I'd become, what I'd done. And it wasn't about to give up its secrets.

It was as if the thing had some ethereal power all its own. The power to lead me to the envelope, make me open it. The colors of the photo looked overbright. Greedy. They wanted more of me, and they would get it.

I racked my brain for understanding. None came.

My initial shock gave way to anger ... bitterness ... and finally, the dread of a soul inevitably bound for hell.

There would be no end to this. To what I'd become.

Strange, how I knew that just from seeing the picture. I can't explain how—and certainly still couldn't fathom the whys. But I knew.

The fist of this reality clutched me for over an hour. I paced from room to room, trying to shake it off, telling myself I could overcome. Eventually the anger returned. I never asked for this. Never expected to be some unwilling and hapless pawn. Was it my fault I was born?

What about the other people on this earth? Didn't I see scarred and struggling slobs every day? They were all around me, fish floundering on a dry beach, shriveling in the sun. If, indeed, a perfect God created the world—was this the way he intended it to be?

Something, somewhere had gone terribly wrong.

I pitched and whirled around my place, cursing God, cursing my own futile existence. Emotions built up inside me until I thought I would explode. My muscles were steel tight, heart ramming against my ribs like a frantic prisoner.

Then—just when I thought my head would burst, I found myself in my bedroom, standing before my closet.

I stared at the door. It beckoned me to open it.

I spread both hands and shook my head. Backed away.

Left the room.

Retraced my steps.

Despairing, I gazed at the door.

My hand went to its knob.

I stood there, feeling the cold, hard metal in my fingers. And a voice in my head whispered, "That's your heart. Cold and hard." But the words were oddly encouraging. They said—*you're indestructible. You can handle this.*

Next thing I knew, the door stood open.

I pushed through clothes to the back of the closet. Stooped to pick up the box.

On my bed I dumped out the contents, books scattering everywhere, some falling to the floor.

And, of course—the fabric.

It beckoned to me.

I picked it up.

The cloth radiated heat into my palms. Soothing, assuring. What an amazing, wondrous feeling! How had I left it in that box for so long? How had I lived these months without it?

Folding it three times, I wrapped it around my shoulders like a blanket. I walked around the room, feeling its lightness and warmth envelope me. This was *right*. This was *good*. Not a curse. This was *life*.

Humanity has its own calls. Out of nowhere hunger hit. I had to eat—*now*, as if that fabric heightened the mortal needs of my body. I ended up in the kitchen, slapping together a roast beef and cheese sandwich with lots of mayo, the cloth knotted around my waist.

I sat down on the couch to eat, staring out the window. Watching darkness fall.

I gulped down the sandwich, my mind entertaining strange and wild thoughts about how lucky I was. How some power in the universe had chosen to give the fabric to *me*.

Sandwich gone, I strode to the kitchen sink and washed my greasy hands, longing to touch the fabric, not wanting to dirty it.

My fingers reached to unloosen it from my waist. But at the knot, they lingered.

How fascinating. I rubbed over the knot's smooth, silky strength. Gazed down at it, marveling. How enticing the green stripes looked, taunting, teasing. Appearing only to disappear, winding in and out over the sleek black background.

Understanding came over me slowly.

A bow was too prettified. Too flimsy. Worse, it had been an afterthought. This fascinating knot could be the act itself.

New tingling warmth spread through me.

When I could stand the knot's beauty no more, I untied it and pulled the fabric from my body. I bunched it to my chest, stroking.

Preparations needed to be made.

From a kitchen drawer I pulled a pair of scissors. Cut a ten-inch strip of the cloth.

Folding the strip, I smelled its silky scent. I headed out to put it in the glove box of my car.

Just outside the door, I hesitated. Logistics and details rolled through my mind.

Back inside, I pulled a pair of leather gloves off the shelf of the coat closet. These I placed in my glove box along with the strip of fabric.

Even as I returned to the kitchen I *felt* that cloth in the recesses of my car. Calling. Singing to me.

The rest of the fabric I returned to the bottom of the box. I covered it with the books and hid the box in my closet.

The rest of the evening was fine. I watched TV. Laughed at sitcoms. I felt right with the world. Properly placed. Worthy of the space I took on the planet, the air I breathed.

By the time I went to bed that night, the strip of fabric in my car had settled down in my mind. Some of its glow had waned. I recalled the sensations of the knot and found the memory pleasant but no longer felt its pull. Sort of like a starving person given food, now satiated.

In fact I felt so right it seemed to me I was done with the cloth. For some reason that strip just needed to be in my car. I wouldn't really do anything with it. Maybe take it out once in awhile, look at it, run it through my fingers. Nothing more.

As for that fascinating knot, just remembering it would be enough.

Yes, just remembering would be enough.

thirty

Kaitlan shivered in the front hallway as she listened to Craig's Mustang turning around in front of the carport. She clutched both arms to her chest, loneliness and vulnerability spinning a web around her head. Every heartbeat banged in her cheek.

Why hadn't Craig killed her?

The sound of his car engine dwindled, then roared once more. Craig was headed down the long driveway.

Kaitlan edged into the living room and peeked through the window. The twin beams of his taillights glared demon eyes.

In a little over seven hours he'd be back.

If only she had a land line phone in her apartment. But she'd been trying to save money, using only her cell. Not that it mattered. Craig would have pulled out the cord and taken it as well.

She turned from the window and focused on the red throw blanket on the back of the couch. The blanket that Craig's last victim had grabbed in desperation as they fought. Kaitlan could never use that throw again. Or sleep on her bed. Or even lie on the bedspread, now stained with the smells of death.

She lowered her face into her hands.

When her grandfather and Margaret didn't hear from her tonight, they'd panic. They didn't even have her address to come looking for her. Only one thing left for them to do: call the police. Some officer on night patrol would come out here. What excuse would she give for her grandfather's worry?

She could think of none except for labeling him an old man, half senile after his auto accident. The thought of such betrayal cut deep.

147 - dark pursuit

Tomorrow Craig would hear that Darell Brooke had called the station. That he was her grandfather. And Craig would know she'd told him. She and her grandfather both would die. Margaret too.

I can't believe this. Craig, what happened to you?

Aimlessly, Kaitlan wandered into the kitchen and guzzled a glass of water at the sink. The forest beyond her window was a black, sucking void.

Her eyes fell to her purse on the kitchen table. No cell phone in its inside pocket. No car keys either. She'd checked the minute Craig left.

The Jensons.

Kaitlan's chin bounced up. Her lips parted as she stared at her purse. Had he checked all through it?

She grabbed her handbag and yanked back the long inside zipper. Thrusting her hand in the deep pocket, she felt around.

Her fingers closed on the key.

With a victorious cry she pulled it out. The key to the Jensons' house. Every few days she took in their mail and watered the plants while they were away. Craig hadn't known.

Her eyes blurred as she slipped the key into her pants pocket. "Thank you, thank you, God."

She ran into the living room and peered out front, making sure Craig was gone.

What if he was hiding at the top of the driveway, waiting? What if this was a trap?

Like she wasn't trapped here anyway.

At her side door Kaitlan eased into the goblin darkness under the carport. Crickets throbbed and sang.

The door sounded loud as she pulled it shut.

She stood there, hugging herself, waiting for her eyes to adjust.

Slowly, listening at every step, she made her way from under the carport and onto the driveway. A weak moon fumbled through high fog. She thought of her grandfather's house on the hill. There the ground-hugging cloud would be thick and chilling.

A shudder ran down her back.

The night plucked Kaitlan's nerves with greedy fingers. Asphalt stretched before her, long and curving, mocking as it disappeared into nothingness.

Was Craig down there?

Kaitlan leaned forward, eyes narrowed, searching the blackness. Did she see the hulk of a car? That shape far ahead . . .

Was it only her imagination?

She hesitated, on the verge of turning back. If this was a test and she failed it, he would kill her.

But how would she get through this long night, worrying about her grandfather and waiting for dawn like some hunted animal in a cave?

Kaitlan took a deep breath and started down the driveway.

After a few steps the crickets' rasping blended with the rhythm of her own body. The beat of her heart, blood whooshing in her ears. Cool air crawled across her skin. She shuddered.

Ten feet from the carport massive sequoias and eucalyptus trees studded the driveway's edge. Kaitlan could see only a few feet beyond them into the woods. Her brain conjured visions of the dead woman's face frozen in horror. Was she buried out there?

Kaitlan neared a bend in the road.

Heart in her throat, she drifted toward the outside edge, craning her neck to view around the curve. After this she'd be able to see the Jensons' house.

Kaitlan's foot hit something hard. She tripped and stumbled forward. Throwing out both hands, she caught herself before hitting the ground.

Chest heaving, she hovered on one knee, darkness pressing against her back.

She pushed her body upright. Looked ahead and saw a faint glow.

Scattered through the Jensons' house were lamps on timers, clicking on at dusk, off at midnight. They'd been strategically placed in front windows, facing the street. Kaitlan now could make out the vague outline of the house's right corner—where the kitchen lay. The light filtered through the kitchen's rear sliding door.

That faint glimmer pushed hope into her soul.

Fastening her eyes upon it, she quickened her pace. All she had to do was reach the Jensons' and get inside to the phone. Call her grandfather for help.

Get to the house, get to the house. The words chanted in her head, driving her steps.

By the time Kaitlan reached the edge of the yard, she was panting. Her heart beat double time. Almost there.

She imagined the sound of her grandfather's voice. Kaitlan didn't even care how grumpy he was, she just wanted to hear it.

Nearing the back of the house, she veered into the yard and picked her way along a stone path that led to the deck off the kitchen and garage.

Her key was to the back garage door.

By the time her hand reached for that knob, Kaitlan trembled all over. Three times she failed to insert the key into the lock. Door finally open, she edged into the garage, even blacker than the night. She felt along the wall that led toward the kitchen.

Kaitlan slipped into the house—and light. Dim, emanating from the front rooms. But to her it was the warmest light she'd ever seen.

With a cry of relief, she flung herself toward the phone.

thirty-one

A loud ringing startled Darell awake.

His arms jerked, head snapping up. He looked around dazedly, the taste of sleep in his mouth. *Who, what? What time is it?*

Kaitlan.

He shoved forward in his chair, groping the floor for his cane, only to remember the phone was a reach away.

A second ring.

Darell snatched up the receiver and punched the talk button.

Dead air. Margaret had answered.

He cursed loudly and slammed down the phone. Danged new systems. Pick up on one extension and you couldn't hear on the next without some fancy button-pushing.

Darell plucked up his cane, positioned his legs underneath him and pushed up with his left hand. On his feet he swayed, seeking balance, then shuffled across the office. He flung open the door. "Margaret! Transfer the—" He growled in his throat. He should have brought the receiver with him. "Never mind, I'm coming!"

"Here, D.!" Margaret's voice filtered from the other end of the house. "It's Kaitlan."

Well, of course it was Kaitlan. Hadn't he known she'd be all right?

Relief flooded his limbs.

As he neared the library Margaret's voice drifted to his ears. "You sure you're okay?"

He thumped across the threshold and over to his assistant. One of his old novels lay on the desk by the phone. Why was that there?

He thrust out his hand. "Let me talk to her."

"Wait, here's your grandfather." Margaret handed over the receiver.

"Kaitlan."

"Hi." She sounded breathless.

"What happened?"

"We went to the party. Chief Barlow threatened me not to say anything that would hurt Craig. I think he knows. And then, um" — her tone turned off key — "Craig brought me home."

Margaret looked on, forehead creased and both hands to her mouth.

"It's him," Kaitlan sputtered. "For sure. He admitted moving the body and everything. First he said he doesn't know why he kills; then he promised it wouldn't happen again."

This wasn't news. Darell had known Craig was the murderer. Still, hearing the confirmation made him want to sit down and take a deep breath. "All right, Kaitlan, calm yourself. This is what we expected." He sidled to his leather chair and sank into it. Margaret moved around so she could watch his face.

"No, it's not what I expected, it's worse! He said if I told anyone, he'd have to 'take care' of that person too, just like he's going to take care of me."

Darell gripped a knobby knee. *Coward.* Arrogant, murderous, lying coward. He would dance a jig — *without* his cane — when Craig Barlow was behind bars.

"And I can't run away. If I do, he'll plant drugs in my apartment. They'll hunt me down and take me to jail — if Craig doesn't kill me first. And with Chief Barlow in on everything, I won't stand a chance, no matter what I say."

Darell felt the rise and fall of his chest—an old man's lungs. He focused on the heavy wooden clock on the wall. Nearly eleven. Anxiety spritzed down his nerves. *Eleven.* He'd been asleep for over two hours. When he was supposed to be creating a plan.

"Grandfather, what am I supposed to do?"

Fear and rage funneled through Darell. "We're going to catch him, Kaitlan, that's what we're going to do."

"How? I have to ... I can't live like this."

"I know. Don't worry, I've been studying on it since you left."

He glanced at Margaret. She gave him a hard look. Darell turned away.

"He told me this body will never be found," Kaitlan said. "So what are we left with? We can't even prove someone was killed, and we have no way to tie him to the other murders—"

"Kaitlan, you've got to calm down."

"I can't! You don't know what it was like. I thought I was going to die. If he finds out I've talked to you he'll kill me. And he hit me tonight. Twice."

Darell's blood drained to his feet. His head buzzed. "He hit you?"

Margaret gasped.

"It still hurts. I'm gonna have a bruise on my cheek tomorrow. He said to tell people I ran into a door."

Darell stared out the window into blackness. A hollow helplessness opened in his gut. He needed a plan *now.* This antagonist wasn't acting as he'd expected. Admitting his crimes, threatening his girlfriend ...

"Grandfather, help me!"

Darell's mind blanked. Utterly emptied. He clutched the phone, heat flushing his face. Not a single thing could he offer her. He could barely even remember the news article he'd read mere hours ago.

Margaret stepped close and held out her hand. "D. Give me the phone."

She knew. She knew he was useless.

Like a child, he held out the receiver.

"Kaitlan?" Margaret backed up two steps. "We don't want you alone tonight. Come stay here."

Darell hung on her every expression. What was Kaitlan saying?

Margaret shook her head. "We don't know yet. But we'll come up with something tonight. He *has* to be caught—there's no other option."

She listened. Her face slacked.

Darell swiped at the phone. "Give it back, what's going on?"

Margaret laid the receiver against her neck. "He took her cell phone and car keys. She's calling from her landlord's house. They're on vacation and she has a key."

Darell struggled to process the information. This didn't make sense. Why had Craig left at all? Why not stay to make sure she didn't go anywhere?

A light snapped on in his brain. "Give me the phone."

"But—"

"Give it to me!"

Margaret handed it over.

"Kaitlan." Darell gripped the arm of his chair. His voice came clipped and intense. "Craig doesn't know you have a key to your landlord's place?"

"No."

"You sure?"

She hesitated. "Yes. Why?"

"I just need to make sure this isn't a setup. That what I'm thinking is correct."

"I didn't see him anywhere around when I walked here."

Darell closed his eyes.

"So what are you thinking?" she asked.

"He could have stayed with you tonight, but he didn't."

"Because he has to be at work early. And he didn't have his uniform with him."

"You think he couldn't have planned ahead and brought it? You think he didn't know he'd have to intimidate you to shreds tonight?"

"I guess. He was different as soon as he walked in the door. All on edge and changing one minute to the next."

"Because he's scared. Because he knows you know, and now he's got to fix it."

And he would — sooner than Kaitlan realized.

Darell could hardly breathe. "He told you the body wouldn't be found?"

"Yes."

"He'd have been too rushed this afternoon to make sure of that. Getting rid of a body takes time, and he was on duty. Besides, it was daylight. He pulled that woman from your apartment, but he couldn't take her far. That's why he left you tonight. Right now he's disposing of the body for good."

And when he finished with that, he'd come back for Kaitlan.

thirty-two

Craig had left only to move the body?

Kaitlan stilled on the chair in the Jensons' kitchen. Her grandfather's words sank inside her like millstones. Her eyes cut to the sliding backdoor as if any second Craig might leap from the darkness. The house felt like a mausoleum. Huge and still and cold. Able to swallow her whole.

"Are you saying"—her voice sounded so small—"he'll come back?"

But she already knew the answer. Of course he wouldn't leave her alone all night. Everything he'd said had been designed to terrify her, keep her from running while he was gone.

"Listen to me," her grandfather snapped. "You have to get out of there."

"I don't have a car!"

"We'll come get you."

"But he told me not to leave. He'll chase me down, and if he can't find me, he'll plant drugs in my apartment."

"That's a chance we have to take. You have no choice now, things have gotten out of hand."

Like they weren't before.

And just what had her grandfather been doing all evening while she followed his advice and went to a party with a killer? "Have you figured out how we're going to catch Craig?" she demanded.

Her grandfather's hesitation screamed.

"*Have* you?"

"I need to refigure it. The situation's different now."

Kaitlan shoved to her feet. "You told me I could count on you! Now look at me. I never should have left your house!" Desperation choked her lungs. She bent over, dragging in air. Craig was coming back to-night—who knew whether to beat her up again or kill her?

She had to get out of here.

"Pull yourself together, Kaitlan," her grandfather snapped. The fear vibrating through his anger heightened her own. "I'm handing the phone to Margaret. She needs directions."

Muffled sounds came over the line as the receiver was passed from hand to hand. Margaret's voice trembled into Kaitlan's ears. She could barely think straight as she tried to spout directions. Twice she blanked on names of streets.

"Okay. Got it." Margaret's words spluttered. "Wait! Your grandfather wants to tell you something."

Kaitlan's fingers cramped around the phone. She grabbed the counter and scanned the void of the Jensons' backyard. Through the line came the sound of her grandfather's rattled breathing.

"You stay in that house now, hear me? Stay down where you can't be seen through the windows. Don't come out until you see us pull up front."

Kaitlan's heart beat in her ears. "Okay."

The line clicked.

She hung up the phone with shaking hands.

The lamps. They would illumine her through any of the front windows. If she turned the living room one off and Craig came back, would he notice?

She couldn't take the chance.

Bent over double, Kaitlan skulked out of the kitchen to find a darkened room to wait in.

thirty-three

"I'm going with you." Darell fumbled around the floor for his cane. Where on earth was the thing?

"No, you're not." Margaret strode for the door.

"Margaret!" He straightened halfway, shooting her back a look to kill. "Stop right now and wait for me."

She turned around, her neck mottled and a tic in her cheek. She clutched the paper with directions as if it might spin away. "I'm *not* waiting for you, D., you move too slowly. I've got to get down there now!" She swiveled around.

"Mar—!"

"You want to help your granddaughter?" She jerked back to face him. "Figure out what we're going to do when she gets here."

"I'm trying."

"Don't try, D. *Do* it!"

She whirled from the library and disappeared.

Darell stood up, agitated and helpless, as her footsteps trotted up the hall toward the kitchen. He heard a faint thud against hardwood like the sound of a purse knocked to the floor. Then her hurried tread down the short hall toward the garage at the rear of the house. A door opened. Slammed shut.

In the silence, air stuttered in his quaking chest.

thirty-four

In the forested hills above town, leaves rattled and hissed like skittish snakes beneath Craig's feet.

His breaths came short and swift. So little time.

He'd blown it at Kaitlan's. Totally blown it. He'd planned to kill her then, get it over with, but when the moment came he just couldn't.

Containment.

No way could he keep her quiet day after day. What did he expect to do, take her car keys and phone every night? She'd end up telling someone, somewhere.

He had to get back to her place. Now.

Fast as he could Craig hurled himself through the darkness. Some fifty yards off the rutted path, he frantically sought the crumbling stone wall. His fingers gripped a flashlight, but he didn't want to use it.

Where was the wall?

He skidded to a halt, neck thrust out, eyes struggling to penetrate the blackness. Slowly he scanned.

Huge trees, only trees.

Craig cursed under his breath.

He slapped the flashlight's beam end against his hand and switched it on. His palm glowed red. Raising the flashlight, he pointed straight ahead.

No wall.

He aimed left. More trees.

Right.

There?

He sidled over two steps and cut the beam through two close trunks. Some twenty feet beyond — the rounded edges of stacked rocks.

Craig turned off the flashlight and hurried in their direction.

His toe found the body before he saw it. Stuffed into a hefty-sized black garbage bag, it gave a slick rustle when he kicked it.

The wall lay just behind.

Why the rocks were there at all remained a mystery. No old cabin nearby, nothing to show a longer barrier had once been there.

Fate.

He'd hauled the woman here this afternoon in the trunk of his patrol car, shock and fear injecting him with near Superman strength. A ditch in the earth just behind the six-foot wall offered what he sought — a natural grave. Spotting it, he'd dropped his heavy load in front of the rocks and sprinted back to his car, terrified that his radio might be going off while he was away.

Not until he'd flung himself back into the vehicle had he realized he should have at least dumped the body in the ditch until he could return.

He needed to keep a cooler head.

Before even removing the body from Kaitlan's bed, he had thought to untie the black and green cloth from its neck. That cloth was long disposed of. Even if by some wild fluke this body *was* found, it would not be tied to the other deaths.

Craig threw down the flashlight and attacked the wall. Yanking up stones he dropped them to one side. Before long his arm muscles screamed and his breath chugged. Sweat beaded down his forehead and plinked into his eyes.

Desperation drove him on. He had to get back to Kaitlan.

When he'd knocked the wall down, he dragged the near-rigid body to the four-foot-long ditch and pushed it in.

Feverishly he shoved stones over the top. When the bag was fully covered, he used the rest of the rocks to build up the height of the wall, now shorter, thicker.

Finished, chest heaving, he snapped on the flashlight for a brief moment and inspected his work.

Good. It was good.

Craig swiped his forehead and rushed through the dark to his Mustang.

thirty-five

Kaitlan huddled on the edge of the bed in the Jensons' front-corner guest room. Right hand pressed against the wall, she leaned forward to peer through the window. Every back muscle strained, her shoulders and neck like granite. The last dregs of light from a lamp post down the street oozed onto the sill in a sickly puddle.

From the entryway a massive grandfather clock's fretting *tick tock* hammered out the seconds.

Where was Craig?

Kaitlan struggled to figure how much time had passed since he left. Seemed like an eternity. But it couldn't have been more than thirty minutes. Maybe less.

How long did it take to dispose of a body? Would he weight her down in the ocean or bay? Bury her deep in the woods?

Kaitlan breathed against the window and the glass fogged. She pulled back.

Maybe her grandfather was wrong. Craig was in bed asleep, the victim's body long ago hidden. He didn't want to kill Kaitlan at all. But now her disappearance would force his hand.

A yowl rose outside the window.

Kaitlan froze.

A second wail pierced the night, mixing pain and anger and defilement. The sound sawed through Kaitlan's nerves.

At the third cry she recognized the sound. *Cat.*

Kaitlan sucked in air, trying to still her shaking limbs.

Long moments passed. Time filled only with the sound of her own breathing, the tick of the clock. Outside—no approaching car. Just echoing, mocking blackness.

Kaitlan tilted her wrist up near the window, trying to check her watch. How long had she been waiting?

The light was too dim to see.

She dropped her hand—and sudden anger welled within her. After all her struggles to overcome her addiction and make a life for herself. Now that she had a baby to think about—this happened. It wasn't fair. And she was not going to let it get the best of her.

Headlights spilled down the street.

Kaitlan jerked up straight. She listed toward the window, eyes glued to the road, waiting to see the car.

A realization punched her in the gut. She'd forgotten to ask Margaret what she drove.

The ghostly form of a vehicle materialized out of the dimness.

Kaitlan grabbed the window sill, willing the car to stop, her muscles tensed to sprint for the front door.

At the edge of the Jensons' property line it slowed.

Margaret! Kaitlan rocketed to her feet.

As she turned to run a sound registered. The rumble of an engine. Far too loud.

Kaitlan stilled. Looked back.

The car passed her window into shadows beyond the street lamp. It was a dark-colored Mustang.

thirty-six

The glove box of my car had a glow around it.

For weeks after I'd put the strip of cloth inside, every time I slid into my car this strange euphoria would settle over me. I'd drive humming. Smile at red lights. Traffic no longer bothered me—I had the cloth for company. Besides, the longer I stayed in the car the better I felt.

I never touched the fabric. Never even opened the glove compartment. But I knew it was there. That's all that mattered.

In one word my life was ... contented. At work. At home. As for that party night and what I'd done—the memory faded.

Had it really happened at all?

If so, it had been necessary. The only right thing to do in such a situation.

I took to driving around just to be in my car.

One Saturday I ended up driving for hours. I found myself on the freeway headed south. After well over one hundred miles I turned around. The pleasant feeling had melted away and my insides had started

to churn. It was barely noticeable at first. I
thought heading back home might help. Maybe my subconscious was simply bored at driving for no reason.

My unease only got worse, like an itch deep
inside me, moving around. Couldn't be scratched.
I shifted in the seat, leaned forward over the
wheel, leaned back. Switched on the radio. The music
sounded out of tune. I smacked it off.

Funny how the hillsides were graying. The sky
muddied. The road, the horizon, everything seemed to
run together. Even the colors of cars faded out.

The glove box heated up.

Its warmth radiated to me, skimming over my
arms, brushing my face. I felt no fright. I wasn't
even surprised. Hadn't I known all along?

My whole body started to sweat.

By the time I got home I couldn't wait to slip
that cool cloth through my fingers. Chill the burning of my skin.

That night I was supposed to go out with some
friends. How to hide my angst? I wanted to cancel
and stay home until it was time. But my rational side
said no. I'd need as much alibi as I could create.

We went to dinner, then had a few drinks at a
bar. Amazing how normal I was able to act. No one
would have known a thing was wrong.

Leaving the bar around midnight, I cruised the
streets. Twice I had to pull over and open the glove
compartment. Feel the fabric.

The third time I hid it under my seat.

I spotted her on a lonely stretch of road. Her
car was pulled over to the side, flashers on. She
stood by the driver's door, feet apart, hands to her
mouth as if beside herself over what to do.

As soon as I got out of my car I recognized her.
The mother on meth. The one who could only say "I
don't know" when asked why she was destroying her
own life and the lives of her kids. At that moment
the universe slid into place, like the final pieces
of a giant frame.

This woman deserved to die.

She didn't remember me until I reminded her. Apparently I'd made little impression on her flighty,
self-absorbed mind. She'd made a big one on me.

No car insurance, she wailed. Now how was she
supposed to get home to her children, just sent back
from their foster home? The policy had run out and
she'd had no money to renew it.

Of course not. Every dime she earned went into
her veins.

Her kids would be better off without her.

I offered to drive her home. "Oh, yes, thank
you!" she cried. I told her to turn off her flashers
and lock the car.

Two miles, that's all I managed. My fingers
branded themselves into the steering wheel.

She was chattering on about what she'd done
to clean up her life since I last saw her. She was
working now at a respectable job. Hadn't used for
months. I didn't believe that. "I have some ideas
for you," I said. "Can we stop and talk a minute?"

"Sure."

I pulled into an alley between two stores. Nobody was around. In one fluid movement I put the
car in park, whipped the cloth from beneath my seat,
and surged toward her neck.

My body caught fire as we struggled, burning up
my desire, her unforgivable sins. Turning them all to
ash. The fabric hardened to steel in my hands.

When she finally slumped over, coolness swept
through my veins.

One thing I knew then. I was born to do this.
All the years preceding this quest of truth were
merely funneled sands of time.

The swelling victory. A long exhale.

My brain notched into logistics mode.

I put on my gloves. Shoved her all the way down
in the seat.

Searching for a place to dump the body, I felt
oddly empty. Only when I'd disposed of it did I numb
out in vast, near-floating relief.

By the time I reached home I knew something
more. It both frightened and excited me. From here
on, things would be different. The next time I
wouldn't wait for death to seek me out.

I would pursue *it*.

thirty-seven

Craig.

Gravity sucked Kaitlan's blood to her feet.

She watched, mind crumbling, as he drove past the house and turned down the driveway leading to her apartment.

The next thing Kaitlan knew she was halfway across the room. She stumbled over the carpet, hands exploring the dark like frantic antennae. She hit the hallway, turned left, trailing her hand down the wall toward the corner so far, far away.

How long before he found she wasn't home? Thirty seconds? What would he do then?

Please, Craig, search the back woods.

Kaitlan reached the entryway and veered left, slipping on the tile. She grunted, thrust upright, and flung herself toward the door.

Margaret would be coming down the street any minute. Kaitlan had to flag her down before she pulled up to the house.

Craig would be turning off his car now. Getting out ...

With melting fingers she fumbled at the deadbolt. Her hands slipped around. On the third try she snapped it unlocked and yanked open the door. She forced herself to close it without a slam.

Kaitlan stumbled across the porch and down the steps. To the sidewalk and swiveled left.

Craig's in the apartment, looking for me ...

The road stretched before her for about a third of a mile, disappearing around a curve. She ran like never before.

In no time her lungs heaved like old billows. She gasped in oxygen, pumping, pumping her arms, blood pounding in her ears. Kaitlan couldn't stay on the sidewalk long. Any time now Craig could careen onto the street, his car beams lighting her up like fleeing prey. But she had to get far enough away from the house to head off Margaret.

He's behind my apartment, calling into the forest. Demanding I come out.

He would be cussing, enraged.

All light from the distant streetlamp behind her faded. There were no more on this rural part of road. Kaitlan pushed through hungry darkness, panic feeding fire to her limbs.

The sidewalk bent uphill. She threw a glance over her shoulder. No headlights. Her legs slowed as she forced herself on, ears cocked for the sound of an engine coming up the driveway. Knowing she wouldn't hear it over the adrenaline rush of her own body, the slap of her feet — until too late.

He's jumping back into his car.

She had to get away from the road.

The curve still lay some distance ahead. She didn't dare try making it.

Kaitlan veered off the sidewalk and crashed into the forest. She tripped and fell with a loud *oof!* The wind knocked clean out of her. She rolled, pushed up to her knees. With effort she staggered to her feet. Feeling her way deeper into the blackness, she slid around trees, scuffing over uneven ground.

She halted. Jerked around. The road lay about twenty feet away.

Terror wound around her throat. What to do? Any closer and Craig could find her. Farther in, and Margaret could pass her by before she got back to the sidewalk.

What if they drove by at the same time?

Lights appeared. Kaitlan peered through the night. Which direction were they coming from?

They brightened. She heard a car engine. A loud one.

Craig.

Kaitlan threw herself to the ground behind a tree. Leaves crunched, the thick, earthy scent of soil filling her nostrils.

The car approached slowly. Kaitlan peered around, wide eyes catching on a large beam gliding through the forest to her right. Headed straight for her.

Craig's police spotlight.

Too late. She had nowhere to go. Kaitlan pressed her cheek to the ground and froze.

The beam cruised nearer, trunks and branches and bushes bursting into light just twenty feet away. She imagined Craig holding the spotlight, jaw thrust forward, eyes like glaciers.

Ten feet.

Kaitlan squeezed her eyes shut.

Every fiber of her being listened to the Mustang, willing it not to stop. Seconds ticked by ... an eternity. Still she heard the engine, steady. Steady.

She opened her eyes to darkness. Turned her head to look the other direction.

The beam skimmed on up the woods.

Kaitlan breathed.

She dropped her head back down, smelling the earth, one hand hooked onto a lumpy tree root. She gathered the energy to get up.

The spotlight disappeared, the rumbling engine now a distant low hum. Craig had driven around the curve.

Kaitlan hefted into a crouch and hung there, listening. Watching. Nothing.

She rose to her feet and fought her way back toward the sidewalk.

At the edge of the forest she halted, neck craned to look up the street for headlights. The minute they appeared she'd have to dash out and flag down the driver. But what if it was Craig? Without the ability to see the car itself, she could only listen for the engine.

Kaitlan leaned forward, hands poised in the air, muscles gathered to spring.

What if Craig came back? He could decide to check the woods on the other side of the driveway.

And *where* was Margaret? She should have been here long ago —

Pale illumination spilled across the curve. Kaitlan cocked her head, straining to hear.

No sound of the Mustang's revved engine.

The glow brightened and gelled into headlights. A car rounded the bend.

Kaitlan jumped into open grass and ran.

thirty-
eight

Darell prowled the house, limbs quivering. He shuffled in and out of the office, his bedroom, then back up the long south hall to the kitchen. Down the north wing into the library. There he found himself staring at the couch where Kaitlan had sat. A pillow in the corner lay tilted, compressed by the weight of her back. He could almost feel her presence, as if her desperate spirit lingered, begging for help.

He shifted his feet, unnerved. If anything happened to Kaitlan, he would never forgive himself.

A plan to catch Craig. He had to come up with something tonight. Time had run out.

What a misstep to assume the body would be discovered quickly. He should have known that Craig would leave no evidence for Kaitlan to use against him.

But what to do without it?

The crush of the sofa pillow pulled at Darell. He stared at it.

Memories of Kaitlan's childhood wafted into his head. Small and unsteady on her toddler feet, tugging at his pant leg. Older and asking if he'd play with her. What was that silly game? Something about climbing ladders. It had been her favorite. Darell had seen her playing it by herself, manning her own pawn and that of an imaginary opponent. Her mother, Sarah, never had time for such nonsense. Neither had Darell.

Sorrow hit him in the chest. Why had he been so busy? Would one game have hurt?

Kaitlan, a preteen, coming to visit, portable CD-player headphones plugging her ears. By then she had drawn away from him, from her mother, pretending to no longer care. The scene fuzzed in his mind. Darell vaguely remembered fighting with Sarah. A screaming match over ... something. That was the last time he'd seen his daughter. Three years later she'd taken off for England, leaving fourteen-year-old Kaitlan with him to raise.

Regret graveled in Darell's throat. If only he'd done it better.

He turned away from the sight of the pillow.

A plan. The tolling bell rang in his head. He needed a plan.

His gaze fell on his old hardback novel, lying on the desk by the phone. He frowned. Why would Margaret be reading that at a time like this?

He thumped over to the desk and picked up the book. *The Neighbor.* His lips bent downward. *The Neighbor.* He wrote that? Couldn't remember it at all. He glanced at the shelves of his first editions and spotted an empty space about nine novels over from the top left. This was his tenth book?

Darell turned it over and read the back-cover copy. Still no memory.

He cursed and slapped the book down on the desk. Turning away, he stomped to his leather armchair. So what? He didn't need long-term memory right now. Just a clear head. And he had that. Just before Margaret left, hadn't his brain been working?

Besides, he had remembered those scenes of Kaitlan.

Darell stacked both palms on his cane, focusing on the rich wooden floor. *Think, now. Think.*

Nothing came.

His thoughts shifted, meandering out the window into the foggy night. There they thickened, soaking in moisture. Clouding covered his brain ...

Sometime later his muscles startled. He looked around. What had he been thinking?

Where was Kaitlan? What time was it?

Darell blinked at the clock, trying to determine when she and Margaret would return. But he couldn't remember when Margaret had left.

Panic bubbled in him.

He gripped the armchair, lips mushing in and out—the mouth of an old man. How he hated himself. Weak and mindless.

Just ten minutes of clear concentration. For that right now he'd give all the years of his fame and fortune.

Darell turned accusing eyes toward the heavens. "Can't you help me for once?"

His fingers slipped off his cane. It fell to the floor with a loud crack. Darell jumped.

Leaning over, he picked it up. He thumped the rubber end against the hardwood floor as if hammering concentration into his head.

Leland Hugh.

Low current shimmied in Darell's mind.

The scene he'd been working on that morning unfolded before him. Hugh, awaiting trial in jail, during a heated session with the defense psychiatrist. Riddled with guilt, yet denying it.

Craig clearly identified with Leland Hugh, down to using the same black and green fabric to strangle his victims.

Darell rubbed the hook of his cane. Why was Craig pulled toward Hugh? What similarity did he see, given that Darell had barely formed his own character? He hadn't even been able to complete an entire scene.

With no evidence to prove a crime, apprehending Craig could not be a chess match of forensics. This would come down to a psychological game.

Leland Hugh.

Darell took a deep breath. What might the man's weakness be? Other than killing, of course. In the core of his being, how did he see himself? What did he want?

What did Craig Barlow want?

The answer hissed up in Darell's brain like a bowling ball spat from its machine. All along it had been coming, he realized, sucked slowly through the invisible tube of his subconscious.

He stilled, a current of thought humming. Ideas began to form.

Yes. This was the right direction. This was *good*.

Darell stared at his feet, thinking.

Pete Lynch would help. The savvy private investigator had been research consultant on quite a few of Darell's books. Darell hadn't seen him since he'd visited at the hospital after the accident, although Pete had called more than once in the past two years to check on him.

At least he couldn't remember seeing Pete since then.

Darell rubbed his lips. Pete would have the equipment they'd need.

Thoughts flitted in and out of Darell's head, like elusive butterflies. He chased after them ... lost himself.

Sometime later he turned toward the clock.

Pete.

It was late for making calls, but no matter. What was time in an emergency?

With renewed vigor he pushed to his feet. In minutes he was back in the south wing, crossing the office toward his Rolodex and phone.

thirty-nine

Kaitlan's legs scissored through the grass, both arms above her head, frantically waving. Gasps spilled from her mouth, stabs of pain in her chest. So short a distance, but the car was coming fast. She didn't dare shout. If Margaret didn't see her in the darkness and passed her by …

The terrible thought fueled her body.

Kaitlan hurtled across the last five feet like she'd been shot from a cannon. The hard slap of her feet against sidewalk sent shock waves up her spine. Her head swung toward the car. It was a mere twenty feet up the road.

Too close. She couldn't stop in time.

The moment spun out. Kaitlan's muscles squeezed, everything within her straining to slow her pounding legs. Her limbs shuddered like machine gears at the throw of brakes. Both hands flung up, pushing against air. A horrified cry grated up her throat.

She sprang across the sidewalk to curb. Margaret wasn't slowing.

I'm dead.

Kaitlan's foot sailed out over the road.

Tires screeched. The car swerved. Not enough.

Her body slammed into the rear door at an angle and bounced off. Kaitlan collapsed in a heap.

She lay on the road, stunned and groaning. Vaguely she registered the car grinding to a stop. Red hazard lights flashed. A door opened. Running footsteps.

"Oh, oh my—" A woman's voice, not Margaret's. A sob. "I didn't see you—what were you—you came so fast—are you all right?"

Kaitlan raised bleary eyes to the dim form of a stranger, bent over her with hands flailing. Short brown hair. Her cheeks and gaping mouth strobed red to black, red to black.

"I ... yeah." Kaitlan's words croaked. "Just ... help me up."

"Oh. I can't believe ..." The woman thrust both hands underneath Kaitlan and pushed her to sit up. "Are you dizzy? Is anything broken?" Her voice shook. "Can you stand?"

Margaret. Craig. "I have to get up. Help me."

"Okay, okay." The woman put her arm underneath Kaitlan's shoulder. "Up you go."

Kaitlan wobbled to her feet, the woman clinging tightly. Kaitlan's mushy brain calculated bodily injuries. Nothing hurt too badly—yet. Shock? Or was she really okay?

"What were you *doing* out here?" Relief and fear pushed accusation into the woman's tone. "You ran right at me!"

"I'm sorry."

The woman blew out air. "Can I take you somewhere? Home?" Sweat on her forehead gleamed in the flashing red. "It's not safe for you to be out here alone at night."

A high-pitched chuckle popped from Kaitlan. "Tell me about it."

The woman peered at her as if wondering at her sanity.

Headlights washed across the curve up the road. Kaitlan fingers sank into the woman's arm.

"What—?"

"Shhh!" Kaitlan held her breath and listened. The car came around the bend. The engine wasn't—

"Out of the street or it'll hit us both!" The woman tugged at her.

Headlights lit them up as Kaitlan let herself be pulled to the sidewalk. She hung on to the woman, breathing hard, nowhere else to go. Panic and hope sparred in her veins. Too late, too late if her ears betrayed her, if this was Craig.

The car skidded to a stop. The driver's door flung open. "Kaitlan!"

Hot relief flooded her. Both knees caved. "Margaret."

The woman held her up. Kaitlan disentangled herself in a half daze, blathering her thanks and sorrys, but her ride was here now and she was fine, just fine. Her unsteady legs moved beneath her, scuffling toward Margaret's car, to safety. Margaret was getting out, hands slapped to her cheeks, her mouth a round O.

"Get out of here fast!" Kaitlan threw back over her shoulder at the woman. "It's not safe."

Uncertainty stalled the woman on the sidewalk. She stared, eyes wide.

"Go!"

The woman's hands flew up and she shook out of her mindlessness, a sudden blur of motion. Jumping into the street, she hustled toward her flashing car to escape the crazed scene.

Kaitlan yanked Margaret's passenger door open and fell inside. She slammed the door shut.

"What hap—?"

"Go, just go!" She scrunched down in her seat, peering over the dashboard. Some thirty feet away the woman had reached the back bumper of her car. "Go around her, don't wait!"

Margaret hit the gas pedal and carved deeply into the other lane. They passed the woman as she slid behind her wheel, the car's overhead light spilling upon her head. For a long second Kaitlan's eyes met hers, the woman's glazed with fear as if recognizing she'd barely escaped some monstrous nightmare.

Kaitlan fell back against her seat. She wiped her forehead. "Where have you been?"

"I got lost."

"Heck of a time to get lost."

"I know!" Air shuddered down Margaret's throat. "I was just *beside* myself. I couldn't . . ." Her head shook in tiny trembles.

The Jensons' house glimmered into view on Kaitlan's right. A sudden, wild knowledge blared in her head. She couldn't go home again anytime soon. And she had nothing with her, not even her purse.

Shouldn't she go to work tomorrow and pretend to the outside world that everything was okay? Craig couldn't hurt her at work.

"Turn into that driveway." She pointed. "I've got to get something in my apartment."

"No! We've to get away—"

"Just do it, Margaret!"

"What about Craig? What if he comes back and finds us there?"

If she only knew how close he was. "I won't be long. But I don't dare go back there tomorrow morning, and my shears are in my car. I can't work without my shears."

"I don't—"

"Turn!"

Margaret swerved.

They tore down the long driveway, every tree alive and closing in on them as if angered at the spray of headlights.

To think she'd walked this alone, in the dark.

"Keep going to the end."

Margaret took the curve fast and soon jerked to a hard stop in front of the carport. Kaitlan jumped out. "Turn off your lights and lock your doors. I'm going inside."

"But you said—"

The door to her kitchen stood ajar. Kaitlan ran inside, mind crackling like wildfire. This was insanity, but she was so close. Better risk it now than in the morning, when Craig would lie in wait for her.

From below the kitchen sink she snatched two plastic grocery bags and sprinted to her bedroom. She threw open her closet door and yanked out three shirts and a pair of jeans. In the bathroom she grabbed handfuls of makeup items and shoved them into a bag. Her brushes, blow dryer. Face cream, shampoo and conditioner.

She hurled back into the kitchen, aiming for the door. At the table she skimmed up her purse, barely slowing. Banging her apartment door shut, she jumped into the passenger side of her Corolla and dug into the glove box for her shears in their case.

By the time she reached Margaret's car it was turned around, ready to flee.

Panting, Kaitlan fell into the back seat. "Let's go!" She dropped the plastic bags onto the floor.

Margaret took off.

Kaitlan thrust herself down in the cloth seat, gripping the edge. They were nearly home free. If they could just get to the end of the driveway ...

She twisted her neck up toward Margaret. The woman's back was ramrod straight, not touching the seat. Her hands clawed the steering wheel like talons.

Kaitlan's body listed as the car swung around the driveway's curve. She held on tighter. "Turn right onto the street. It's longer to the freeway, but Craig could be circling back."

"Circling *back*?"

"He was here. About two minutes before you came. I hid in the woods. He drove right by me with a spotlight."

"Are you kidding? And you had me bring you back here?"

Kaitlan felt the car turn onto the road. "See any other headlights?"

"No."

Cautiously she raised her head. "Go left at the next road, then the second left after that. After about a mile you'll see a sign to the freeway."

Kaitlan whipped around toward the rear window. Only blackness. *Come on, come on.*

She collapsed against the seat, utterly spent.

The car turned ... turned again.

Kaitlan lifted her chin. "See the freeway sign?

Margaret hesitated. "There it is."

In another minute they hit 280. They'd done it.

Kaitlan sank her cheek against the seat and closed her eyes. For the first time since barreling into that woman's car she realized how much her body hurt.

forty

Nothing but panic and fury were left in Craig's veins. They ate at him like acid, bubbling and gurgling all reason away.

If he'd just done what was needed. If he hadn't been so *stupid*.

But no, this was not his fault. She hadn't listened.

Craig cruised the dark rural streets, recklessly panning the woods with his spotlight. He didn't even care who saw, who might ask questions. He just needed Kaitlan silenced.

Long, long, he looked. Way past when he knew it was hopeless. Where had she gone?

Defeat hurled fire in his belly.

Fingers curled into the steering wheel, lungs like stone, he smacked off the searchlight and threw it on the passenger seat. He screeched around in the middle of the road and aimed toward Kaitlan's apartment for one more search — even though he knew she wasn't there.

On the way he gulped oxygen, forcing his head to clear.

Minutes later he swerved into Kaitlan's driveway.

All right. Okay. All wasn't lost yet.

Craig Barlow was a policeman. He could contain this. He *would* contain it. He just had to think what to do. Reason through things.

He pulled up behind Kaitlan's car.

Tomorrow was another day. For now he'd scared her sufficiently. Just because she'd fled didn't mean she'd told someone. What was there to tell? There was no evidence of a murder. None. That woman would be reported missing. But without a body . . .

And nearly twenty people had seen him and Kaitlan at a party tonight, acting just fine.

Slowly he tapped the steering wheel.

He could only hope she'd be scared enough to show up at work tomorrow, like he'd warned her to do. The longer she acted like nothing was wrong, the harder time she'd have trying to prove anything had happened.

Besides, if she tried that, his irate father would shut her down in a hurry.

If she'd already told someone, and that person believed her ... Craig closed his eyes. He had to keep his father out of this.

Containment. At any cost.

Jaw set with determination, Craig got out of the car to search Kaitlan's apartment one more time.

forty-one

"Where's Kaitlan, what took you so long?" Darell pounded his cane against the kitchen floor, his cheeks heating with anger born of relief.

"She's right behind me, just getting her things." Margaret looked flustered and shaky. She dropped her purse on the counter, hands fluttering about. "I got lost. Couldn't see the street signs in the dark—the lamp posts are so far apart out there. I thought I'd have a heart attack. And then—there she was. On the street."

"On the—"

"Grandfather!" Kaitlan drew out the greeting, as if she'd thought never to see him again. She dragged in from the hallway, threw some plastic bags and a purse beside Margaret's, and came at him, arms out. Before he could say a word, she wrapped him in a hug.

Kaitlan hung on. He could feel the shiver of her body. Or maybe it was his own. How many years had it been since a family member had hugged him like that?

Darell's left hand lifted and found its way around her back. He patted her gently.

She drew away, hands sliding to his shoulders. Her eyes glistened.

Her face.

Darell's jaw sagged open. He touched her left cheek. It was purple red with multiple small abrasions. Streaks of dirt ran down to her chin. Pieces of leaf and twig were stuck in her hair. "This where he hit you?"

His voice was gruff. Rage popped around in his chest like oil in a wet pan.

Kaitlan winced. "Does it look bad?"

"Oh, my." Margaret looked sick. "I hadn't noticed in the dark." She plucked a broken leaf from Kaitlan's scalp.

Kaitlan backed up, rubbing her arms. Exhaustion pulled at her mouth. "I fell. And I had to hide in the forest so ..."

Darell stared at her, searching for words. What on earth had happened? His rage spattered higher, its heat turned up. He would trap Craig Barlow if it was the last thing he did. If he had to die in the process.

He inhaled deeply. "Let's sit down in the library so I can hear what happened. And I will lay out our plan."

Margaret's eyes rounded as though she was shocked he could come up with anything. He threw her a look.

Kaitlan's gaze cruised the cabinets as if she'd only half heard his words. "I need some water."

"I'll get it." Margaret fetched a glass and started to fill it from the refrigerator.

"No, just tap." Kaitlan ran a distracted hand through her hair, picking at the debris.

"Okay." Margaret stepped to the sink.

Kaitlan murmured "thank you" and guzzled the water. She set down the glass and swayed against the counter. Margaret reached out a hand to steady her.

"I'm okay." Kaitlan waved her away. "I'm just ..."

"Exhausted." Margaret huffed. "And I'll bet you've hardly eaten."

Kaitlan shook her head. "I couldn't. That dinner with Chief Barlow threatening me—no way. Not knowing what Craig was going to do when we left. And the smell of the food ..." She scrunched her nose. "I've felt sick all day."

Her eyelids flickered, as if she'd let something slip. She firmed her mouth.

A warning bell sounded in Darell's head. Was there something she wasn't telling him? An illness? "Why, what's wrong with you?"

Kaitlan's tired eyes fixed on his. She swallowed, defensiveness falling across her face in pale shadow. The moment stretched, as if she considered what to say.

A sigh escaped her. Both shoulders sank. "I'm pregnant." She closed her eyes. "There. I've said it."

"Oh." Margaret's fingers lifted to her lips.

Darell felt the blood drain from his head. Everything he'd planned in the last hour rose before him in a new, tainted picture. "You telling me Craig's the father?"

Kaitlan focused on the floor. Her chin rose and fell in a tiny nod.

No.

Darell's fingers tightened on his cane. His head pulled back, eyes narrowed. "How far along are you?" Disdain coated his voice.

Kaitlan bit her lip. "About six weeks."

"Good. You've got plenty of time to get rid of it."

Kaitlan's eyes rose to his face in shock. "I don't want to get rid of it."

"Of course you do."

"No, I *don't.*"

"Kaitlan." His tone snapped and he didn't care. "What are you thinking? We want the world and especially *you* rid of this man. How do you expect that to happen if he's the father of your baby? Forever, Kaitlan, you'll be tied to him, whether you want to be or not. You want to raise a child who came from that? Whose daddy is a convicted killer on death row?"

Kaitlan's face flushed. She thrust two steps forward, an arm flinging out. "I don't *care* who her father is! What I care is that I'm the mother." She jabbed at her own chest. "I care about loving this baby the way my mother never loved me. I want to raise her and be there for her."

"With what means? You haven't got a penny to your name."

"I'll find a way! What's it to you? You want me to kill my baby just because I'm not rich like you?" Tears sprang to her eyes. "I want a family, don't you get that? It's more important to me than anything."

"But Craig is the father."

A tear spilled down her cheek. "When he's in jail he won't have any part of my baby. I'll go to court if I have to. Or maybe I won't even tell him it's his. I'll say I was with someone else. She won't tie me to him. My daughter will be *mine*."

"You don't know it's a daughter," Darell retorted inanely.

"Son then. Either way, I'm not having an abortion."

Darell backed up and leaned against a counter. This was too much. He should sit down.

Margaret cleared her throat. "Could I just—"

"*No*," Darell spat.

"Stop it!" Kaitlan's tone shrilled. "Why are you so mean to her? Just because *you* never cared about family."

The words bit deep. "Fine, then." Darell hit the hardwood floor with his cane. "You two talk all you want. Apparently you don't need me, and I'm tired. I'm going to bed."

"What, you can't go to bed!" Margaret caught his arm. "You said you have a plan. This news doesn't change anything for tonight; we can deal with it later. Right now we've got enough to think about."

Darell yanked his arm away. "She said she doesn't need me."

"She never said that."

Kaitlan bent over, hands hiding her face. Just folded like a rag doll. A sob pressed through her fingers.

Margaret shot Darell an accusing look. "See what you've done?"

The crying squeezed Darell's heart. He gawked at Kaitlan. "*I* didn't do anything. She brought it up."

"D." Margaret's green eyes moistened. "Kaitlan could have died tonight. Craig came back before I got there, and she had to hide in the woods. She got hit by a car—"

"What! Hit by a—"

"On top of everything she's pregnant and sick. Now you want to tell her what to do with her own baby?"

Kaitlan's breathing shuddered then quieted. She lifted her head to gaze at him dully.

Darell buffed his forehead. "You got hit by a car?"

She tilted her head. "Actually, I hit *it*."

His face scrunched.

Kaitlan waved a hand—*doesn't matter*. Her gaze slid into the distance. Exhaustion and defeat trailed across her brow.

Margaret raised her eyebrows at Darell.

He scratched his ear, nonplussed. "Come into the library." He turned to thump out of the kitchen with all the dignity he could muster. "Heaven knows I've waited for you long enough."

Sudden music sounded. Darell halted. "What's that?"

Kaitlan's stunned gaze pulled toward the counter. Dreamlike, she crossed to her purse and opened it. The music turned louder.

"It's my cell. He gave me back my cell." Her hand slipped into a side pocket in the purse and withdrew a phone. "This is Craig's ring tone."

"Don't answer," Darell commanded.

They stared at the phone as if Craig himself might crawl from it.

After a moment the music stopped.

Kaitlan set the phone on the counter. "No message."

"Evidence. He wouldn't be so foolish." Darell gestured with his chin. "Turn it off." The location of a live cell phone could be traced.

She held down a button. Notes sounded, then the phone went silent.

"If he did that . . ." Kaitlan checked in her purse again. "Hah!" She pulled out a car key. "Look. He gave this back too. Why would he do that?"

Darell's mind chugged. He frowned at the key.

Margaret shifted. "Maybe—"

"Quiet!" He massaged his jaw, frowning at the floor.

The answer surfaced.

Darell's head came up. "He was afraid you'd gotten to someone for help and would tell what's happened. The only thing he could do was make you look crazy. With no sign of the body you claimed to find, and your keys and phone in your purse where they should be . . ." Darell lifted his hand and shrugged.

Kaitlan's eyes rounded as if she couldn't believe Craig's cunning. "What about the bruise on my face?"

"He'd claim to know nothing about how you got it." Darell's gaze roamed over her cheek. The scrapes were redder now. "Your fall hasn't helped matters any. Now it would be hard to prove the bruise didn't come from that."

"Oh. Of course." Kaitlan's expression flattened. Shoulders slumped, she put the key back in her purse, then pressed her palms to her temples. She looked like an orphan, hollow-cheeked and lost.

Her gaze drifted to the cell phone. She scooped it up with a sigh and dropped it into her purse. Turning away, she did a double take. She leaned over the handbag. "What ...?"

Reaching deep inside, she pulled out two white rectangles. Kaitlan turned them over. Her skin blanched white. She cried out and shook the objects from her hands as if she'd been stung. They landed on the floor face up.

Photos.

Darell squinted. What were they of?

Margaret's wide eyes locked on the pictures. She cut a glance at Kaitlan, then edged over to pick them up. As she bent down, her face registered horror. Air seeped up her throat. She hesitated.

"Give them to me!" Darell thrust out his arm.

Gingerly she picked up the photos by one corner and shoved them into his hand. He peered at them.

The victim's body.

One was taken from the right, one from the left. Vivid color shots of her ghastly frozen features, the black and green fabric around her neck. Clear in the photos were the surroundings. A bed, a cheap wooden headboard, walls and furniture.

Kaitlan's bedroom, no doubt.

forty-two

You think you have problems? Your issues are nothing.

After that second kill my life plummeted. Or did it soar? I couldn't tell. One minute I'd feel free as I'd ever been. The next I'd be eating dust.

The killing itself was the soaring part. The rightness of it. The seductive call of the fabric, the way it felt in my hands. Its power to take life—just like that. A living, breathing human choked to a deserving, sudden end.

Then out of nowhere fear would drive me to my knees. Utter chest-constricting fear of getting caught. It would descend at the most unexpected of times. When I was at work. Watching television. Taking a shower. On the phone. The thought of friends, family, society at large knowing what I had become petrified me. They would never understand. They would hate me, judge me.

Punish me.

I *can't* go to jail. Not me. That happens to other people. Criminals. People not so smart.

When the panic is at its worst my brain swells like a rushing river. Visions of being apprehended roil and plunge, dragging me under. The worst thought is of being separated from my black silk fabric with green stripes. From its touch and smell. Its comfort.

I'd be undone. Purposeless.

In those horrific moments I tell myself I won't kill again. I've succeeded undetected so far. Why push it?

But deep inside I don't believe my own words. Because even then the fabric calls to me.

The very same night of that second killing I cut another strip of cloth.

Sliding it through my fingers, I remembered the knowledge that had surfaced within me. That I would soon pursue death, not wait for it.

When you first ingest something sweet you get the full effect of the sugar. But sip perfectly sugared coffee, then follow it with candy. The next drink of coffee will no longer taste sweet enough.

We humans always want more.

Where did our craving come from? Why are we never satisfied? Why couldn't I, of all people, be content, hoarding the incredible gift of life the fabric had given me?

Three weeks after that killing I found my next target.

I was reading the paper at the breakfast table, a piece of toast in my hand. My eyes grazed the woman's name in some small article—one I would have ignored. The letters leapt off the page.

The fabric in my car's glove compartment switched on. Waves of heat radiated through the car window, into my kitchen. Caressed the back of my neck.

I stared at the name. Why this one?

That day at work I heard the name again. Gossip. Talk around town of the woman's lurid past—one she denied. An abandoned baby. Three abortions.

And she claimed to want to serve the city.

I had little time. The cloth lulled me, sang to me. Then foreswore all pretense and downright demanded me. I would either break in two or answer its siren song.

Through diligence I learned where the woman worked. Her habits. I planned what must be done—detailed, schemed, clever plans that demanded forethought.

And I struck.

As soon as the deed was done, blessed relief descended once more.

The feeling was short-lived.

It wasn't my fault. Sometimes even the best-laid plans go awry.

I have entered new waters, far deeper than I ever intended. They are dangerous and icy, and will demand of me actions I hadn't expected to take.

But take them I will. Desperation drives the best of us.

Before I knew it a new strip of fabric was cut. Strange, but I don't remember doing it. The hours were too full of anxieties and details.

Something else. I am no longer two people in my mind. The days of barely remembering the killings—gone. I now tread the center divide, blessedly aware of Who I Am and ever so cautiously hiding it from the world.

The cost of being chosen.

I wear the fabric on my body, carefully folded, tucked into a pants pocket. There it clings to me like sucking tentacles.

This is my salvation. I can no longer function apart from it.

Death—at my fingertips.

forty-three

"Help me, God." Slumped on the couch, Kaitlan whispered the words toward the library ceiling. She had to believe they'd rise up to heaven. God had listened before. He could save her again.

Visions of Kaitlan's old life reignited in her head. Stretched out on a ratty floor, coming down from cocaine in a room full of traitorous friends. Turn her back and they'd steal from her, lie to her. Anything for their own fix. She would have done the same.

With God's help, she'd overcome all that.

Despite her prayer, defeat sucked up the air around Kaitlan in a noxious cloud. Hadn't the three of them been here hours earlier in the very same positions? Scheming how to outwit Craig? Lot of good that had done.

This is real, not a novel, she'd told her grandfather. Yeah. And in real life, even *with* prayer, the good guys didn't always win.

"Sit up and listen to me, Kaitlan." Sternness edged her grandfather's voice.

"But he has pictures of her. Dead—in my bedroom! Now that I've disappeared he'll use them against me."

"I doubt he wants to do that. They're evidence of the murder he's trying to hide."

"Great, they're just back-ups—in case he doesn't kill me first." Kaitlan covered her eyes with both hands.

"Listen to me, girl, those photos are a point for our side. That was a major misstep for Craig."

"You said you had a plan, D." The hope in Margaret's tone sounded forced.

"I do. Kaitlan, sit up."

She rubbed her forehead and dragged herself up straighter. Whatever her grandfather said, it wouldn't work. Every corner they turned, Craig was already ahead of them.

Darell Brooke perched in his chair, legs spread, cane planted between them. Shocks of white hair stuck this way and that, straggly brows hanging in his eyes. His gaze gleamed like some wild and weary Einstein.

"I am catching Craig Barlow tomorrow," he announced. Glancing at the clock, he drew his mouth in. "Make that today."

It was after midnight. Kaitlan sighed. So much terror and no sleep.

Her grandfather pointed at her. "You won't go to work. In fact you will not leave this house until he's caught."

That would be a nice thought.

She lifted a hand. "We have no evidence to catch him, even with these pictures. They only point to me."

"Not true about the pictures, and evidence exists." Her grandfather shrugged. "The police just haven't found it yet. More likely, the chief knows and is doing everything to point away from it. Craig bought the fabric. That transaction can be traced. Likely he still has the cloth in his house. Now he's taken photos. He may well have taken pictures of the other victims too. They would be his trophies. Perhaps fibers have been found on the victims that will match the carpet in the make and model of his car. Maybe a hair."

"What if he's gotten rid of everything?" Margaret rubbed her knee in small, nervous circles.

"Doubtful. But even if he tried, down to erasing the pictures from his memory card, a skilled technician could recover them. I'll bet Craig doesn't know that. The digital card is like a computer hard drive that's been erased. Old photos can still be found."

"So what do we do tomorrow?" Kaitlan asked.

Her grandfather eyed her with the satisfaction of a cat conning a mouse from its hole. "The King of Suspense is about to make one local fan's day."

The meaningless words floated down inside Kaitlan, weightless as feathers. But they reached bottom with the thud of stone. Understanding puffed up like dust. "You're going to call Craig?"

"More than that. I'm going to invite him to the house."

Margaret gasped.

Kaitlan's lips parted. "No way!"

"You got a better idea?"

"No, but—"

"Then I suggest you listen to what I have to say."

"You can't." Kaitlan shoved forward on the couch. "It's dangerous! What if it doesn't work? What if he gets here and realizes he's been set up—"

"It'll work."

"But the minute he sees me ..."

"He's not going to see you. Or Margaret. He won't know anyone else is in the house. It'll just be him and me."

Kaitlan stared at her grandfather. Determination and stubbornness hardened his features. She knew the look all too well. No matter her arguments, he would not be stopped.

But he had no idea what he was getting into.

She folded her arms. "You *cannot* be alone with him. I'll go back to my apartment and meet him myself before I let you do that."

"You can't!" Margaret cried.

"No, you won't." The sereneness in her grandfather's expression astounded her.

In that instant his soul shimmered, then blazed before her, as if the sun itself chased away its shadows. Kaitlan went weak.

He knew exactly what he was doing. He understood the danger. And that was a chance he was willing to take.

For *her*.

She died so easily.
Sure she fought. And I had a time ye...
...ere I wanted. But when it comes right down to
...oking the life out of them, I've learned some-
...hing. The li... between death and life—that final
...reath—is painfully ... ... this realit...
As before, the days leading up to it were intense.
... about my business, then wham. Days a...
... more. It called wit...

Part 3

deception

forty-four

Margaret opened her eyes to sickly dawn.

Her night had been fitful, plagued by wraithlike dreams not fully formed. As she gazed blearily at the ceiling she couldn't remember a single detail, but they haunted her just the same.

The clock read 6:45 p.m. Four hours of sleep. Her head felt like mush.

She and D. and Kaitlan had talked past 2:00 a.m., discussing D.'s scheme. There wasn't much to it, really, and that's what petrified Margaret. Yet he insisted it would work.

They could not unequivocally prove Craig did the murders. But they could gather enough circumstantial evidence for the California State Police to be forced to take a look at the situation.

Especially with the media involved.

Craig's biggest mistake was hacking into D.'s manuscript—and using Leland Hugh's black and green fabric for the killings. D. had already gathered information from some key phone calls. The hacking was likely on his own computer, he reported, not the online data storage site, which would employ heavy encryption to guard against such theft. The house's internal wireless network had long been secured, but it wasn't completely infallible. Still, the hacker would have faced the challenge of "pushing" a Trojan Horse or some other kind of spyware onto D.'s computer.

Margaret could believe his own computer was the vulnerable point. He wouldn't let her on it, and likely he hadn't kept up with security updates.

He could prove the hacking with the help of a savvy computer crimes technician, D. said. The tech would need a couple hours to run his software, looking for the spy program. The harder issue was tracing where it had come from, but thanks to brand-new technology that could now be done.

D. would present this proof to Craig, threatening to call the Sheriff's Department over the theft unless Craig admitted what he'd done and promised to stop. Craig's confession would be secretly filmed by a local TV reporter. A copy of that tape and D.'s manuscript—along with the photos Craig had so thoughtfully chosen to give them—would be taken to the state police. Kaitlan would tell them her full account. They would have to investigate. With the TV station blowing the story wide open, the Gayner chief of police wouldn't be able to keep the lid on evidence they hadn't pursued. Public pressure would mount to find the truth.

"But why would Craig admit to the hacking in the first place?" Kaitlan had pressed. "He knows that manuscript could tie him to the fabric."

D. smiled sagely. "But he doesn't know *I* know about the fabric. He has to meet my demand and confess in order to contain me. If I pressed charges, the media would be all over the story. Every point of my manuscript—including the fabric—could be made public. And some homicide detective on the Gayner police force would wonder at the coincidence."

Amazing, Margaret had thought—that D. had been able to logic through all this.

Kaitlan thought the plan absurd. "So you tell him that's why you really brought him here, get his confession, and see him to the door. And you expect this maniac, the guy who wants to kill me, to just go along with it?"

D. reared back his head. "I write dialogue for a living, girl! I'll finesse the conversation. I'll look at his manuscript first and give him some pointers. When I bring up the hacking it'll be with disappointment, not anger. Just an unfortunate detail I choose to deal with quietly, between him and me. He'll do what I ask because he'll want to keep it that way."

"Something will go wrong."

"No, it won't."

"You don't know that!"

D.'s features blackened. "How many evil antagonists do you think I've created in my lifetime, girl? You think I can't keep a step ahead of this one?"

"This isn't a book!"

"I *know* that!"

The argument boiled over. D. and Kaitlan shot points back and forth, back and forth. Margaret didn't say much—Kaitlan covered it all.

D. pounded his cane. "Unless you come up with some other bright idea, I'm through talking about this!"

"But I don't want to end up on TV!" Kaitlan burst. "Everybody will be looking at me, my privacy gone."

D. growled. "Don't be a fool, Kaitlan. You lost your privacy the minute you found that body on your bed. What do you think—Craig's going to be arrested and tried in secret?"

That did it. Kaitlan was beaten down. Margaret could see the fight drain from her limbs. Besides, D. was right—they had no other plan.

Feet on the couch, Kaitlan pulled her knees up and buried her face.

D. looked utterly spent. He slumped in his chair, piercing the floor with an angry stare. Soon it smoothed to hollow-eyed blankness.

Margaret hadn't liked the plan then. Now in the light of day it seemed nothing short of insane. A frail elderly man facing down a killer one third his age?

She had to talk D. out of it.

Throwing back the covers she slid from bed.

She showered and dressed by rote, her mind on the list of arguments to abort the plan. Too much could go wrong. They had no fallback. All three of them could get killed. The more she envisioned Craig Barlow here, in this house, the more her muscles tied in knots. By the time her makeup and hair were done, she vowed to go to the police herself rather than let D. carry out his harebrained idea.

Except she had no absolute proof yesterday's murder ever happened. What if they believed the photos had been staged—all for publicity for a has-been writer?

The news.

Margaret slapped down her brush and trotted over to turn on the television, weak hope floundering in her chest. If by some miracle the victim at least had been found . . .

She punched the remote to Channel Seven, where *Good Morning America* would cut away at intervals to a minute or two of local news.

Commercials.

Margaret massaged her neck and waited. *Come on, give me something.*

The familiar face of local anchor Matt Hagerty appeared. He clipped through stories of an Oakland attorney indicted for trying to bribe a judge, a string of home burglaries in San Francisco's Marina District. Traffic conditions on local freeways. "And now," he nodded, "back to *Good Morning America.*"

Margaret's shoulders fell.

Punching off the TV, she strode to her desk in the far corner of her room. It was less likely the papers would carry anything about the murder this quickly, but she'd look anyway. She turned on her computer, idling with impatience as it booted. She clicked to the *San Jose Mercury News* website and scanned its headlines.

Nothing.

Margaret returned to Google and searched for "Gayner homicide victim"—the same words she'd run yesterday for D.

No breaking stories. Only those of the last two victims.

She typed in "Gayner missing woman." Her heart leapt at the returned hits, but again none of them linked to current news.

Who was this woman, that no one had even reported her missing? Margaret made a face at the computer. This was useless.

As she exited the bedroom she left the computer running.

In the kitchen she made coffee and choked down some toast. The house screamed the silence of a tomb. Darell had instructed her to wake him at nine.

Margaret prowled the kitchen, coffee in hand, unease a leaden block in her chest. How to convince Darell to change his mind? When the man decided something his feet set in concrete.

And even if she did convince him—what then? They'd be back where they started, with Kaitlan trapped here, helpless.

Toting her coffee cup, Margaret returned to the computer. She refreshed the *San Jose Mercury* page for updates. Nothing new.

She stared out the window into thick fog. The backyard lay obliterated.

Maybe she should go back to perusing D.'s old novels. Yesterday she only read the opening chapters of the first ten. How driven she'd been. But that strong urge had been swept aside amid the events of last night.

Perhaps within one of the books lay an idea not to help Darell catch Craig Barlow after all, but to talk him out of trying.

As Margaret considered that possibility, the urge returned.

She pushed back from the computer. Eight-twenty. She had forty minutes—enough time to scan through the openings of ten or so novels.

In the kitchen Margaret refilled her coffee mug. With purpose she headed to the library and planted herself before the bookcase holding D.'s first editions. An empty space spoke of the novel she'd been reading last night.

Margaret fetched the book from the desk where it lay and returned it to its place on the shelf. She stared at the next novel, D.'s eleventh. *Out of Time.*

Appropriate title.

Breathing a prayer, she slipped it off the shelf.

forty-five

In and out of fog Leland Hugh ran, chased by phantoms. Cloud wisps wound around his head, squeezing his thoughts to cotton. Somewhere he'd lost his way. He saw nothing, heard nothing, felt no earth below his feet. His muscular arms pumped, pumped . . .

Both biceps crumbled. His fingers turned inward, gnarled, the legs beneath him now wobbly and stiff. His mind thickened, and he didn't know what to do, where to go, his thoughts gauzy and white, while something, *something* snatched at his hand, calling him, pulling him—

"D." A voice out of the ether.

His hand jiggled.

"D., wake up."

Darell's eyes opened. He lay in bed, Margaret standing over him. Anxiety tangled her expression.

The dream roiled in his mind. Leland Hugh. The fog. The confusion.

He blinked.

"It's nine o'clock," Margaret said. "Time to get up."

Memory poured over him. *Craig Barlow. Kaitlan.*

Darell pushed up on one elbow and tossed back the covers. "Okay. Right."

Margaret stood back as he finagled his feet to the floor. Detritus from the dream drifted fitfully in Darell's mind like sand settling after the tide. Hugh, lost and alone, becoming *him.*

Why?

A sense of urgency rose within Darell. So much to do. So many details. He reached for his cane, throwing Margaret an impatient glance. "Go on, I don't need your help. I've got to make that call right away."

She folded her arms, determination etching her face. "D., I don't want you to do it."

"Huh?"

"You're not going to lure that killer here."

What a way to put it. He gawked at her. "Have you gone mad, woman?"

"It's too dangerous."

"I have to save Kaitlan."

"We'll find another way."

"You got a better idea?"

"Yes, let the police handle it. Like we should have done in the first place."

"Oh, right. They're doing a real good job."

She shook her head impatiently. "I was reading your old novels, thinking one of them might give us an idea of what to do. That's why one was lying out in the library last night — "

"What are you blathering about, woman?" One of his books off its shelf? He had no memory of any such thing.

"See?" Margaret hunched forward as if she'd scored a major point. "You can't even remember that. Yet you think you can outwit this killer — "

"I know I can outwit him!" Darell waved his cane.

"D. — "

"Stop talking to me like I'm an old man!" He lurched to his feet. "My only grandchild needs saving, and I'm going to do it."

Margaret stood her ground, vertical lines puckering around her tightened lips. "Is this really about Kaitlan? Or is this about proving yourself—to *you*?"

The words stabbed to the core of him. Darell's face went hot. He threw back his shoulders and stalked around her with all the dignity he possessed. "Out of my path, woman, I've got work to do."

She reached for his arm. "D., please—"

He yanked from her grip. Stepped sideways to push his face into hers. "Do not say another word!"

Darell jerked around and steamrolled for the bathroom. Once inside he slammed the door.

Rage rattled in his chest. He glared at himself in the mirror, seeing nothing but a grizzled man, his eyebrows moldy gray bundles of straw, white hair tufted and wild.

He had *not* seen a book out of place in the library last night. Margaret was making things up just to confuse him.

How dare she question his abilities? Even worse, his motives?

Leland Hugh materialized in his thoughts. Hugh in the fog, lost. Turning into him.

"Aah!" Darell thwacked the mirror with his palm and wrenched away. Bent over his cane, he fumed at the beige tile floor. Hugh was turning into more of a mystery than ever. Darell's last hope for finishing his book could well lie in Craig Barlow's manuscript. Tonight before he trapped the man if he could just glean some insight . . .

Hugh's voice echoed in his head. Joined by Margaret and Kaitlan and Craig. Soon all four clamored, jumbling Darell's brain. Concentration started slipping, slipping . . .

Darell buffed his face. What was that first thing he had to do?

His eyes rose to twin blue towels hanging on their gold rack. He frowned at them, through them . . .

Tonight's meeting. He had to call Craig to set it up.

Just like that a moving pathway in Darell's mind cleared. He stepped upon it. But as he rode along, purpose morphed to fear. What this day would demand of him.

At the sink he splashed his face, dried his hands, his movements jerky, nervous. By the time he left the bathroom his heart thwacked his ribs.

Ridiculous. This is only the phone call.

Margaret had moved across the hall to plant herself in the office doorway. Her face still scrunched with worry, one hand pressed to the side of her neck. "D., I'm sorry. I'm just . . . scared."

"You ought to be. Sorry, I mean." He made a move to brush around her but she stayed firm. He threw her a withering look. "Let me by."

She slapped both palms against the doorposts, blocking the entrance. "Remember your book *Over the Waters*? About the couple on a cruise ship and the wife disappeared?"

"No. I don't. Now move before I make you."

"One of the stewards was involved. The husband knew it and set this elaborate plan to catch him. And the whole thing went awry—"

"That's a story, Margaret!" He banged his cane so hard against the floor shock waves jittered up his arm. "This is real!"

"I know. But what if—"

"Get out of my way!"

Movement in Darell's peripheral vision turned his head. Kaitlan stood halfway down the hall, shoulders drawn inward, round-eyed. Her clothes looked thrown on, her hair mussed.

Margaret followed his gaze. The vibrations from her smoothed out, as if she'd been caught making a scene. Her hands fell from the doorposts. "Good morning, Kaitlan." She forced a wan smile.

Kaitlan approached warily, head half turned, looking at them askance. "What's going on?"

Darell glared sideways at Margaret. "We were just discussing today's plans."

"Nothing's changed, right? We're going through with this insanity?" Kaitlan pulled up beside him, hugging herself. Her cheek mixed deeper shades of purple and red, streaks down to her chin. The scrapes she'd taken from her fall stood out angry and rough.

Margaret sucked in air at the sight of her.

Kaitlan touched her fingers to the area and winced. "I know. I look terrible."

Her vulnerability ripped at Darell's chest. What Craig had done to her. And her cheek screamed only of the surface pain.

He would get her out of this.

"Absolutely no change, Kaitlan." Darell planted a hand on Margaret's shoulder and firmly pushed her aside. "I'm calling Craig right now as a matter of fact. And I need total silence" — he hitched his eyebrows in a glower at Margaret — "from the two of you."

Nose in the air, he thumped his way across the office with rank determination. His heart rat-tatted — and that infuriated him.

He reached his desk, feeling like a prisoner approaching the noose.

forty-six

Darell sank into his desk chair and surveyed the phone. He could feel the eyes of the two women at his back. Margaret and her dread of his failure. Kaitlan's life dependence on his success.

Calm yourself, man. Collect your thoughts.

He picked up the receiver. Mentally he scrabbled for last night's reasoning about his plan.

How serendipitous that Craig Barlow had possessed the nerve to hack into his manuscript. For once being thought old and infirm had worked to Darell's advantage. The kid wouldn't have dared such a thing three years ago, when Darell's work was still being published.

Darell half turned. "Kaitlan, do you know the number to the Gayner Police?"

"No. I would just call Craig on his cell phone."

"Okay, doesn't matter."

But somehow it did. That small unknown — a portent.

Darell dialed 411 and requested the number to the Gayner Police Station.

"Is this an emergency?" the operator asked.

Only my granddaughter's life. "No, the front desk will be fine."

As the computer-generated voice intoned the seven digits, he wrote them down, then disconnected. He stared at the receiver in his hand.

For Kaitlan.

Darell dialed the number.

"Gayner Police." A woman's voice.

"Good morning. This is Darell Brooke. I'm trying to get through to Officer Craig Barlow."

Stunned hesitation vibrated the line. "*The* Darell Brooke? The author?"

In that inopportune moment it all flooded back. The adulation. The reputation he'd once wielded. How he missed it.

"That's correct."

"Wow! Hello! I've read *all* your books. This is amazing; how *are* you?"

"I'm well, thank you."

"That's great. Great! Are you writing again? I can't wait to read a new book from you."

That would make two of us.

"Yes, I'm writing. In fact, that's why I'm trying to reach Officer Barlow. I need to ask him some research questions about police procedure."

Silence behind him. He pictured Margaret and Kaitlan holding their breath.

"Oh." Hesitation coated the woman's response. "Uh, you sure you don't mean the chief?"

"No. His son, Craig."

"Oh, okay. He's on patrol. I can contact him with your phone number. I'm sure he'll call soon as he can. He's a fan too."

No kidding.

"That would be great." Darell gave the woman his number. "Tell him I'm stuck on this manuscript until my questions are answered. I'd appreciate talking to him as soon as possible about setting up a meeting for tonight."

"I will. So nice to talk to you!"

"Thanks. You too."

Darell hung up the phone — and exhaled. His hands trembled.

"What happened?" Margaret blurted.

Darell started. Turning stiffly he threw Margaret a look. "I left a message, all right? That's all I can do at the moment. Now stop gnashing your teeth and fix my breakfast."

He hoped he could eat.

Margaret's hand rose to her chest, all argument beaten out of her. Besides, it was too late. Events had been put in motion.

"I . . . Okay." She gave Kaitlan's shoulder a harried pat as she drifted away.

Kaitlan sidled over the threshold, her arms still clutched and brows knitted. She leaned against the wall, eyes begging Darell to tell her all would be well.

He firmed his expression into that of a poker player sure to win. "Trap set." One side of his mouth tugged upward. "Now for the prey to come along."

forty-seven

Craig smacked his cell phone shut and hurled it into the passenger seat.

Linda at the station's front desk had been so excited about Darell Brooke's call. One day ago, he would have been too.

This "research" meeting was a sure setup.

What in the world did the old man think he could do?

Blood simmering, Craig stared out the windshield of his patrol car at Kaitlan's garage apartment. Morning sun filtered through the trees, spotting the front stoop, the gray-painted wood. Birds chirped in the forest, and a squirrel scampered by, cheeks bulging. The sun went down, the sun came up, forest creatures slept and woke. How perfectly the world continued to turn.

Nature taunted him. His containment had failed.

Sudden rage drove his flattened palm against the steering wheel. Again and again he hit, cursing with each blow, pulse pounding in his head and heels dug into the floor. His life was unraveling. Fate threatened to swallow him whole, and he *hadn't. Been. Able. To. Contain it!*

Spent, he threw himself back against the seat, chest puffing.

His police radio crackled. Dispatch was calling an officer out on a domestic disturbance. The exchange brought Craig back to focus. He closed his eyes. He had to pull himself together.

Clamping down his breathing, he listened to the skid of his heart.

It was bad enough that Kaitlan had escaped last night. Even worse when he'd returned to find she'd sneaked back and snatched her purse and toiletries. He should have known then she wouldn't show at work this morning. But he'd clung to hope.

Now this.

Craig pressed his knuckles against his forehead. Now the containment would be harder. Messier. He could get caught.

No. He would never be caught.

Their bodies must not be found.

Craig hadn't thought Kaitlan would go to her grandfather. Clearly, they were estranged. He'd talked about Darell Brooke numerous times, trying to draw her out, but she'd never admitted their relation. And Craig hadn't wanted to admit how thoroughly he'd checked up on her when they first started dating. Computers could do a lot these days. He'd been amazed to discover her connection to Darell Brooke. But Kaitlan had stuck to her story—she had no family. Her only living relatives, including her mother, had thrown her out of their lives.

Recently, when Craig's father had run Kaitlan Sering through the system, he hadn't dug past her mother's name change to discover Kaitlan's connection to Brooke. Craig had kept the knowledge to himself, afraid that his father or Hallie would let it slip to Kaitlan.

How glad he was of that.

More chatter from dispatch. Craig's unit was being summoned for back-up to the domestic disturbance call. He radioed that he was on his way. How normal his voice sounded.

Officer Craig Barlow performed a perfect two-point turn in Kaitlan's driveway and took off. As he rounded the curve, the idea dawned. What he must do this afternoon—for containment.

A humorless smile bent his mouth.

How ironic.

forty-eight

Eleven o'clock. Kaitlan hunched at the breakfast table, nibbling saltine crackers and drinking mint tea—Margaret's suggestion for her icky stomach. Her eyes felt gritty and her chest made of stone. Not to mention every muscle in her body hurt. She must have hit that car last night at sixty miles an hour. And her side where Craig had kicked her throbbed.

She hoped the baby was all right.

Margaret was furiously sponging down the already spotless refrigerator.

The crackers sat like sawdust in Kaitlan's mouth. All the same her nausea was beginning to settle.

Before she collapsed into bed at 2:30 a.m., Kaitlan had left a message at the salon. She was sick and throwing up. She wouldn't be in the following morning—please reschedule her appointments.

It wasn't far from the truth.

She picked up another cracker.

Craig hadn't called yet. Dread lolled in the pit of Kaitlan's stomach.

They'd counted on him to return the call quickly. As soon as the meeting was confirmed they had to call the computer technician, the private investigator, and the reporter. Those people had to travel here and meet with them over details. The tech had to run his diagnostics and leave. The entire setup could take hours.

Why hadn't Craig phoned?

Maybe he was out on a call right now. As soon as he was done and could check his cell for the message ...

He had to be incensed at her disappearance. He'd probably checked her apartment a half dozen times—

The phone rang. Kaitlan jumped.

Margaret's back stiffened, her sponge poised in the air. "D. has to answer."

Kaitlan's eyes riveted to the receiver, her skin tingling. The mere thought that Craig could be on the other end of the line made her want to run and hide.

No second ring.

Her head snapped around. "I have to hear what's happening."

"Don't let your grandfather see you!"

Kaitlan was already scurrying out of the kitchen.

On cat feet she crept down the hall toward the office. The door stood open, her grandfather's voice drifting from the room. At the edge of the threshold she flattened herself against the wall, pulse fluttering. She closed her eyes and steeled herself. If she was this bad now, what would it be like with Craig in the house?

"Yes," her grandfather said. "It shouldn't take too long. But I'd like to sit down with you and lay out my scenario."

A pause.

"Yes, I know he's the chief of police. But you're the one I want. To tell the truth, I'm killing two birds with one stone. Some time ago a friend of yours on the force emailed me saying what a fan you are of my books. He asked on your behalf if you'd be able to meet me. My memory is vague but I think it was around the time of your birthday, and your friend was holding out wild hope to set it up as your present. I know I'm a little late, and granted now I need *your* help, but if you're willing ..."

Is Craig buying this? Why would he have reason to doubt?

"I'm sorry, I can't remember his name."

Kaitlan held her breath.

"You are? Good for you. Writing that first novel is a difficult thing." Her grandfather's voice tinged with excitement. "Tell you what, Craig, in return for your help, if you'd like to bring a chapter or two I'd be happy to look at it when we're done."

Surely Craig's head was swimming over his good fortune. For one minute at least he wouldn't be thinking about finding her.

"I was thinking of seven o'clock."

Kaitlan peeked around the corner. At his desk chair her grandfather hunched over, clutching the phone. The hard jut of his knuckles captured her eyes. So white. Not the hand of a confident man.

"I see. How much earlier?"

"Oh." His voice wavered. "Three o'clock."

Three? Craig would finish his shift at two. That gave him plenty of time to go home, change clothes. But that was way too early for *them*. What if they couldn't get everything in place by then?

Her grandfather rubbed the phone hard with his thumb. His right hand rose and gripped a thatch of his hair as if to pull logical thought from his brain. Kaitlan could see him struggle to refigure, to get things back on track. Her eyes widened. Surely he wasn't considering this.

Come on, come on, tell him it has to be later!

His head turned and she saw her grandfather in profile, unshaven jaw working. He looked so feeble, so old. For a terrifying moment his face went blank.

Kaitlan's heart skidded to her toes. He couldn't do this. He'd never pull it off with Craig, never. Craig was too smart.

Her grandfather took a deep breath and managed to recharge himself. "All right, if that's your only time."

No! She wanted to run into the room and wave her arms. *Stop* him.

"Three o'clock it is. Let me give you directions ..."

Kaitlan's eyelids sank shut. They'd never make it.

forty-nine

Darell set down the receiver and stared at it. His left fingers flexed, trying to loosen. Elation and fright and dread tumbled around in his gut. He was really going to do this. He would trap this killer—for Kaitlan.

And he'd get to read some of Craig's manuscript!

Somewhere in the back of his brain a warning bell feebly chimed. Three o'clock. Darell checked the time. Less than four hours away.

Last night's phone conversations popped to mind. *Four hours.*

What had he done?

Clothes rustled behind him. Darell jerked around. Kaitlan stood inside the door, hands to her mouth, face ashen.

"Three?" She looked about to throw up. "You'd better start making calls."

Defensiveness chafed him. Darell growled in his throat. "You and Margaret, refusing to trust me." He made a face. "Get out of here, I've got work to do—for *you*."

Turning his back on her, he snatched up the phone.

fifty

Craig was coming—at three?

Margaret leaned both hands on the kitchen sink. *Lord, help us.*

Kaitlan hovered nearby, her forehead crisscrossed with lines. Desperation rolled off her in waves. "I don't think he even realized what he did until he hung up."

Margaret wrung out the sponge and threw it down. She should have stood her ground with D. and made him stop.

"Please tell me he can do this." Kaitlan's eyes glimmered. She touched her bruised cheek as if it were a mere token of what Craig would do to her if the plan failed.

Reality squeezed Margaret's lungs. This had to work for Kaitlan's sake. Not another lick of energy, not another second could be spent on worrying or last-minute changes. It was too late. D. would need all the help she could give to make it work.

Margaret placed her hands on Kaitlan's shoulders, willing the fright from her voice. "Of course he can." She pulled back and took a deep breath. "I'll go see what I can do to help. You should get dressed."

She bustled from the kitchen.

In the office D. was hanging up the phone. He turned at the sound of her footsteps. "Pete will be here within an hour."

Margaret nodded, studying him. His eyes looked alert, back straight. Energy chugged from him like a warming engine. It wasn't likely to last long, especially given his lack of a full night's sleep. "Does he think he can set up by three?"

Defensiveness flitted across D.'s face. "Pete can. The computer tech he set me up with—name's Martin Something-or-Other—wasn't supposed to be available until midafternoon. I told Pete to tell him I'd pay him triple."

D.'s expression gave him away. He'd indeed forgotten the detail of the tech's availability when he talked to Craig. Margaret refused to let her dismay show. Without proof of the hacking, where would they be? "And the reporter?"

"I've got to call him right now." D.'s face slacked. He shuffled through papers on his desk. "Where is that number . . ."

"Right here." Margaret pointed to a yellow sheet of paper he had shown her and Kaitlan last night. Ed Wasinsky, from Channel Seven.

"Yes, yes, I see it." Darell waved her away.

The reporter—and cameraman he'd bring along—had no idea what they would be filming. Ed knew only that he'd been offered an "explosive exclusive" story, if he would trust Darell Brooke. If it weren't for Darell's reputation, Margaret had no doubt the station wouldn't have released him and a cameraman to come.

But would they be available so many hours earlier than expected?

D. focused on the paper and started dialing. Margaret held her breath.

Within minutes D. was able to speak to Ed Wasinsky. He and his cameraman couldn't leave San Francisco until around one-thirty. That would put them here at two. It was barely enough time to be briefed and get into place.

D. shot her a stubborn look. "They'll get here. Stop worrying."

"I just—"

The phone rang. He plucked up the receiver. Margaret could hear the gravelly voice on the other end. It was Pete, saying Martin Schloss would do his best to leave his house by noon.

D. hung up the phone triumphantly. "See? Everything's falling into place."

Maybe. If nothing went wrong. If there was no traffic . . . "Yes, D., it'll be fine."

Out of tasks, D. took a sharp breath and looked around, as if not knowing what to do next. His chest caved, and he sagged in his chair. His gaze wandered to the floor.

Margaret touched his arm. "You've got time now to shave and clean yourself up. Maybe rest a little."

He blinked up at her. "Yeah. Okay."

Not even an argument about resting. For once Margaret wished he'd snapped at her.

D. reached for his cane and struggled from the chair. "When Pete and the rest of them come they'll be setting up in the library."

Her eyes rounded. "D., no! It's all the way on the other side of the house."

"It's the best choice. The upstairs floors squeak. And my bedroom's too close. One noise from any of you in there could filter across the hall."

"That's not what you said last night! You made me think we'd be right next—"

"I didn't say what room; you just assumed it."

"But you'll be alone with him. If something happens—"

"Shut up, Margaret!" He thumped his cane against the floor. "I'm tired of your arguments!"

He stalked from the room.

Margaret opened her mouth to lash out again, then snapped it shut. Fighting with him would only rile him up more, and right now he needed to rest. Pete would have to persuade him.

D.'s bedroom door banged shut.

She brought a hand to her forehead. It sounded like he was beyond rest already.

A *skreek* nearby made her jump. Margaret's gaze cut to the window behind D.'s desk. A scraggly oak branch scratched the glass like the twisted fingernail of a hag.

Beyond, the fog had barely lifted, gnarled trees on the front lawn grayed and ghoulish.

What if Pete and the others couldn't find their way?

The branch screeched again. Margaret shivered.

Abruptly she strode from the office and headed for the north wing. The vague hiss of water ran through pipes. Kaitlan must be taking a shower upstairs. Margaret turned the corner into the library and stalled, not sure why she'd come. Her eyes flitted over the room. The leather sofa and armchair, D.'s cherry wood desk and phone. Far as this was from the office, D. had a point. Sound wouldn't carry easily from here to there.

She pictured the men with their equipment. They would need an extra table for Pete's monitor. Margaret didn't want the desk scratched.

Hurrying back up the north wing hall, she swerved toward the garage. If she remembered correctly, she'd seen a square folding table there.

The garage smelled faintly of oil and dust. Margaret's footsteps echoed as they clipped over the concrete floor. She passed D.'s black Mercedes in the first parking space, her own Subaru in the second. The third space remained empty, as did the fourth. Pete and the tech could park here, leaving the reporter and cameraman to hide their car just outside the garage. Craig Barlow was to remain in the front part of the house, unable to see the visitors' vehicle in the rear driveway.

At least that was the plan.

In the storage closet at the far side she found the folding table.

It took her three trips to carry the table and its four chairs into the library. Only when she'd set them all up and stood back, hot and anxious-ridden, did she realize there was little chance they'd need the chairs.

Sweat itched her forehead. Snatching a tissue from the desk, she wiped it away.

She started to fold the chairs up and return them to the garage. Then she thought better of it.

Margaret wandered the room, hands clasped and pumping up and down, praying. Her nerves thrummed.

She envisioned Kaitlan's cheek, the terror in the girl's every move last night. The ghastly face of the dead woman, a black and green cloth knotted around her neck.

The man who caused all that would be here in three hours.

Margaret's eyes grazed over the wall clock. A minute before twelve.

The news. She swerved toward her suite. Grabbing up the remote from her bed, she switched the TV on.

Margaret shifted on her feet while endless ads ran. She jabbed in another local channel. A pretty Asian woman behind a news desk flicked on.

Pacing, Margaret suffered through stories about a fire in a San Francisco warehouse, a three-car accident on Freeway 580 in the East Bay. "After this break—" the anchor announced, "a woman is reported missing in Gayner." A close-up of a smiling brunette filled the screen.

Margaret's breath hitched. That had to be her!

She tossed down the remote and ran from the room. Down the hall, across the entryway and up the stairs to the first guest suite on the right. "Kaitlan!" She banged on the door.

"Yeah?"

"The news is about to report on a woman's disappearance. Come see in my bedroom!"

"Oh! Coming!"

Margaret swiveled back toward the stairs. Behind her she heard a door open, followed by hurried footsteps. She glanced back to see Kaitlan in jeans and a T-shirt, a blue towel wrapped around her head.

By the time they pulled up in front of her TV, the news show had resumed. Kaitlan's head towel leaned like the Tower of Pisa. Distractedly, she shoved it upright.

"And now disturbing news from Gayner." The anchor's large brown eyes gazed into the camera. "Forty-four-year-old Martina Pelsky, a local woman running for a seat on the town council, has been reported missing."

The brunette's face returned to the screen.

"That's her!" Kaitlan hunched forward, one hand fisted at her mouth.

"Pelsky, a nurse at the Redwood City Kaiser and an avid cyclist, is reported as last seen by a neighbor yesterday afternoon as she took off on her bike to leave her campaign flyers door to door throughout Gayner. This morning she failed to appear at a court hearing regarding her pending divorce from her husband, Richard Pelsky, from whom she has been separated for the past four months. Martina's attorney, Edwin Rastor from San Mateo, contacted Gayner police this morning after phoning Martina Pelsky's home repeatedly to no avail. According to police her supervisor at Kaiser reported Pelsky didn't show up for her evening shift yesterday.

"A search of her apartment showed her purse and car had been left behind, with no sign of her bike in the garage. If you have information regarding this woman's whereabouts, please call the Gayner police."

"Martina Pelsky." Kaitlan whispered the name.

Margaret had never heard it before.

The news shifted to another story, now mere noise. Margaret turned off the TV. She looked at Kaitlan, who was still staring at the blackened set.

"It's her, Margaret. And she looked so ... alive."

Kaitlan sank down the bed, head hanging. A tear pushed onto her cheek. Margaret sat beside her and rubbed her back.

"It's so hard to believe." Kaitlan dragged in a breath. "Yesterday her life was just going along and now she's dumped out there somewhere like trash." Kaitlan brushed the tear away. "I didn't even know her, but it feels ..." She shook her head. "And you know what? Even now I want to believe Craig didn't do it. Not because I want to be with him anymore." She shuddered. "But because of my baby. I never had a father. Now neither will she."

Margaret massaged harder. "I'm sure you'll meet a terrific man who'll take your child as his own."

Kaitlan shrugged. The gesture tugged at Margaret's heart. So much pain this girl had experienced. "You know, Kaitlan, you don't have to go through all this alone."

"God, you mean? I know. I haven't told you how I ... found Him when I was kicking the drugs. I know He saved my life then. Gave me a fresh start. Even brought me back to this house."

Margaret smiled wanly. "I'd been praying for that since you left."

Kaitlan's face lifted toward her. "Really?"

"Yup."

Kaitlan looked away and nodded, as if affirming to herself the prayers accounted for her return. She swallowed and lifted her shoulders. "Martina Pelsky. We have to tell Grand—"

From the entrance hall the gate's bell sounded.

Margaret jumped up, nerves buzzing. "Pete's here."

fifty-
one

As Margaret pushed the button to open the front gate for Pete, Kaitlan ran upstairs. For one minute she blow-dried her hair, then ran a comb through the wetness. It would have to dry the rest of the way on its own. Her heart skipped around and her fingers shook. Craig wasn't even here yet and look at her already. So much at stake.

So very much.

She eyed herself in the mirror. The purple-red stain on her cheek now clawed at her nose and stained under her jaw. With no makeup and fear glazing her eyes, she looked like a beaten waif.

But she was far from that.

Downstairs a short muscular man with a huge belly hanging over his jeans was hauling two leather black bags through the front door. Margaret stood by, hands clasped to her chest.

"Hi." The man's throaty voice greeted Kaitlan as she bounded off the bottom stair. His gaze riveted to her cheek. His eyes were mud green and deep, his shoulder-length brown hair pulled back in a ponytail. His long-sleeved blue shirt hung baggy. Pockmarks bit into his face and a one-inch scar jagged under his left eye. He looked like a boxer way past his prime. On a bad day.

Where had her grandfather found this guy?

"You must be Kaitlan." He studied her bruise, his expression mixing sympathy and indignation. An aura of confidence and grit wafted from him, as though he'd experienced all the world could throw at him and survived.

"Yeah."

The expanse of what this day would bring swept over Kaitlan. Her life would never be the same. If it all worked right, if Craig was caught, she would end up on TV, exposed. Millions of people ogling pictures of her purpled cheek. Would they judge her for ever dating Craig? Would they dig into her background and label her a drug addict?

Pete nodded and his eyes tightened as if he read her soul. "No worries. We'll fix it." He turned down the hall and strode heavily toward the office.

Kaitlan threw Margaret a glance and scurried after him. Margaret followed.

In the office Kaitlan's grandfather stood scowling at a bookcase in the front far corner of the room. "How do you propose to hide that thing on here?" Irritation singed his voice.

Kaitlan probed her tender cheek.

Pete set his bags on the square table across from the computer desk. He shoved thick-fingered hands on his hips and surveyed the shelf. "We need a plant on top."

"Margaret," Kaitlan's grandfather snapped, "go get a plant!"

She melted out the door and soon returned with a large philodendron. "Here. From the dining room."

"Perfect." Pete pulled a chair over to the bookcase to stand on. Margaret thrust the plant into his hands. He set it on top.

For fifteen minutes Pete finagled his high-tech equipment into place. First the camera complete with microphone, no bigger than three inches square, was set on a rotating stand. Hiding it in the green leaves, Pete aimed it at a designated chair at the table. The chair with its back to the wall, facing the front windows.

There, Craig would be sitting.

Pete switched on a laptop. As it booted up he pulled a black oval contraption from its case. It resembled a video game control with an upright lever like a gear shift.

Kaitlan's grandfather watched Pete's efficient movements with the keen eye of a hawk tracking a mouse.

"Everything's wireless." Pete leaned over the laptop and typed. Kaitlan, her grandfather, and Margaret all edged closer to see the screen.

The empty chair appeared.

"Hah!" Kaitlan's grandfather leaned in eagerly. The camera's angle would give them about a three-quarter shot of Craig's face, and her grandfather's profile.

"Now just in case the camera's not aimed quite right ..." Pete nudged past Margaret to the black control. "Watch." He gently manipulated the lever. The picture on the screen shifted to a close-up.

"Good, good." Her grandfather looked victorious.

Kaitlan hugged herself. Could this work after all? If her grandfather could just keep his wits about him ...

Pete jerked up straight and checked his watch. "We gotta move. What room are we setting up in?"

"The library, in the north wing." Kaitlan's grandfather threw a warning look at Margaret.

She focused on Pete. "Will your wireless go that far?"

"It'll go a lot farther than this house."

Margaret looked disappointed. "But we won't be close to this room. In case something goes wrong."

Pete's eyes bounced from Margaret to Kaitlan's grandfather. "Nothing's going to go wrong. Our target will never know we're here, right? That's the plan. He'll have his meeting with Darell, leave, and be none the wiser." Pete spread his mouth in an evil grin. "Until the law comes knocking on his door."

He is *the law.*

Sudden anger at her grandfather sprayed through Kaitlan. Stubborn old man, thinking he could pull this off. She'd never known him to listen to anyone.

Pete jerked his thumb toward the front yard. "I've got to get the monitor out of my car to hook to this computer. I wanted the reporter to have a bigger screen to film." He rolled toward the door.

"When you're done you need to move your car to the garage." Margaret hurried out behind Pete to show him the way.

With Pete gone, the room fell quiet. Kaitlan turned to her grandfather. He stared hollow-eyed at the door. Kaitlan's throat dried out. Great, he was already losing it. "You okay?"

He blinked and shook his head. "Yes. Yes, of course." He pushed up his spine and gave her a stern look. "Why wouldn't I be?"

She bit her lip.

His gaze ambled to Pete's laptop screen, the empty chair upon it. Anticipation lit his eyes. "Craig Barlow's going to help me with my manuscript." He mumbled it half to himself.

"What?"

"That's my plan." He rubbed a thumb against his cane.

His mind *was* going. "What are you talking about?"

"His character's based on mine, you know — on Leland Hugh. I need to jumpstart my plot. Craig's bringing a chapter or two. I'll take from them whatever I can use."

Shock took hold of Kaitlan's stomach and dragged it inside out. Her mouth dropped open. Suddenly the crazy things her grandfather had said yesterday — needing a twist, not disappointing readers — made eminent sense.

"You're bringing Craig here — because of your *book?*"

Her grandfather's head jerked, as if he'd let something slip. "Well, no, of course not — "

"Then why did you say he's going to help you?"

"Because ... I haven't ..."

"Haven't what? Been able to write?" Kaitlan surged three steps away from him. "I don't believe this!" She swiveled around. "So my coming to you for help was perfectly timed, is that it? Help a granddaughter, get a story."

Her grandfather pulled back his head. "What nonsense are you accusing me of?"

"You just said it. You're using me to get you a plot!"

His cheeks flushed. "I am *not* using you!"

Kaitlan jabbed a finger toward Pete's laptop. "This plan of yours will never work. But you don't care, you just want your book."

"It will work!" Her grandfather waved his cane. "I've thought through—"

"Even if Craig leaves here not knowing a thing, the state police will never listen." Kaitlan paced, panic biting her heels. They'd been through all this last night, but she'd been tired enough to stop fighting. Now they were done for. Out of time and everything was crumbling away.

"Girl, don't be an idiot," he spat. "They will listen. With our proof they can tie Craig to the fabric—"

"Stop it, just stop it! None of this matters. The guy who wants to kill me is going to be here soon—and what are you thinking about? Your book!" Kaitlan thrust both hands in the air, her throat tightening. "That's how it's always been with you—your work. You don't care about anybody else or any other thing—just you. The King of Suspense and his writing!" Kaitlan's hands slid over her eyes. She was going to cry, and she hated herself for it.

"What on earth?" Margaret's astounded voice came from the doorway.

Kaitlan raised her head. Her grandfather's eyes were burning coals. "Go ahead, tell her."

He pointed his cane at Kaitlan. "I ought to throw you out of here, you ungrateful little brat."

The world blurred. So it was back to this. "Maybe I just want to live! Maybe I just want to believe that you care about my safety more than your writing."

"I do care about your safety, or you wouldn't be here!"

"It sure doesn't sound like it!"

Margaret's hands fluttered to the base of her throat.

"He just wants a plot." Kaitlan flung a hand toward her grandfather. "Figures he can get it from Craig's manuscript. He told me."

Margaret's eyes cut to Kaitlan's grandfather. "What's she talking about?"

"Nonsense, that's what." Her grandfather snorted.

Margaret looked from him to Kaitlan like a referee considering how best to calm a fight. "Kaitlan. Arguing now will only tire him."

"But he—"

"Do you want Craig caught?"

Kaitlan tipped her head back and sighed. Tears rolled out of her eyes. She just wanted to run and hide.

Pete barreled into the room. One look at their faces and he pulled up short, palms rising, as if apologizing for his interruption of a family argument. He cocked his head at Kaitlan's grandfather. "It's ready."

"Good."

Awkward silence tremored.

Weariness flushed through Kaitlan, sweeping her anger away. She turned eyes on her grandfather, seeking one sign that she should trust him.

He glared at her, thin shoulders rising with each breath.

Pete's cell phone rang. He pulled it from his belt holder and checked the ID. "Yeah, Martin." He listened, then drew a deep breath. "Come on, man, we need you."

Kaitlan swiped at a tear. The overhead light threw shadows on Pete's pockmarks, digging them deeper.

"I know you thought it would be tonight, but—" Pete's eyes squinted. "Tell you what, his offer just went up. Five times what I told you." He threw a glance at Kaitlan's grandfather, who nodded.

Kaitlan could vaguely hear Martin's voice, ticking through further excuses. Something had come up, no way could he leave work right now. This wasn't what they'd agreed.

Pete argued and upped the payment two more times. He argued some more. Finally he heaved a sigh. "All right, man. Later."

He snapped the phone shut. "The tech can't come."

fifty-two

Don't think I will be taken. Don't believe for a minute I will be tricked.

They think they are so clever. That I can't see.

Let me ask you—who is more ruthless? More driven?

I didn't choose this gift, it chose me. In anyone else's hands the black and green silk is just cloth. It takes cunning, ingenuity, the ability to shed light where there is none, to give it Purpose.

I don't regret what I have done.

I will protect myself at any cost.

Try me, you'll see. I welcome it. I can't wait for it.

You think you can heal me? Redeem me? Like this is some curse to be rid of?

So little you know. And you claim to be enlightened.

What I have is freedom. And no one will take it from me.

I am ready. Strong.

My hands itch.

fifty-
three

Darell sank into a chair at his office table. His limbs wobbled from the brunt of Kaitlan's anger.

The brat. Thought she knew everything.

He frowned. What had just happened? Something gone wrong ...

His mind churned like a wheel in mud.

The answer surfaced. Pete's computer tech couldn't come.

So what? Darell could do this without details of the hacking. They knew Craig did it—that's what counted. He'd pretend he had the proof.

Darell's gaze fell on Pete's laptop. Screensaver photos rolled—Pete and his Great Dane on the beach, cuddling a little boy in a white cane rocker. Pete was crazy about his grandkids.

"Now what?" Kaitlan's voice accused. Her eyes darted from Darell to Pete.

Darell sighed. "It's fine, Granddaughter, fine." His mouth dragged downward. Would she even be thankful when this was over?

"But how—"

"I don't need the proof right now, all right? We'll get it soon enough. Pete, call the tech back and tell him to come tonight."

"Yeah, okay." Pete nodded. "So you wing it. It's all in the presentation."

"But without proof stuck in front of him, Craig won't admit it," Kaitlan cried. "We'll have nothing."

"Then let him deny it!" Darell smacked the table. "When we get proof I'll press charges and the police will still have to investigate. That'll lead to everything else."

"But—"

"*Quiet!*"

Darell seethed at the laptop. A new picture rolled in. Pete, feeding a pink-clad baby with a bottle.

Darell shook his head, clearing it. Time he took back charge of this situation. "Pete, I want to see what you've done in the library." He pushed out of the chair, glowering at Kaitlan. "And I don't want another word out of *you.*"

fifty-four

Margaret and Pete trailed her grandfather out of the office. Kaitlan refused to follow.

Left alone, she stalked the hardwood floor, insides roiling.

None of this would work. The plan was stupid, stupid. Margaret knew it too. But would Kaitlan's grandfather listen? Oh, no. He just wanted to write his book.

Fear and dread clumped in Kaitlan's lungs. She passed a window and stalled, gazing into the fog. A wind sent swirls of mist dipping, turning, whisking ghost fingers against the pane.

She pictured the dead woman's silently screaming face and shuddered.

The clock read 1:40 p.m.

Kaitlan fretted her way out of the office and up the hall. She found herself in the formal living room on the other side of the entryway. All muted colors of browns and beige, everything perfect. She could remember when her grandfather would hold grand parties here. When wine glasses clinked and women trilled laughter and men tried to emulate the great King of Suspense, standing straighter in his presence, working their eyebrows.

Once, even, her mother had come.

Kaitlan slid onto the corner of a couch, brought her knees up, and hugged them. When this plan failed she would have to flee the area, she and her unborn baby. Go ... somewhere.

But in what car—with Craig's ability to track her license plate? The gate's bell sounded. *The reporter.*

Margaret's footsteps clicked up the hall. Around the corner, unseen, Kaitlan listened dully as she answered the bell.

"It's Ed Wasinsky."

"Yes, good! Come on up."

Kaitlan wandered out to the entryway as her grandfather and Pete appeared. Soon two men were at the door, a notepad in the reporter's hand, a camera balanced on the shoulder of his partner. Ed Wasinsky was tall and broad-chested, thick blond hair parted on the side. Wide lips, a Grecian nose. Booming voice. The guy had TV written all over him.

He looked at Kaitlan's face, and his eyelids flickered.

Her gaze dropped to the floor.

Sam, the cameraman, was a bald guy with a bulldog face and one gold loop earring. "Where can I put this?" He jerked his head toward his equipment.

"In here." Pete gestured toward the north wing, then led him down the hall.

Ed shook hands with Kaitlan's grandfather. "So good to meet you, sir. I'm a big fan."

Of course. Wasn't everybody? The man who lived to write.

"Thank you. Glad you could do this."

They chatted about books for a moment—pure insanity to Kaitlan. A killer was coming here in less than an hour, and the world just turned on. Her grandfather had thrown back his shoulders, trying to stand straight, but Kaitlan saw the strain on his face. He was tired, too tired, and he hadn't had enough sleep, and besides he was half senile, and *this would never work.*

She pressed against the wall, sick to her stomach.

"You need to move your car," Margaret told Ed. "Follow the driveway on around back. I'll open the garage door."

"What's up?" Ed tapped his notebook against his leg, looking to Kaitlan's grandfather. "You told me this was good."

"Oh, it's good all right. And it'll only get better."

Ed's gaze cut to Kaitlan. Curiosity shone in his eyes, mixed with something else. Empathy?

"This involve you?"

She hesitated, then nodded.

"What happened to your cheek?"

Kaitlan stared back defensively. *Reporters.* But for some reason she didn't want this man to think badly of her. "I got hit—twice. And I fell. Running from a madman."

His eyebrows rose. "What madman?"

"The one you need to help us catch. If this works. Which it won't."

Her grandfather huffed.

Ed cocked his head, as if considering which question to ask next. "And if it doesn't?"

"I'm dead."

He flinched. "What—"

"You really must move your car," her grandfather said. "Immediately."

The cameraman and Pete reappeared. Margaret's hands flitted about as she reopened the door. Ed stepped out onto the porch, then turned back. His eyes found Kaitlan's. "Come with me."

She drew back like a frightened child and shook her head.

As he retreated down the porch steps, she hurried to the kitchen for a drink of water.

Placing the glass in the sink, she thought of Craig, and last night, and a half dozen red roses. Suddenly she felt his presence, right behind her, reaching for her throat.

With a cry she whirled—to see only an empty room.

She sagged against the sink, fingers to her lips. She wouldn't survive this. Just the thought of being in the same house with him. If anything went wrong, if he somehow found out she was here . . .

The door from the garage clicked open. Margaret and Ed passed by in the short hall. Kaitlan flung her head up, trying to look normal, knowing she failed badly.

Minutes ticked, ticked away toward Craig's arrival, and the next thing Kaitlan knew their group was gathered in the darkened library, its lights off and shades drawn, her grandfather pointing to the monitor, explaining to Ed what he would see. "Keep your camera on the monitor," he told Sam. "Close up."

"Wait a minute." Ed held up a hand. "This guy doesn't know he's on camera?"

"No."

"I have to check with the station then. That's secret taping—"

"You're not taping him," Pete said. "I am. You're filming *me* filming him. You're okay."

Kaitlan's grandfather nodded.

He'd actually thought of this?

Ed scratched his jaw. "Who is the guy?"

"Craig Barlow." Kaitlan's grandfather spoke the name with disdain. "A Gayner police officer and son of the police chief."

"A policeman?"

"More than that. The killer of the three women in Gayner."

Sam cursed under his breath.

Ed's jaw sagged. "What ... there's a third woman dead?"

"One's missing. You'll hear about it soon."

"You mean the gal running for town council? Martina Pelsky?"

Kaitlan's grandfather shot up his eyebrows. "You heard?"

"Oh." Margaret brought a hand to her cheek. "It was on the news this morning, D."

"Why didn't you tell me?"

"I didn't have a chance—"

"I'm trying to catch her killer, and you didn't even give me this *very important* information?"

Like he was going to bring it up to Craig.

"I'm sorry, we didn't have time."

Kaitlan's grandfather glared at Margaret, the confidence he'd displayed seconds ago rippling from his face. "Anything else I need to know?"

"No, you're fine."

A pitiful laugh escaped Kaitlan. *None* of this was fine.

Ed blinked at her, then her grandfather, as if the whole lot of them was crazy. "How do you know Pelsky's dead?"

"Because I found her," Kaitlan blurted. Her voice sounded shaky, off-tune. She crossed her arms and pulled in her shoulders. Ed gawked at her, and for some reason that made her mad. "She was on my bed, in my apartment. Craig is—was—my boyfriend. He killed her, he buried her body where it won't be found, and now he's trying to keep me quiet, and because I ran from him, now he's trying to kill me too. And he doesn't know Darrel Brooke is my grandfather, so he has no idea this meeting's about *him*. There. That enough for you, Mr. Reporter?"

Silence. Ed's shocked expression mirrored Sam's. Ed pulled out of it first, the experienced calm of a reporter in crisis smoothing his brow. Sympathy pulled at the corner of his mouth. "Craig's the one who hit you?"

Kaitlan's defensiveness dwindled away. She nodded.

The gate bell sounded.

Everyone froze.

"That can't be him!" Margaret burst. "It's only two-thirty."

"It has to be him." Kaitlan's grandfather paled, as if reality suddenly hit. He pushed himself into motion. "I have to answer it."

He shuffled up the north wing hall as fast as he could go, Kaitlan and everyone else chuffing behind him. In the entryway, her grandfather hesitated, visibly pulling himself together. The rest of them crowded around, muscles tense, eyes riveted to the intercom.

He pushed the button. "Hello?"

Kaitlan fisted her hands to her mouth.

"Hi, it's Craig Barlow." A car engine rumbled in the background—too quiet for his Mustang. "Sorry I'm early. And I thought I'd be late." He gave a nervous laugh. "At the last minute I had to put my car in the shop and borrow my sister's SUV."

SUV?

Her grandfather motioned for everyone to remain quiet. "That's all right, Craig. I'm opening the gate for you. You can park in front of the house."

"Thank you."

There was nothing wrong with his car last night ...

The distant clank of the gate filtered through the intercom. Sam started to move and Margaret caught his arm. "Wait," she mouthed.

The engine surged as Craig drove through the gate.

Seconds later the intercom fell silent.

"Go, all of you!" Kaitlan's grandfather snapped. "Into the library! And don't come out no matter what. Remember, he thinks we're alone."

Margaret shot him a final desperate look. "I could send him away, tell him you're sick."

"Go!"

She hung there, uncertain. Then she turned and trotted for the hall. Pete and Sam followed.

"Come on, Kaitlan." Ed grabbed her elbow.

"No, wait!" She yanked her arm away and swung back to her grandfather. "Something's not right. Why would he have such a big car?"

Her grandfather swiped a hand in the air. "Get out of here!"

"But I don't believe him."

"Go, Kaitlan, before he drives up and hears you!"

"Listen to me—"

"Get *out* of here!" Her grandfather thwacked his cane against the floor. "Ed, take her!"

"No—"

"Come on, there's no time." Ed clamped a hand around her shoulder and pulled her toward the hall.

Kaitlan's head twisted back for one last look at her grandfather before the corner of the hallway shut him from sight.

fifty-five

A heady business, meeting a murderous antagonist face to face.

Fascination trickled through Darell's fear.

Craig Barlow stood on his doorstep, clad in a brown sport jacket over jeans. He carried a soft-sided black leather portfolio case, presumably with his manuscript chapters inside. If you didn't know him for what he was, you'd think him a good-looking kid. Perfect face for a killer. Women would never guess.

"Come in, come in." Darell stood back, ushering him into the web, the spider to the fly.

Craig stepped inside. His gaze cruised the entryway as if cataloguing details. "This is just such an honor, Mr. Brooke. Thanks again for inviting me."

Darell surveyed him. A keen confidence overrode his air of faux humility, although no doubt he didn't think it showed. It was in the tilt of his head, the firmness of his mouth. Most telling were his eyes. In their glacial blue Darell saw the depths of the man's calculation. They were eyes that could look straight at you, sheening with sincerity while he lied.

Leland Hugh.

"Thank you for coming." Darell led him down the hall.

Like an old fluorescent light, Darell's brain hummed as he rounded the corner into his office. Weariness pulled at him even as adrenaline

239 ~ dark pursuit

coursed through his veins. So many details to remember. So much he had to get right.

"Please." Darell indicated the chair upon which the hidden camera was fixed. "Sit."

"Thank you." Craig put his black case on the table and settled in the offered chair. Resting his forearms, he laced his hands, torso bent forward, body language exuding the picture of eagerness to help.

Taking his time, Darell positioned himself, resting his cane on the floor.

"So." Craig smiled, and the grooves in his jaw deepened. Such model good looks wouldn't keep long in jail. "What research questions did you want to ask me?"

"Let's talk about you first. Tell me about your writing."

"Oh. Well, I started about a year ago. Have maybe half a book done."

"What's it about?"

He looked chagrined. "It's a suspense novel. A detective investigating a string of homicides."

"Really." Darell raised his eyebrows. "Well, that's right up my alley."

"Yeah." Craig reached for his portfolio and unzipped it. He stuck his hand inside. "I brought some chapters, like you asked." As he pulled out pages, he glanced at the top one. Immediately dismay creased his face. "Oh, no." He slapped down the papers and leaned over to shuffle through the stack.

He looked up at Darell, embarrassed. "I stuck the wrong ones in here."

"That's all right. I'll look at whatever you've got."

"No, no, I—these are an older draft. I had everything in my own car and then had to transfer over when I borrowed my sister's. What I want is probably on the passenger seat. Mind if I go get them?"

Darell started to push back from the table. "Not at all."

"No, just sit." Craig was already on his feet. "I'll just let myself out and come right back."

"No, I'll—"

"Please. I don't want to put you out."

Before Darell could pick up his cane, Craig whisked up the papers, stuffed them into his portfolio, and hurried from the room.

fifty-six

In the library, Kaitlan gasped. "He's going to look through the house!"

On Pete's monitor, her grandfather was cranking his torso around, trying to peer out the office window. Opposite him, Craig's empty chair mocked.

Kaitlan flung a horrified look at Pete. "What if he comes in here?"

Sam swung his camera toward her. She turned away.

"Shh," Pete hissed. "Just wait." He sprang from his chair at the folding table and stepped toward the door. His right hand hovered at his waist.

Hunched over, muscles about to crack, Kaitlan strained with all her might to listen. In the frozen silence she could hear Margaret breathing.

Sam's camera panned to Ed.

The faint metallic click of an opened door latch spun to Kaitlan's ears. Craig had gone outside.

Pete's forefinger came up—*hear that?*

Kaitlan locked eyes with Ed. He nodded grim reassurance. If the reporter hadn't believed them to this point, her fear had clearly rubbed off on him. He stood some six feet away, spine ramrod straight, fingers clasped to the back of a folding chair.

An interminable minute later the front door slammed.

"He's back." Kaitlan's eyes darted to the monitor. Pete returned to watch the screen. His hand remained at his waist.

Sam refocused his camera to the monitor—and the empty chair.

Craig reappeared onscreen.

He tossed down the black case and seated himself, puffing a little. "Sorry about that." Over the microphone his voice sounded a little tinny and distant but clear enough. "They were on the front seat."

"Glad you found them." Kaitlan's grandfather placed his palms on the table.

Pete sat down in his folding chair and reached for the gear shift on his console. Watching the monitor beside him, he nudged the control forward and slightly to the left. Craig's body edged into a close-up.

"So let's have a look." Kaitlan's grandfather's voice, offscreen.

Kaitlan and Margaret locked eyes.

"Okay." Craig opened the case. "Only now I'm really nervous. My writing's probably horrible."

"You have to start somewhere."

Craig slid the pages across the table until they disappeared from the screen.

A pause.

"Your first chapter's in the detective's point of view?"

"Yes."

Silence.

Craig watched. His lip began to curl.

Ice melted down Kaitlan's back. "Look at him."

She pictured her grandfather's head down, focused on the manuscript. Unaware of the transformation taking place.

Pages rustled.

Pete zoomed in even closer on Craig's face. Kaitlan saw the hard, cold look in his eyes. The smugness. The same killer expression he'd used to terrorize her last night.

Margaret sucked in a breath.

Abruptly Craig's smirk vanished. Chased by a small, pleasant smile. The drastic change chilled Kaitlan to the bone.

"Your detective is—"

"Mr. Brooke, you didn't really bring me here just to see my manuscript, did you?"

"Well, no, I have questions to ask you."

"Then why don't we get to them?" That pleasant look hung on, but Craig's tone edged.

Kaitlan's muscles turned to wood. *He knows something's up.*

Her grandfather hesitated. "What, are you pushed for time?"

Craig leaned forward, his smile gone and eyes narrowed. "Let's cut to the chase, shall we, Mr. Brooke? Why did you really bring me here?"

fifty-seven

Margaret swiveled to Kaitlan, feeling sick. "This isn't right."

"Shh." Pete flung up a hand, eyes riveted to the monitor. "If something goes wrong, I've got a gun."

Surprise flicked across Kaitlan's face. She looked at Margaret and swallowed hard.

So what, Margaret thought, *we're too far away to help!* She swung away, a hand thrust to her scalp. Why hadn't she stopped this?

Her focus landed on the bookcase of Darell's first editions. Ratcheted up to the top shelf.

Over the Waters. The cruise-ship story, with the protagonist's plans to catch the killer gone so awry. The warning was right there this morning, if only she'd made Darell listen—

Life After Death. The next novel in line. The title leapt out at her.

Margaret stared at it.

Vaguely, she registered Darell's voice on the monitor.

Life After Death. The title screamed.

Dreamlike, Margaret drifted to the bookcase, already knowing. Ancient memory bubbled like lava, her nerves singeing hot, so hot. Her arm reached up to the top shelf, to the book she would have read next if she hadn't stopped too soon, if she hadn't been so terribly, utterly *stupid* ...

She slid out *Life After Death.*

Craig's and Darell's voices were arguing. They barely registered.

Sam, Pete, somebody in the room uttered a curse.

Margaret opened the hardback book. She skimmed the first page. The second.

Darell's story of years ago — the homicidal ER doctor, the hospital on a far-flung island.

In Margaret's mind, the lava-memories boiled higher and plunged over a cliff.

"Ah!" Kaitlan cried.

On the third page Margaret found it. The fabric. Black silk with green stripes. The cloth the doctor used to strangle his victims.

The novel slipped from Margaret's fingers and slammed to the floor.

fifty-eight

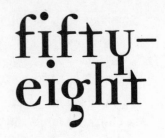

Darell stared at Craig Barlow. What was happening here? And how *dare* the kid talk to him like that?

He tossed down the manuscript papers. "What makes you think I have another reason?"

"'Cause I don't buy the one you gave me."

"That so?"

Craig lasered him with his eyes.

Okay, if this was the way he wanted it. "You sound guilty to me, boy."

"Guilty? About what?"

"About stealing from my work, that's what."

Craig's face scrunched. "Huh?"

"That's right. You hacked into my computer. Don't think I don't know."

"Are you crazy?"

"Not half as crazy as you. I had a computer tech out here. He found your little spy program and traced it straight to you."

Craig sneered. "You don't know what you're talking about."

"I was going to handle this more delicately, till you flew off the handle. Just admit it and promise not to do it again, and I won't go to the police."

"I *am* the police."

"How about the Sheriff's Department? This house is in their jurisdiction. Or the state police. I have some good friends there."

"You can't have half the friends in the state police that my father does."

A rank sense of injustice scissored through Darell's head. Its blades shredded the last of the script he'd hoped to use.

All right then—Plan B. He was ready.

"This is about you, Craig, not your father. About how I'm going to prove what you've done."

"That I'm stealing your work?" Craig laughed derisively. "What's to steal? The way I hear it, you can't even write any more."

Darell slammed a palm against the table. "Do I look like somebody who can't plot a suspense? Who doesn't know how to figure out things? I can tie your hacking to the murders!"

Craig stilled. His blue eyes burned white hot. Slowly he leaned forward, a snake positioning to strike. "Say again, old man?"

"You want to see what this 'old man' can do?" Darell spat. "I'll connect you to the black and green fabric. The cloth you used to strangle three women. Yes, three. You were stupid enough to take pictures of the last one."

Craig shoved back and jumped to his feet. His chair bounced against the wall and clattered to its side. "I knew this was a setup." He slid a hand into his jacket and pulled out a gun. "Call Kaitlan in here. Right now."

fifty-nine

At the crack of the book against hardwood floor, Kaitlan jumped. She jerked around to Margaret and saw the woman hunched over with hands to her head. *What—?*

Craig's seething low voice yanked Kaitlan back to the monitor. Pete had zoomed out his camera to show both men, her grandfather's face in profile.

"Say again, old man?"

Kaitlan's breath hitched. "Somebody do something!"

Sam filmed on, Ed standing with his feet apart, arms folded. Pete's hand hung above the console even as he pushed back his chair and slid to its edge, ready to rise.

"This can't work." Margaret blurted. "He read it in a *book*."

What was she—

"... you were stupid enough to take pictures of the last one."

Kaitlan's fingers clapped to her mouth. Her grandfather had careened off course. Totally lost it.

She ogled his profile, seeing fury—and something else. Grim determination.

In that horrifying second, understanding steamrolled Kaitlan. *The filming. He hadn't lost it.* He'd planned for this. If Craig wouldn't cooperate, her grandfather's accusations were designed to push him over the edge.

Had he known all along this is what it would take?

Craig shoved backward and jumped to his feet with a gun. "Call Kaitlan in here. Right now."

"No!" Kaitlan and Margaret both cried. Kaitlan swung toward the door.

Pete heaved from his chair.

Ed jumped in Kaitlan's path and caught her hard by the arm. "You can't go out there."

"Let me go!" She pounded him in the shoulder with a fist.

He wrapped his arms around her and hung on.

Pete lumbered around the folding table, right hand pulling up his baggy shirt. A gun poked from a holster around his waist. He grabbed it. "Stay here, everybody—and keep filming." He opened the door and ran with muted long steps.

"Kaitlan!" On the monitor Craig bellowed her name toward the office door, eyes fixed on her grandfather. The old man hadn't moved. "Get in here, or I'm shooting!"

"She's not here," her grandfather snarled.

"Kaitlan! I'll give you ten seconds."

"Go on, shoot me, you coward."

His own murder, on tape—that's what he wanted. To save her from Craig.

"Let me *go*." Kaitlan struggled to break from Ed's iron grasp.

He clung tighter.

She squirmed around to watch the monitor. Onscreen Craig's head jerked as if he'd heard a noise. He sidestepped toward the office door, out of camera range.

Margaret surged closer to the table to see, cutting off Kaitlan's view.

Crack. Crack.

Gunshots.

No!

Ed started at the sound. His hold on her momentarily loosened. Kaitlan shoved him away and ran.

"Craig!" She screamed his name as she barreled out the door, veering right. "Craig, I'm here!" Stumbling, she sprinted down the eternal hall, the office so far away, never, ever fast enough to save her stubborn grandfather.

sixty

Kaitlan screamed before Ed could stop her.

Who got shot—Pete or Craig?

Ed's eyes cut from the monitor to Kaitlan's fleeing back. As she hit the door and vanished, he took out after her.

She screeched her way down the hall. Ed chased, nerves pinging.

Everything within him wanted to yell for her to *stop*. But he didn't dare. He would tackle Kaitlan, pull her into another room ... If Craig was still alive he didn't know Ed was here, another man to fight.

"Craig!" Kaitlan wailed.

They passed the living room on their right. Far ahead, across the entryway and in the opposite hall, heaped a body.

Pete.

At the edge of the entrance hall, Ed snagged Kaitlan's shirt. He yanked hard, pulling her backwards. She stumbled and fell against his chest.

From the office—Craig's voice. "Stay here, Brooke."

Ed swerved toward the kitchen, dragging Kaitlan with him.

sixty-one

Heart bludgeoning his chest, Sam stood his ground, camera trained on the monitor. He'd been brought here to film, and veteran that he was, he'd film to the end.

Margaret flailed two steps and collapsed to her knees.

"Get up!" he hissed. "Shut the door and come work the remote control."

"But—"

"Do it."

"I have to help—"

"You *can't* help out there. You want that man caught; this tape's the key."

Crying, Margaret pulled herself toward the door.

"Does it lock?"

"Yes, but they—"

"Lock it."

"What if they need to come—"

"Lock it."

Onscreen Sam couldn't see Pete. Or Craig. But he'd heard Craig's voice, commanding Darell to stay put.

Darell Brooke was pulling to his feet. In four steps he was off-camera. He'd headed not toward the door but across the office.

Was he calling 911?

Margaret floundered back to the table.

253 ~ dark pursuit

"Move the camera around, see if you can pick up Darell."

She put a shaky hand to the console and pushed too far. The camera zoomed in on a blank wall. She gripped harder, panning slowly. To the right, Darell's leg appeared, moving toward the doorway.

"Follow him."

Margaret filmed him until he disappeared around the office threshold.

Her breath caught. She swiveled around toward the desk. "I'm calling 911."

"He may have already done it."

"I'm not taking any chances."

Sam heard her snatch up the phone and punch three numbers. Her voice trembled as she gave the address. "Hurry. I think someone's already been shot."

She banged down the receiver. "I have to open the gate."

The gate. Sam had forgotten.

Nothing on the screen. The action had moved elsewhere.

He needed to get it on film.

Sam turned from the monitor. "Stay here, I'll do it. Lock the door behind me."

sixty-two

Darell yanked open his desk drawer and extracted his gun. A Glock 17—possibly the same model Craig wielded. It was fully loaded. Darell had inspected it this morning when he moved it from his bedroom nightstand where he kept it.

He transferred his cane to his left hand and clutched the gun with his right.

Darell hurried from the office. Pete Lynch lay in the hallway.

Darell stopped and cranked his body into a stoop. He reached out his gnarled hand holding the Glock, hovered his knuckles in front of Pete's nose.

No air.

With effort he straightened. He cast desperate looks around the body. No sign of Pete's gun either. Craig had taken it. He was after Kaitlan.

Idiot girl had been screaming like a banshee. Where had she gone?

Darell turned around to peer at his bedroom door. What if Craig was hiding in there?

No. He'd have followed the sound of Kaitlan's voice.

Darrel shuffled around and hurried up the hall.

Had Sam gotten everything on film? Craig, pulling a gun. It wasn't a murder, but it should be enough.

With perfect clarity Darell saw Craig's immediate plan. Wouldn't Darell have his antagonist do the same, if he were writing the scene? Craig couldn't just shoot them. First he had to squeeze names out of them—who else had they told?

How long before Craig discovered others in the house?

In the distance, somewhere off the entryway—a noise.

Kaitlan.

"Craig Barlow!" Darell thumped over the hardwood. "You want to kill somebody, here I am!"

sixty-three

On her knees in the kitchen, Kaitlan huddled with Ed behind the cooking island. Ed was crouched down, ready to spring. He'd grabbed a frying pan off the cook top, as if that would do any good.

Craig would be here in seconds. They wouldn't get out of this alive.

She'd seen Pete's body down near the office. If Ed hadn't pulled her back, Craig would have already gotten to her. She hadn't cared then. She'd only been driven to save her grandfather.

"He's okay," Ed had whispered, dragging her away.

Pete. Kaitlan wanted to mourn the man, but she felt strangely empty. She had no time to feel.

If only they could get Pete's gun.

Somewhere down the south wing, her grandfather yelled for Craig.

No. Kaitlan's eyes squeezed shut.

Crack-crack-crack. Gunshots rang from the north wing.

Ed stiffened. Kaitlan pressed against him.

A stifled yell. Something heavy crashed. The news camera?

Sam.

Ed's chin dropped, as if he guessed the same.

Deathly silence followed.

Kaitlan pressed a fist to her mouth, breath roughening her throat.

Footsteps entered the kitchen.

sixty-four

When the shots fired, Margaret knew. Sam hadn't made it up the hall.

It should have been her. If he hadn't gone in her place ...

A sob caught in her throat. Was everyone else dead?

Through blurry eyes she checked the monitor. The office remained empty.

She flung toward the desk and grabbed the phone to call 911 again. How would the Sheriff's Department get here with the gate locked?

No dial tone.

She punched the Talk button off, on, off, on.

Silence.

Margaret dropped the phone and did the only thing left to do. She prayed.

sixty-five

Craig approached the kitchen, muscles taut.

A gun in each hand, he'd run up the long hallway in seconds flat, the trained, fit policeman chasing his prey. He was the good guy, Kaitlan the bad. He had to view it that way.

He was in this now. No alternative but to see it through.

Passing the TV room he'd had the presence of mind to veer inside and stuff the gun from the man he'd just shot under the pillow of a couch. He didn't need it; he had plenty ammunition himself. Not to mention backup if absolutely necessary.

On a table near the sofa where he'd hidden the man's gun, Craig spotted a phone. He knocked it off the hook.

Then, calmly, he proceeded to find Kaitlan.

When she last screamed it had been from somewhere near the entryway. Then — poof. Gone. She couldn't have made it to the stairs.

The entrance area spilled to a hall leading toward the back of the house. Through a wide door Craig glimpsed tiled floor, the edge of cabinets. Kaitlan could have gone without his seeing her.

He headed toward it.

Sudden motion to his left. He pivoted, gun pointed. A man was running up the long wing from the other side of the house. With a *news camera*.

Craig pulled the trigger three times. The man tumbled to the floor. His camera crashed and skidded.

A newsman. Craig's breath bottled in his throat. What had Darell Brooke done?

Craig started for the equipment, thinking to find the film and rip it out. Four steps down the hall he turned back. He would take care of it later. First—Kaitlan.

The minute he'd hit the kitchen Craig heard Brooke calling his name from down toward the office. *Yeah, yeah, old man. Wait till you see your granddaughter die.*

He stepped onto the tile.

sixty-six

Kaitlan pressed her palms to her thighs, every muscle gathered to run. She could see Ed's knuckles whiten around the handle of the frying pan.

Frying pan. A hysterical giggle birthed and died in her throat. How insane, this scene.

"Kaitlan." Craig's voice sounded hard and cold. "I know you're back here somewhere."

She glanced at the short hall leading to the garage. He wouldn't know if she had gone that way. He'd have to pass the cooking island to check.

"Hear your grandfather calling for me?" The footsteps came closer. They stopped near the other side of the island. "Come out now or when he gets here, I'll shoot him. I figure you got about thirty seconds."

No.

Kaitlan rose. Just like that. Craig stood a mere seven feet away, gun pointed.

She nudged Ed with a foot—*stay down.*

"Well, there you are." Craig smiled, so cool, so good-looking in his brown sport jacket. Or so she once would have thought. "You've led me on quite a chase."

"How did you know? That he's my grandfather."

His lips curved to a smirk. "I've known since the beginning."

Kaitlan searched for words and found none. Her mind had blanked to white.

She gripped the slick tile of the counter. Maybe if she told him she was pregnant ... But that wouldn't stop him. Not now.

Sound filtered from the hall—a muted shuffle. Her grandfather, trying to be quiet.

In a casual move Craig turned and fired.

"*No!*"

From outside her line of sight came her grandfather's wrenching "hngk!" She heard him fall.

Kaitlan screamed. Blindly she shoved back from the island. *Run, run to him!* she told her feet, but they cemented to the floor.

Craig lunged around the island for her.

Ed leapt up, whipped back the frying pan like a baseball bat, and swung. He smashed Craig square in the cheek.

"Ah!" Craig dropped to the ground. The gun flew from his hand and spun around on the tile. Ed threw down the pan with a clang and heaved toward the weapon.

Dazed, Craig thrust himself up on one elbow and caught Ed's ankle. Ed dove toward the floor, chin first.

Kaitlan screamed again and jumped from their path. Ed landed half on top of Craig, and the two men grappled. They clutched, seeking hold, punching each other's heads. Kaitlan's eyes jerked with their movements, trying to find the gun. Neither held it.

They rolled to one side, Ed on the bottom. Black metal poked from beneath his thigh.

Kaitlan stumbled forward, reaching shaking fingers for the gun. The men rolled again. The gun disappeared.

Ed slugged Craig in the temple. Craig's head ricocheted to the side. Rage flamed his face red, a vein throbbing in his forehead. He slapped his hands around Ed's throat and squeezed.

Ed's mouth sagged open. His eyes widened, his fingers clawing talons at Craig's deathly grip. He dug a foot against the floor and pushed. His body jolted a few inches backward.

The gun popped from beneath his legs. Kaitlan grabbed it.

She flew up straight, weapon glued to both hands, pointed down. Trying, trying to aim at Craig, but she'd never held a gun before, and what if the bullet went through him to Ed?

Craig's teeth clenched, spittle at his mouth. He shifted his knees to either side of Ed, clamped his fingers tighter. Ed's face purpled. Desperation glazed his eyes.

Kaitlan folded over, rammed the barrel into Craig's side, and pulled the trigger. The explosion was *loud*. Her arms jolted.

Craig convulsed and jerked up. His face slackened, his hands falling from Ed's throat. Shock quivered across his features like the shedding of snakeskin. Slowly, dumbfounded, his head rotated to Kaitlan.

Their eyes met.

Craig's rolled up. His neck flopped to one side.

Ed shoved him hard in the chest. Craig slid off him and collapsed.

Kaitlan threw down the weapon and ran to her grandfather. He lay on his back in the hallway, feet facing the kitchen. Not moving, his face waxy. Blood stained his left shoulder. Vaguely Kaitlan registered a gun some feet away.

Kaitlan threw herself beside him and cradled his head in her hands. "No, no, please." A sob wrenched from her lips. "Grandfather, listen to me. Please don't die!"

Behind her—an animal cry of rage.

Something wrapped around Kaitlan's throat. Yanked her from her grandfather. She caved sideways and slammed onto her back.

Above her, upside down, Kaitlan saw Hallie Barlow's fury-drenched face.

sixty-seven

All breath cut off.

Time stalled, the world jerking into slow motion. Kaitlan's hands floated to her neck, fumbling at the thing around it. *Cloth...*

The scene warped into normal speed.

Hallie wormed around to Kaitlan's chest, lifted her head, and deftly wrapped the fabric strip twice. Kaitlan glimpsed a flash of black and green.

"You killed my brother." Hallie grated the words, inhuman. "He tried to help me, and you *killed* him."

From far in the back of her head, a logical voice cried out. *The front door.* Craig left it unlocked for Hallie to come in. She'd heard the shots.

Kaitlan's jaw crunched open, her lungs seeking, craving oxygen. For a wild second she saw herself as Ed on the kitchen floor beneath Craig's stranglehold. Kaitlan's hands scrabbled through thick air, scratching at Hallie's face.

"Why'd you come home yesterday, huh? Why'd you have to spoil it?"

Someone screamed. *Margaret.*

Hallie's stone fingers tied the cloth ends once and pulled opposite directions. The world faded gray.

Thudding footsteps on the tile. Ed braying a cry, and Margaret screaming again—where *was* she?—and Hallie's head swinging up,

263

her hands firm on the cloth, mouth cursing, shouting, "No, no, get back!" and still there's no breath, and Kaitlan's lungs shriveling, the ceiling spotting black-red—

Hallie's face whisked away.

Something hit flesh with a wet smack.

A body thudded.

The cloth loosened—not enough, not nearly enough. Kaitlan hands slashed at it, tearing, her lips racked apart and gurgling air.

Ed's face appeared—"Stop, I'll get it." He thrust her fingers off, and his went to work, untying, unwinding, and Kaitlan's throat expanded, her windpipe hawking, gusting in oxygen. Her head lolled, and she saw Margaret looming above Hallie, aiming a gun with iron hands, tears streaking her face.

Margaret with a gun, how crazy is that? Kaitlan thought, and then the hallway whirled into a black hole and voided to nothing.

Part 4

Truth

sixty-eight

For the fourth day in a row, Kaitlan sat in the ugly orange armchair at her grandfather's bedside. The hospital room smelled of steel and emptiness. A setting sun slanted through half-drawn blinds, lining the floor with streaks of yellow. Feet tucked beneath her, temple resting on her fist, Kaitlan fought to keep her eyes open.

She couldn't seem to get enough sleep. Not that the world wanted to give her any.

She'd had two long interview sessions with the San Mateo Sheriff's Department. Not to mention dodging the media everywhere she went. And the public in general.

No charges would be filed in her shooting of Craig Barlow. Self-defense, they said.

But it wasn't just a lack of rest. Kaitlan felt a deep tiredness in the marrow of her bones. She carried it around with her, a stone in her chest. Yesterday Margaret said it would pass eventually—that Kaitlan had lost much and been through multiple levels of shock, and that didn't heal overnight. Margaret was still reeling herself.

They both agreed they and her grandfather were alive only by the grace of God.

More than once they prayed together for their own strength and healing. "Get us through this, God," Kaitlan had promised Him, "and I'll give my life to You. All of it."

She wasn't quite sure what that would mean. But it was a bargain she intended to keep.

Sighing, she changed positions.

Craig lay in this same hospital, under guard. The bullet had torn through his upper intestine, missing his heart and lungs. With all the evidence against him, he had confessed. When he was discharged, it would be to jail. He faced two counts of first-degree murder, other counts of aggravated assault, plus tampering with evidence and other charges regarding his disposing of his sister's final victim.

Under interrogation, her brother wounded, a barely controllable Hallie Barlow had melted. She related in detail each murder, including her sinister planning of the third one. Kaitlan still could hardly believe the story. How could Hallie have done this? And if someone seemingly as nice as Hallie could be so black inside, what did that say about the human race?

Kaitlan had turned these questions over and over in her mind.

Unlike the first two random murders, Hallie Barlow had targeted Martina Pelsky. Studying her habits, Hallie learned Martina was bicycling the town every afternoon, leaving campaign flyers at houses. Martina was meticulous about this project, sectioning the town into grids. But Hallie didn't want to risk an outside killing in daylight. She watched until Martina's task took her near Kaitlan's neighborhood. What better place to lure Martina than Kaitlan's out-of-the-way garage apartment?

In preparation Hallie managed to "secretly borrow" Craig's key to Kaitlan's apartment — just long enough to make a copy.

The day of the murder Hallie drove past Martina as she biked not far from Kaitlan's home. Hallie stopped and invited Martina to "her place," expressing an interest in helping with the campaign. "No worries, I'll bring you back here," she smiled. Hallie was such a likable person. Without a second thought Martina left her bike in the woods and climbed into Hallie's SUV.

Hallie tried something else new — bringing a camera for pictures. She would have plenty of time afterward to haul the body away and straighten Kaitlan's place.

But fate intervened. While Hallie was taking the photos, Craig showed up, bearing a half dozen red roses to leave as a surprise for Kaitlan. Shocked out of his mind at what he stumbled onto, he swung into frantic protection mode for his sister. He had Hallie call the salon to make sure Kaitlan was there—only to learn she'd left early and was on her way home.

In sheer panic Craig and Hallie fled before she could spot their cars.

The roses.

Kaitlan had cried many tears over them. To think Craig had bought those flowers for her hours before he picked her up. Before, driven and desperate, traveling a dark streak of his own, he turned into a monster for the sake of his sister.

Didn't he feel bad about what he was doing to his girlfriend? a detective asked him.

"Anything for family," Craig had replied.

Now behind bars, Hallie was reportedly grief stricken and suicidal. She'd been placed on special watch.

A search of her apartment turned up the fabric, hidden at the bottom of a box of books in her closet. Plus scrapbooks full of old photos of Hallie's and Craig's mother. Authorities searched for one picture in particular that Hallie had mentioned—a full-length shot of her mother, dressed in black pants and a green blouse. The day her mother walked out of her life, Hallie told detectives, the woman had been wearing that outfit.

Most important, detectives found Hallie's journal that had recorded her downward spiral. Quite appropriately, she'd titled it *Obsession*. So far only a few of its pages had been released to the media, but what Kaitlan heard had been heart-stopping.

On TV talking-head psychologists were going wild with the story. Childhood abandonment issues, they said. Bitter anger welling up when Hallie happened to read Darell Brooke's novel *Life After Death*—about a murderous doctor using fabric of black silk with green stripes to kill. The women Hallie strangled were representations of her mother, the psychologists surmised. Each victim Hallie perceived as a poor mom, abusive to children. Not worthy of life.

Hallie reportedly sees none of this. Her answer to why she killed? "I don't know."

Such sensationalized publicity for the King of Suspense. All copies of *Life After Death*—an apropos title for a book now thirty-five years old—sold out almost overnight. The publisher had rushed a large reprinting.

But this kind of publicity Kaitlan's grandfather did not enjoy. Beyond his closed hospital room door a private security employee posted himself in a straight-backed chair. No reporters allowed. Except for Ed.

Kaitlan stretched and blinked at the wall-mounted TV. It was on but muted. Commercials.

In his bed her grandfather was sleeping.

He was scheduled to go home tomorrow. It could have been sooner after the surgery to remove the bullet in his shoulder, but he'd lost a fair amount of blood and struggled with weakness. Except for his tongue. Kaitlan had seen her grandfather send more than one nurse scurrying.

The door cracked open. Ed stuck his head inside. Kaitlan smiled and motioned for him to come in.

Ed entered, closing the door quietly behind him. "He asleep?" he whispered. He soft-footed it over to sit in a wooden chair beside Kaitlan.

"I was until you bothered me," Kaitlan's grandfather crabbed. Beneath the covers his legs shifted. He opened one eye. "That you again, Wasinsky?"

"Yes, sir."

The eye closed. "Don't think you're fooling me, coming here every day. It's not me you're wanting to see."

Kaitlan's face flushed. Which no doubt looked terrific on her mud-yellow cheek.

"Ah, don't give me that." Ed rose to stand by the bed. "I want to see you too." His fingers grazed her grandfather's hand. "How are you?"

"Spiffy."

"Well, good."

Her grandfather heaved a sigh. "Where's Margaret?"

"Home," Kaitlan said. "Cleaning the place up. Getting it ready for you. She'll be in to see you soon."

He grunted.

They fell silent. Her grandfather's eyes slipped shut once more, and Ed wandered back to his chair. He regarded Kaitlan with raised eyebrows—*how are you?*

She tilted her head.

Kaitlan's gaze pulled to her grandfather. His wizened jaw relaxed but his lips were closed, further hollowing his cheeks. His wild eyebrows needed trimming.

Guilt and gratitude panged her heart. Crazy old man. Willing to give his life for hers. She'd tried to express her overwhelming appreciation—more than once. "Thanks for what?" her grandfather retorted. "Coming up with a cockamamie plan that near got us killed?"

"No, for—"

"Couldn't even remember one of my own stories. Not to mention misreading the entire crime. What a mind I got."

"But you did it for me. You purposely pushed Craig—for *me.*"

He'd batted a hand at Kaitlan. "Girl, you're talking nonsense."

Ed rubbed his forehead. "I went to Sam's funeral this afternoon." He spoke in low tones.

Kaitlan's eyes welled. Man, she was crying a lot lately. Yesterday she and Margaret had waded through reporters to attend Pete Lynch's memorial service. The private investigator had left behind an adult daughter and two grandchildren. "I'm so sorry about Sam."

"Yeah. Me too. We'd worked together for five years." Ed's gaze fixed beyond her. "Guy filmed to the end."

Including Craig pulling the trigger on the first bullet that hit him.

Kaitlan caught a tear on her knuckle. She wiped it on her jeans.

Ed's eyes lowered to hers and held. In them shone caring and kindness. His mouth curved in a sad smile.

Kaitlan looked away.

Ed was thirty, with a great job and TV looks. He was clearly interested in her, which was beyond belief—but he didn't know. And she didn't know how to tell him. She was pregnant with Craig Barlow's baby. A baby she loved. When Ed found that out, he'd stop coming around.

He cleared his throat. "Hear about Chief Barlow?"

"Hear what?"

"He's resigning. Well, taking early retirement."

"Oh. Wow." But Kaitlan wasn't that surprised. Under his leadership, investigations of the murders had been badly handled. And his children . . .

He hadn't known, Russ Barlow was insisting. He'd had not the slightest suspicion of his own daughter. Despite how hard-nosed he'd been to Kaitlan, she could believe that. Who would have suspected Hallie?

But how ironic—the chief's worry that Kaitlan would be the one to ruin his son's life.

What a broken man Russ Barlow must now be.

The door swished open and Margaret entered. She smiled at Ed, no hint of surprise at his presence. "Whoo, it's warm in here."

Kaitlan gestured toward the bed with her chin. "He likes it that way."

Her grandfather kept his eyes closed. "When you getting me out of here, woman?"

"Tomorrow, D. You know that."

He sniffed. "I think you like me stuck in here. You're probably running around free as a breeze, painting the town red."

"You're right." She laughed. "That's what I do best." Margaret patted his arm. "How you doing?"

"Why does everybody keep asking me that?"

"Probably because you're lying in a hospital bed."

"Well, stop it."

"Okay." She rolled her eyes at Kaitlan.

Her grandfather scratched his cheek. "I got to get home; I got work to do."

"Oh? What work?"

"Writing, what else?"

"You been lying here thinking of a plot for Leland Hugh?"

He made a sound in his throat. "Something like that."

"That's great." Margaret's face lit. "That's really wonderful, D."

The King of Suspense gave her a look. "Don't sound so surprised, woman. It *is* what I do for a living."

sixty-nine

On a Saturday afternoon Darell stood before the mullioned windows in his office, brooding at the Pacific Ocean. Was it only five weeks ago he'd been in this very spot, brewing with frustration over his fight to plot a book?

It seemed like eons.

Beyond the closed door he could hear Margaret calling Kaitlan. He could swear his assistant's voice sounded lighter, happier. How lonely she must have been in this house with only him for ... hardly comfort. More like harassment.

Darell pushed up his lower lip and sniffed.

Margaret called again. Fool woman. So much for quiet in the house. Didn't she know he was setting to work today?

Imagine what writing's going to be like with a baby around.

His lips relaxed, then hinted at a curve.

The computer called.

Darell glared at it. Leland Hugh sat in there as silent and enigmatic as ever. No thanks to Craig Barlow, who'd proved no help at all with Hugh's motives.

Now Hallie Barlow's journal — that was a different story.

In the hospital Darell had spent day and night trying to slough the mud from his brain and plot the manuscript he so wanted to finish. The one that would rejuvenate his career. Sure, it was great that sales of his backlist were soaring — though for all the wrong reasons. People no

275 ~ dark pursuit

longer had forgotten Darell Brooke. But he wanted to write *now*. Give his fans something new.

Nothing worked.

As the sun dared rise three days ago, the King of Suspense finally gave up.

In that nascent light Darell had stared at his white bedroom ceiling and seen his life. Blank. Vain emptiness. Oh, he'd built a career, a worldwide reputation. His books were still selling. He'd made all the money he'd ever need. But he trampled over people to get it. Worse, he'd trampled over family.

In that moment of stillness, a profound knowledge pierced Darell as surely as an arrow: *It's your fault that you've been alone.*

Why hadn't he seen this before? How does one miss the ocean from the beach or stars in a clear night sky?

Perhaps he'd known all along and refused to see. And he'd thought himself so clever.

On the office door a knock sounded. Darell turned. "Come in."

Kaitlan timidly stuck her head inside. "I'm so sorry to bother you—"

"Kaitlan." He gazed at her with intensity. "You are never a bother."

Surprise crisscrossed her face, followed by a slow smile that yanked at Darell's heart. "Okay."

Two weeks ago Kaitlan had returned to working at the beauty salon. She missed it, she said. And salacious-minded people were finally beginning to leave her alone.

She hung in the doorway, eyes roaming the office as if seeing it for the first time. Impatience gurgled inside Darell. "You wanted something?"

"Yeah. Just to tell you Margaret and I are going shopping."

Darell shrugged. "Fine." He surveyed her. "What about tonight? You seeing Ed?"

Her eyelids flickered. "Yeah. It's time I ... we need to talk."

That they did.

She took a deep breath. "You okay by yourself for a while?"

"Of course. I have writing to do."

Kaitlan grinned. "Good. That's *so good*."

The computer pulled at Darell like a magnet. He'd been thinking this through since his epiphany—and now he was ready. More than ready. Anticipation popped through his veins.

Darell raised his eyebrows. "Remember, you promised to help me."

"I know. I will."

"You sure you understand what it will mean? How thoroughly I'll have to interview you? Reliving difficult events is never easy."

Nor was baring one's soul.

"I know. But I'm ready."

He read the thought she would not express. She needed to do this, as he did.

"Good." He waved a hand at her. "Now get out of here. I have to get to work."

"Okay, bye!" The door closed.

Darell shuffled to his desk and sat down. The desktop page gleamed so empty. So frightening.

Writing would still be difficult, even if he didn't need to plot. He'd have to fight his wandering concentration constantly. But he would prevail.

Write a page a day—and you have a book in a year.

Darell took a deep breath and reached for the mouse.

"Help me on this one, God."

The prayer blurted out, surprising him. Quite the first in his writing career. But apropos. Necessary.

This book would be from his heart, with his own chapters in first person. It would be his penance. His coming clean. Not that it wasn't an amazing story. But to tell it with truth, every detail the way it really happened, required airing his own weaknesses and destructive pride. It meant admitting the lifelong dark pursuit that had cost him so much.

When all was said and done, his reputation as the formidable King of Suspense would be forever tarnished.

So be it.

Darell opened a new file.

Kaitlan had come home. Next year she'd present him with a great grandchild. But somewhere in England he still had a daughter—Kaitlan's mother—whom he had driven away. Who he hoped would read this book. And *hear.*

The white page awaited.

How far would he get in his work today? Anticipation pulsed through him at the thought. At least the first few pages were already written.

Settling himself, poising fingers over the keys, Darell Brooke typed his cover page.

Dark Pursuit

by

Darell Brooke

For my daughter,
Sarah Sering,
with love

chapter 1

"Ever hear the dead knocking?"

Leland Hugh watches the psychiatrist ponder his question, no reaction on the man's lined, learned face. The doctor lists to one side in his chair, a fist under his sagging jowl. The picture of unshakable confidence.

"No, can't say I have."

Hugh nods and gazes at the floor. "I do. At night, always at night."

"Why do they knock?"

His eyes raise to look straight into the doctor's. "They want my soul."

No response but a mere inclining of the head. The intentional silence pulses, waiting for an explanation. Psychiatrists are good at that.

"I took theirs, you see. Put them in their graves early." Deep inside Hugh, the anger and fear begin to swirl. He swallows, voice tightening. "They're supposed to *stay* in the grave. Who'd ever think the dead would demand their revenge?"

From outside the door, at the windows, in the closet, in the walls—they used to knock. Now, in his jail cell the noises come from beneath the floor. Harassing, insistent, hate-filled, and bitter sounds that pound his ears and drill his brain until sleep will not, *cannot* come.

"Do you ever answer?"

Shock twists Hugh's lips. *"Answer?"*

The psychiatrist's face remains placid. The slight, knowing curve to his mouth makes Hugh want to slug him.

"You think they're not real, don't you?" Hugh steeples his fingers with mocking erudition. "Yes, esteemed colleagues." He affects an arrogant highbrow voice. "I have determined the subject suffers from EGS—Extreme Guilt Syndrome, the roots of which run so deep as never to be extirpated, with symptoms aggrandizing into myriad areas of the subject's life and resulting in perceived paranormal phenomena."

He drops both hands in his lap, lowering his chin to look derisively at the good doctor.

The man inhales slowly. "Do you feel guilt for the murders?"

"Why should I? They *deserved* it."

He pushes to his feet.

~~He pushes to his feet.~~ He slumps back in his chair.

~~He slumps back in his chair.~~ He aims a hard look

Darell Brooke ~2

~~He aims a hard look~~
~~The psychiatrist.~~
~~Hugh's hands fist,~~
~~He cannot~~
~~He can only~~
~~He~~
XXX

"Aaghh!" I smacked the keyboard and shoved away from my desk. All concentration drained from my mind like water from a leaky pan.

The characters froze.

I lowered my head, raking gnarled fingers into the front of my scalp. For a time there I'd almost had it—that ancient joy of thoughts flowing and fingers typing. In the last hour I'd managed to write three or four paragraphs. Now—nothing.

Absolutely nothing.

King of Suspense. I laughed, a bitter sound that singed my throat. Ninety-nine novels written in forty-three years. Well over a hundred million copies sold. Twenty-one major motion pictures made from my books. Countless magazine articles about my career, fan letters, invitations to celebrity parties. Now look at me. Two years after the auto accident and still only half-mobile. And wielding a mere fraction of the brain power I used to have.

What good is an author who can't hold a plot in his head?...

Darell Brooke ~3

Violet Dawn

Kanner Lake Series

Brandilyn Collins

Something sinuous in the water brushed against Paige's knee. She jerked her leg away.

What was that? She rose to a sitting position, groped around with her left hand.

Fine wisps wound themselves around her fingers.

Hair?

She yanked backward, but the tendrils clung. Something solid bumped her wrist.

Paige gasped. With one frantic motion she shook her arm free, grabbed the side of the hot tub, and heaved herself out.

Paige Williams slips into her hot tub in the blackness of night — and finds herself face to face with death.

Alone, terrified, fleeing a dark past, Paige must make an unthinkable choice.

In *Violet Dawn*, hurtling events and richly drawn characters collide in a breathless story of murder, the need to belong, and faith's first glimmer. One woman's secrets unleash an entire town's pursuit, and the truth proves as elusive as the killer in their midst.

Softcover: 978-0-310-25223-8

Pick up a copy today at your favorite bookstore!

Dread Champion

Brandilyn Collins

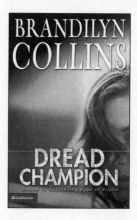

Chelsea Adams has visions. But they have no place in a courtroom.

As a juror for a murder trial, Chelsea must rely only on the evidence. And this circumstantial evidence is strong — Darren Welk killed his wife.

Or did he?

The trial is a nightmare for Chelsea. The other jurors belittle her Christian faith. As testimony unfolds, truth and secrets blur. Chelsea's visiting niece stumbles into peril surrounding the case, and Chelsea cannot protect her. God sends visions — frightening, vivid. But what do they mean? Even as Chelsea finds out, what can she do? She is helpless, and danger is closing in....

Masterfully crafted, *Dread Champion* is a novel in which appearances can deceive and the unknown can transform the meaning of known facts. One man's guilt or innocence is just a single link in a chain of hidden evil ... and God uses the unlikeliest of people to accomplish his purposes.

Softcover: 978-0-310-23827-0

Pick up a copy today at your favorite bookstore!

Eyes of Elisha

Brandilyn Collins

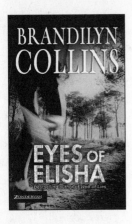

The murder was ugly.

The killer was sure no one saw him.

Someone did.

In a horrifying vision, Chelsea Adams has relived the victim's last moments. But who will believe her? Certainly not the police, who must rely on hard evidence. Nor her husband, who barely tolerates Chelsea's newfound Christian faith. Besides, he's about to hire the man who Chelsea is certain is the killer to be a vice president in his company.

Torn between what she knows and the burden of proof, Chelsea must follow God's leading and trust him for protection. Meanwhile, the murderer is at liberty. And he's not about to take Chelsea's involvement lying down.

Softcover: 978-0-310-23968-0

Pick up a copy today at your favorite bookstore!

Hidden Faces Series
Brandilyn Collins

Brink of Death

Terror rocks Grove Landing when a woman is murdered in her home. The victim's young daughter, Erin, witnessed the crime but is too traumatized to give a description. Desperate detectives ask neighbor Annie Kingston, with a background in art, to interview Erin for a composite. But what if Annie's lack of experience in forensic art leads Erin astray? The detectives could end up searching for a face that doesn't exist, leaving the real killer to stalk the neighborhood.

Softcover: 978-0-310-25103-3

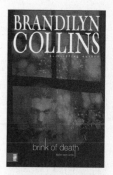

Stain of Guilt

For the highly succesful TV show American Fugitive, forensic artist Annie Kingston agrees to draw the updated face of Bill Bland, a cunning fugitive wanted for a double murder committed twenty years ago. In studying the man and his crime, Annie knows she must descend into the mind of a killer — a mind of greed, darkness ... and death. Book Two in the Hidden Faces Series.

Softcover: 978-0-310-25104-0

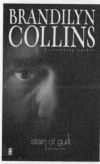

Dead of Night

The Redding, California, area is terrorized by a serial killer with an unusual method for murder. Annie Kingston is called in to draw sketches of the victims' faces so they can be identified. As the body count rises, the pressure increases to find this heinous killer. The Sheriff thinks he's close — maybe too close. How can Annie — and her son — stay safe as the killer closes in? Book Three in the Hidden Faces Series.

Softcover: 978-0-310-25105-7

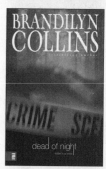

Web of Lies

In the fourth and final book of the Hidden Faces Series, Annie Kingston and a new ally — Chelsea Adams from Eyes of Elisha — are drawn into a terrifying battle against time, greed, and a deadly opponent.

Softcover: 978-0-310-25106-4

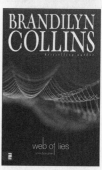

Share Your Thoughts

With the Author: Your comments will be forwarded to the author when you send them to *zauthor@zondervan.com.*

With Zondervan: Submit your review of this book by writing to *zreview@zondervan.com.*

Free Online Resources at
www.zondervan.com/hello

 Zondervan AuthorTracker: Be notified whenever your favorite authors publish new books, go on tour, or post an update about what's happening in their lives.

 Daily Bible Verses and Devotions: Enrich your life with daily Bible verses or devotions that help you start every morning focused on God.

 Free Email Publications: Sign up for newsletters on fiction, Christian living, church ministry, parenting, and more.

 Zondervan Bible Search: Find and compare Bible passages in a variety of translations at www.zondervanbiblesearch.com.

 Other Benefits: Register yourself to receive online benefits like coupons and special offers, or to participate in research.